"This collection of stories is refreshingly honest and daring in its treatment of Singapore's history and quotidian life. The stories disturb; they are painfully truthful. This kind of storytelling is what is missing in Singaporean literature."

—Lily Rose R. Tope,
Professor of English, University of the Philippines

HEAVEN
HAS
EYES

HEAVEN HAS EYES

Stories

PHILIP HOLDEN

First North American edition published 2026 by Gaudy Boy.

The North American edition includes four new stories: "Letters from London," "Pigeons and Doves," "The Strange Machine of Dr Goh," "Questions for a National Therapy Session, 9 August 2030" © 2026, by Philip Holden.

Original title: *Heaven Has Eyes*
© 2016, by Philip Holden.
First published by Epigram Books, 2016.
Published by arrangement with Agence littéraire Astier-Pécher.
All Rights Reserved.

Published by Gaudy Boy LLC,
an imprint of Singapore Unbound
www.singaporeunbound.org/gaudyboy
New York

For more information on ordering books, contact jkoh@singaporeunbound.org.

ISBN 978-1-958652-22-0
eISBN 978-1-958652-23-7

Library of Congress Control Number: 2025940765

Cover design by Flora Chan
Interior design by Jennifer Houle
Proofreading by Chamois Holschuh

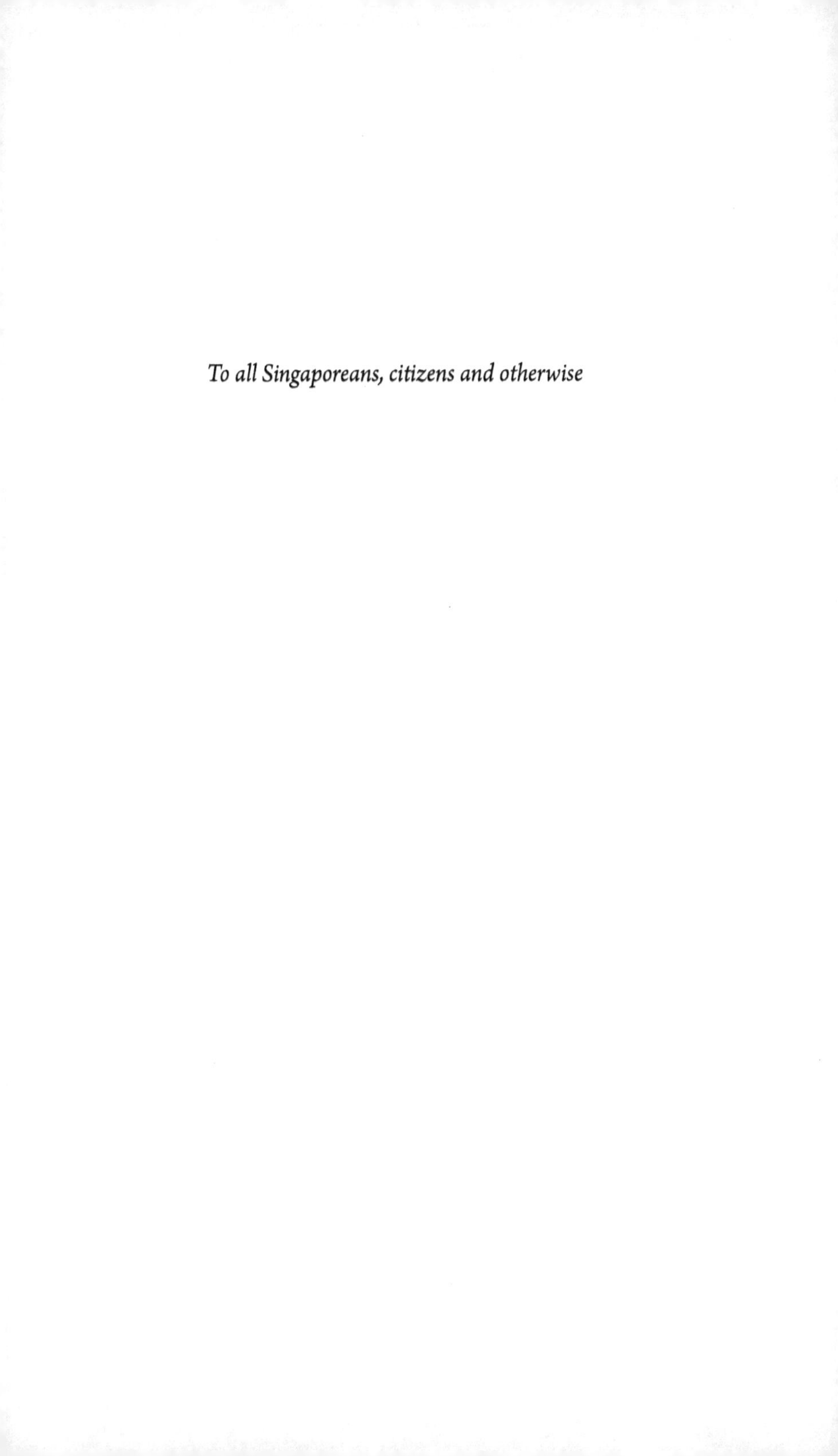

To all Singaporeans, citizens and otherwise

Contents

Preface

The story behind this book begins in Changsha, Hunan Province, China, in September 1986. I arrived at Hunan Normal University with a freshly minted MA in English Literature from the University of Florida to teach literary studies to graduate students older than I was, several of whom had returned to the university after the nightmare of the Cultural Revolution. On the day I arrived, I was driven from the airport through the city, over the bridge across the Xiang River—which I later learned many of the university's faculty had built with their own hands—and up the hill and through the university gates to the Zhuanjia Lou, the Foreign Experts' Building, at what was then the top of the campus, next to the concrete water tower.

In the first few days before the semester started, I got to know others who lived in the building. Below me, on the second floor, was a large apartment inhabited by a Canadian couple, Edward and Margaret Berry. Edward was a professor from the University of Victoria in Canada, a Shakespeare expert and close to retirement. An American who had migrated northwards, he would often talk to me about Vancouver and in particular the University of British Columbia, surely the most beautiful campus in the world: on a peninsula at the edge of a continent, surrounded by tall trees and jutting out into what he then called the Strait of Georgia, but which we now call the Salish Sea.

On the third floor, there was a smaller apartment, inhabited by two undergraduate sisters from Singapore, whom I knew as Zhang Hong Ying and Zhang Hong Nian, and whom everyone called, rather unimaginatively, the Singapore girls. Their father, Mr Zhang, taught at the Railway University across the river and would visit from time to time. They introduced him to me, and on weekends we talked over tea about London, the city where I had studied as an undergraduate, and about British Labour Party politics. As the weather grew colder, we discussed decolonisation, democracy, political failures, and hopes for the future. Our conversations condensed on another city, Singapore, the island from which he was exiled and to which his daughters and later he himself would return near the end of his life. Gradually, from conversations with faculty and from my own reading after I left Changsha, my companion's identity emerged. He was Eu Chooi Yip, who had been Secretary of the Malayan Democratic Union, Singapore's first political party, in the 1940s and later a leader in the Malayan Communist Party. He had taken a very different path in history from his classmate at Raffles College in Singapore in the 1930s, Goh Keng Swee, or his journalist friend and post-war political associate, Sinnathamby Rajaratnam, both of whom joined the People's Action Party, the political party that came to dominate post-independence Singapore politics.

I did not realise it at the time, but the topography of much of my future life was mapped out through the conversations in that simple room in the Zhuanjia Lou, with its misaligned window screens that could never quite keep the bugs out and its shower heater that gave you a salutary shock in the morning if the arc of falling water above your head completed a circuit. I sipped tea from Dongting Lake in a covered cup that I opened only after all the leaves had fallen from the surface of the water. I began my lifelong struggle to learn Mandarin Chinese. At the same time, I was immersed in conversations about three cities: London, the city I had left but would never return to as a Londoner, and the cities of my future, Vancouver and Singapore.

I arrived in Vancouver three years later, in September 1989, to study for my doctorate at that university among the trees on the promontory, up the hill. I came by train from Toronto, across the Canadian Shield, the Prairies, up through the Rockies, and down along the Fraser Valley. I spent my first night at the youth hostel in Jericho. In the evening, free from my heavy suitcase for the first time in days, I walked out onto the jetty at sunset and looked in wonder at this golden, glowing city, cupped by mountains. The next morning, I took the trolleybus up the hill to the University of British Columbia, into the mist and a new life.

In August 1994, my doctorate completed, I flew into Singapore during a rainstorm. It was the National Day holiday: I hunkered down in the Novotel Orchid on Dunearn Road, now long demolished, and took a shuttle bus to Lucky Plaza for dinner. The next morning, I climbed another hill, to the National Institute of Education, situated on the same Bukit Timah campus where Eu Chooi Yip had studied over half a century before, to report for work. I wore a new shirt, pants, and leather shoes that I'd bought at Eaton's Department Store in Vancouver a few days before my departure. The shoes chafed, and at the end of the day I hobbled back to my room to sleep. I sent my clothes to the hotel laundry and belatedly realised that I had left my keys in one of the pockets. I called the reception, and a young member of the hotel staff came up to my room and proceeded to take off his clothes. I gently showed him out. A few days later I went to Punggol to eat seafood with a friend I had met in Vancouver. We ate prawns at another long-vanished restaurant by the sea. At some point the juices spattered over her hair. I found myself brushing them off, very gently, the tiny globes of light shattering and falling. Another story began.

The stories in this collection emerged from my life in Singapore, as an academic who would eventually teach Singapore and Southeast Asian literatures in English, as an HDB (Housing and Development Board) dweller, as a member of an extended Singapore Chinese family, but above all as some-one who made Singapore his home. Some simply take a moment from this life, settle there, and go deeper. Others make connections to those other two cities that I still visit and have lived in for short periods, whether by necessity or choice. Returning to these stories after a decade and adding new ones, two more themes have become important to me. The first is returning to Singapore's history of decolonisation and to those who were leading actors in this process. The space of fiction, I hope, enables me to go back to forgotten moments and place them in stories that are neither hagiographic nor condemnatory, but which incite curiosity about the way in which the past speaks to us in the present. The second concern that surfaces for me might loosely be called mental health, while leaving open the fact that ideas of health and sickness are culturally situated and critically generative. This concern comes from my lived experience in the last decade: exploring a mental health diagnosis and finding it wanting, discovering different languages in which to talk of distress, searching, eventually training as a mental health professional, yet not entering professional practice. Singapore is often seen as a place of pure rationality, but it is perhaps also a place of certain kinds of strange and wonderful madness which can be traced out into the world and back into history.

Stories of migration and belonging, some part of me wants to say, should have easy endings. They should be about arrival, about finding home. But stories are recalcitrant: they lead you to places of discomfort just when you think you have reached a conclusion. They heal, but they also leave scar tissue. The stories here are about finding a home in the world, even as they are also about belonging in difference.

Dramatis Personae

While most of the characters in the collection are fictional, the following historical figures appear from time to time in the stories.

GOH KENG SWEE

Often thought of as independent Singapore's economic architect. Studied at Raffles College in colonial Singapore, then at the London School of Economics for both his undergraduate degree (1948–1951) and his doctorate (1954–1956). Minister for Finance after Singapore achieved self-rule in 1959. Later, as Minister for Education, Goh oversaw the introduction of the streaming of pupils in Singapore schools based on academic ability and language proficiency.

LEE KUAN YEW

Founding member of the People's Action Party (PAP) and Singapore's first Prime Minister, serving from 1959 to 1990. Studied law in England (1946–1950), initially at the London School of Economics (LSE), then at Cambridge. Began using his Chinese name, Kuan Yew, rather than his English name, Harry, on his return to Singapore. Visited Vancouver in October 1968, as part of a two-month sabbatical visit to universities in North America "to refresh my spirit".

LIM CHIN SIONG

Founding member of the PAP. He and Lee Kuan Yew flew to London as PAP representatives at the multiparty constitutional talks with the British in 1956. Imprisoned by the British later in the same year and released in 1959. Led the left wing of the PAP to leave the party and form a new opposition party, the Barisan Sosialis, in 1961. Imprisoned again in 1963, this time under a PAP government: lived with depression and suicidal ideation while in prison. Released in 1969 after agreeing to renounce politics and go abroad in exile. Returned to Singapore in 1979 after a decade in London.

SINNATHAMBY RAJARATNAM

Often thought of as the architect of Singaporean multiculturalism. Born in Ceylon and raised in Seremban, Malaya. In 1935, departed to King's College, London, to study law. Spent twelve years in London, eventually abandoning his studies to become a fiction writer and journalist. Continued journalistic career after his return to Singapore in 1947 and became one of the founding members of the PAP. Served as Minister for Culture and, after Singapore was fully independent in 1965, as Singapore's first Minister for Foreign Affairs. Stepped down from government in the late 1980s. Lived with dementia from the middle of the 1990s until his death in 2006.

PIERRE TRUDEAU

Prime Minister of Canada from 1968 to 1979 and 1980 to 1984. Briefly studied at LSE in 1948 before embarking on a year of travelling in Europe and Asia.

HOME

Aeroplane

Jin Jin, not now. Later we can fold a paper plane. But now we all have things to do. Your grandmother is watching her movie on TV. I've got something I have to write. Do your Chinese homework. Look, you can sit here at the table with me. Put a cushion on the chair, so you can reach. No pencil? Ask Yati, she's sure to have one.

Outside, a light breeze before the rain. When the music from the television fades, sounds from beyond the house gather again. The wash of traffic on the recently widened road. Voices, raised, anxious, but too far away to understand. The sealing wax palm in the garden stirs. We wait for the patter of water on tiles, on the roof of the car, or, soon enough, the rattle of a bolt drawn back and the creaking open of the gate. First Jin Jin's mother, my sister-in-law, then other family members, settling like migratory birds at my mother-in-law's house in that golden hour before sunset, before dinner.

妈妈，你在看什么电影？

She's watching *Air Hostess*, my mother-in-law tells me in Mandarin. Look! Watch Ge Lan, see how she tilts her head when she smiles. See what she tells her mother, tells Ah Xiang, tells the boring boyfriend. She has thought about this career move deeply. She wants to take off, to fly into the blue sky. She does not want to be a canary in a cage, no matter how sweetly she can sing. And she can sing, very beautifully. Later, we will have the

"Oh Calypso" song. But now it's only the background music that swells. Miss Kang steps out, leading her new recruits proudly onto the apron. They wear high heels, pencil-slim skirts, and tiny blue-grey berets that nestle miraculously on their heads. Behind them are the waiting planes, white as birds flocking beneath the green of mountains.

I turn back to the table. Opposite me, Jin Jin hovers over her homework, head down, elbows sticking out, her exercise book ruffled by the fan. On my laptop are photographs and documents that I need to lay out, one by one, into a story. A portrait of a young man with a trilby and a cheap suitcase, standing by a waiting plane. No mountains here, only a flat expanse of grass. Then PDFs of colonial office records, their folder covers turned a deep brown with age: even here, on the screen, you can almost recall their musty smell, how you were afraid they would fall to pieces in your hands under the watchful cameras of the reading room. I shift on the chair, trying to catch the breeze of the fan. Newspaper columns with bold titles: ANOTHER YEAR FOR DETAINEES; FREEDOM AT LAST; THE BIG SPLIT; OPPOSITION LEADERS DETAINED; SUICIDE ATTEMPT IN PRISON; EXILE OR DETENTION: PM'S OFFER TO LIM CHIN SIONG; RELEASE TO GO ABROAD FOR STUDIES. Below the march of headlines, the print diminishes to the size of ants, trailing away into the darkness. Academic articles are much easier to read: bright, angular, and solid, their references marshalled as neatly as the air hostesses on the tarmac.

It's even easier to watch the movie. Ge Lan is on her first flight. The propellers turn, slowly at first, then fast enough to seem as if they are spinning backwards. The plane lumbers along, impossibly heavy, and gathers speed for take-off. The music returns: the aeroplane seems to float in a blue sky empty of anything but clouds. In the cabin, the passengers behave much as expected. There is a terrified woman who clutches Ge Lan's hand and will not let go, a lecherous middle-aged man to be engaged in conversation and then avoided, a greedy passenger who wants two bowls of soup and wants them now.

Uncle?

Jin Jin, one minute, I'm working.

Can I ask you a question?

Okay.

Your legs, why so hairy?

Because I come from a country very far north, very cold in winter. So I need to be warm.

Like a polar bear?

Yes, very like. Now do your homework. Write out those characters. If you don't practise over and over again, your writing, your 笔画, will be as bad as mine. Look, you've hardly started.

I turn back to the screen. This shouldn't be taking so long. Short entries, the dictionary's editor told me. We'll pay you per word but only up to a certain limit. There's a knack to this, to summarize the lives of those opposition leaders who are only footnotes in history, to give them a beginning, a middle, and an end. But history takes you on detours. It keeps you waiting; it never arrives on time. Look at this photograph and its description: "Riot at Nanyang University". Three earnest young students hold a banner next to a ceremonial arch. Where is the riot? How did the photograph, consigned to the archive, come to be attached to the caption? What kind of story is being told here? A story about the future, surely. Be quiet. Do your homework. Wait, work hard, and the future you want will be delivered to you. But what if you look up every now and then? The future has arrived, you notice, by express delivery. Each year there are bigger and bigger packages. More things. They crowd around your desk. You do not open them; you return to your work. At some point, perhaps, you suspect they are not quite what they seem, and you open one, only to find there is nothing inside.

Mother-in-law turns and calls for her helper. An ad break. I turn to her. 葛兰呢？空中小姐的生活过得怎么样？

It's not easy, she tells me, an air hostess's life. Did I see the last few minutes? When Ge Lan promised she'd come back for her mother's birthday? Not really her mother, of course. An actress whose name she can't remember. In this movie, Ge Lan plays the role of Lin Keping. Keping wants to come back to celebrate with her mother in Hong Kong, but the flight is cancelled. The mother waits by the window, the rain pouring down outside, with her birthday cake untouched. 被 pang pui ki, Mother-in-law tells me. She's switched to Hokkien.

My Mandarin flaps awkwardly, shuffles, and sometimes takes flight. Hokkien's something else, a darkened landscape seen from above, with little islands of light: *mee sua, lay dio, pang sai, jiat png*. Mandarin is abstract, refined, pure thought. Hokkien is tied to the body: the food that goes in, and the fluids that come out. Mandarin has four tones, which I know well. Hokkien, apparently, has seven. Some people say eight. All I can do is listen and then repeat.

妈妈, *Pang pui ki* 用华语怎么讲？

Pang pui ki 就是放飞机.

Pang pui ki, then, is to fly an aeroplane, to stand someone up. To say you'll do something, my mother-in-law elaborates, and then not do it. To say you'll meet someone and not arrive. Quiet, now. The movie is starting again.

Uncle, my hand hurts.

Don't press so hard, Jin Jin.

She hops down from the chair and comes over to my side of the table, under the flickering shadows of the fan.

Who's that?

Who?

The man in the photo on your computer.

He's Mr. Lim. What do you think?

I think he's going on a journey, a very long way.

How do you know that?

There's a plane behind. He's got a suitcase. It looks like it's empty. Maybe his mother gave him it. I don't think he has much money.

And his clothing?

He doesn't look . . . comfortable. Like he's wearing it for the first time. And a long, long time ago. Like my grandparents' wedding photos.

Where is he going?

She shrugs her shoulders, holds up her hands.

Look again.

A hat and a coat. Somewhere far away, very cold. Polar bear land? Will he see the polar bears?

No, he won't see polar bears. A few ageing wolves, perhaps, across a table.

Can we make the paper plane now?

Ten more minutes.

Promise?

Don't worry. I won't 放飞机.

Eh?

Ten more minutes. You can watch the clock.

I assemble the pieces of the story quickly. This first flight in 1956, to that other island in the north, to the negotiations for self-rule, was a good one. Slow, of course, and uncomfortable. He was different from the others who went with him: he found it difficult to share their jokes or their laughter, their ease with English and Englishmen. In the northern island, in that great grey city, in a season that for some unknown reason they called spring, he must have felt alone. But I can leave that out. At all those talks on Singapore's future, he was on the sidelines, waiting. This was his job for now: to listen, to express his opinions, but above all to wait, until history composed itself in his and his country's favour. But history has a way of not keeping appointments. There was a second flight for him, years later. No cameras this time; no photographs in the newspapers. A short transfer from prison, then the journey. In this northern city, there were no service apartments waiting in Westminster, no chauffeurs, no ceremonies of welcome. Only a fruit stall in Bayswater, the patter of rain. It was summer, and someone special to him had accompanied him. Yet he found it difficult to recompose his life. He went for treatment. The psychiatrists were puzzled; after a while, they called on a young houseman from his part of the world, who listened and paraphrased. Later, perhaps, he saw a psychotherapist in training, and his words came back to him, like an echo from a well.

Music again, from the television. Ge Lan has discovered that the darkly handsome, brooding pilot, Lei Daying, so remote and authoritarian in the air, has a soft side. After the flight, he sidles up to her and asks her what she is thinking about.

"A problem that isn't clear to me."

"What problem?"

"A person."

"What person?"

She hesitates, smiles, and walks on, leaving him with a single word.

"You."

Another break. My mother-in-law stirs and looks impatiently up at the clock.

Jin Jin, it's time. We can fold the plane now. No, don't use your homework paper. Take another sheet. That one.

Like this?

Correct. Like that. Fold lengthwise. Make sure you get it right at the beginning. You can't afford to be like Ge Lan's friend in your grandmother's movie: the one who was stuck doing ground service. She said she failed at the first step. That's right. Now press down with your nail, make the fold as clear as you can. Two tri-angles. Like this. Press hard. And then two more. Fold it back, then on each side. Good? It doesn't look like a plane now? Like egg prata? Wait. Pull here. Do you see it now? Not like the planes in the photo or the movie. Thinner, sleeker. Like SAF fighters before National Day, the ones you hear first and only then look up.

You want to try it now, in the alleyway? You don't want to watch the movie? Your grandmother says this is the best part. Singapore in 1959. The prison doors for Mr. Lim and his companions are about to open, but we do not see this. The plane passes over the Cathay Building and lands at Paya Lebar. Lin Keping and Lei Daying go sightseeing. There's Raffles on his statue, brooding over the Padang. The Sultan Mosque at Arab Street, Nanyang University, the central building just completed, the earth still raw, and the gardens bare of trees. The aquarium by Fort Canning. Finally, the Esplanade. They look out onto the great harbour, full of the world's ships. This is a lost city that neither of us has ever known. Only your grandmother knows.

You really want to go? You don't want to wait for Ge Lan to sing "Oh Calypso"? Let's go, then, before it's dark, before your mother comes. Put on the outside light. Wear your shoes. There's no wind now; I don't think the rain will come. Unlock the gate. Wait now, let's ask your grandmother one more thing.

I can remember the sounds of the Hokkien phrase she told me but not the tonal pattern.

妈妈，放飞机用福建话怎么讲？ In Hokkien, how do you say "fly an aeroplane"?

Pang pui ki.

The sky is still light, as blank as the future. The lane is still empty.

Come, Jin Jin, let's fly the plane. Before dinner, before your mother comes. Pang pui ki. These moments are golden, aren't they, when someone doesn't arrive on time? We have to take them when we can. They are places where stories can begin, where even words can take flight.

Heaven Has Eyes

Zi Qiang felt little surprise when the news headlines announced the election date. The ground had been prepared for months. At Chinese New Year, citizens had been showered with what was described as a prosperity package; as always, small but significant sums were added to their state retirement and medical accounts. This time, in a further gesture, each of them had been given national shares, tiny virtual financial stakes in the country with an interest rate that, they were promised, would shadow GDP growth. A week later, the annual upward revision of public transport fares was postponed indefinitely. And at Zi Qiang's housing estate, a long-delayed covered walkway to the Mass Rapid Transit station materialised almost overnight, gleaming in steel and glass.

He turned the page of his newspaper, weighing one corner down with his cup so that the wind from the fan wouldn't blow it away. Early morning in the coffee shop: the tables had just been wiped, and thin, persistent arcs of water lingered on the surface, to which newsprint stuck obstinately. He peeled the paper away. On the second page was a map of the constituencies. Almost the entire lozenge-shaped island was coloured in the white of the ruling party, with two lonely opposition wards near its centre peeping out like twin eyes, one red and one gold. On the facing page was a calendar of dates, neatly colour-coded. One week to nomination day, when the candidates had to declare themselves, then nine days—the minimum legislated campaigning period—before election day at the beginning of the following month.

"Always like that," said Adelyn when he mentioned it that evening. "What do you expect? And it's only a couple of weeks since they changed the electoral boundaries. They want to catch the opposition off guard."

She shuffled in fat slippers to the window. Evening closed in quickly on the housing estate, and lights were coming on in the living rooms of the opposite blocks of flats. Although they were on the sixteenth floor, noise travelled upwards from the playground below: the high voices of children crying out to each other, the thud of the ball from the adjoining basketball court, a second's silence, followed by cheers as—he guessed—the ball landed in a basket.

"What's the time?"

"Almost seven-thirty."

She smiled. "Shall we?"

"*Heaven Has Eyes*? Do you really want to?"

He reached for the TV remote. The green light below the screen winked back at them as they settled onto the couch.

Heaven Has Eyes was the longest-running drama serial on television. Channel 8, of course; the Chinese channel productions, although derivative, were much better than the gauche English-language imitations on Channel 5. The programme was filmed locally but with a significant leavening of imported foreign talent from the region. It had been running for several seasons, long enough for most viewers to forget how it had all started. Zi Qiang had read that the show's producers employed a panel of consultants from the university to ensure that any new episode by a young screenwriter unfamiliar with the past did not wander too far off the rails of history. The plot revolved around a family of three generations living under one roof and running a business founded by the patriarch when he'd negotiated a buyout at a substantial discount from previous owners, who had retreated in the face of an uncertain political situation. The old man was both charming and ruthless; through a series of mergers, acquisitions, and a total elimination of the competition, he guided the family concern to ever greater heights. The genius of the series was that you could never fully like or dislike him. You wanted to be him, to identify what he stood for, yet you had the nagging suspicion that something was missing in the relentless pursuit of progress he had bequeathed to his descendants. In the last few seasons, he'd receded from view. Zi Qiang pictured him as a fat spider, motionless and invisible at the centre of a huge web of his own devising. But Adelyn said no, he was more like one of those bugs in those re-runs of *Star Trek*, the kind you ingested that then took up residence around your spinal column, embracing it so intimately that you were unaware of their presence. Much more effective if you worked through that kind of love.

The family, indeed, seemed uncertain how they might inhabit the house the old man had built for them. At first, they moved through the rooms like some strange, transparent species, exploring the confines of a cave in which they had long been sealed off from the outside world. The eldest son, Yee Siong, was groomed for succession but succumbed to the inevitable cancer that always made its entrance at a strategic point in such dramas. Family conflicts shifted from the house to his hospital room. Tears, laughter, curses, and apologies volleyed over the bed where he lay silent, past the screens that registered every murmur of his body, over cannulas nestled into his flesh so closely no one could figure out where machine ended and body began.

After Yee Siong returned home as an invalid, a mild-mannered uncle watched over the company as a caretaker CEO. When the heir recovered and finally took the helm, things were more fractious than before. A third generation, less tractable than the last, ventured beyond the high gates at the end of the drive and brought back found objects, dirt, and misshapen play-mates from the world outside. As teenagers, some turned their attention to the house and its garden. They found a forgotten cellar full of damp stacks of newspapers, photographs smudged with fungus, and, in a drier area, the desiccated carcass of some unidentified cat. In the corner of the garden a grand-nephew discovered—and partially unearthed, until he was prevented from continuing—a solitary grave, its headstone curved like a tortoise shell, the characters worn indecipherable with age. When they were young adults, this generation ventured further afield and returned or simply passed through the house with things: lacquered laptops left casually on tables or counters, plasma screens bigger and brighter than the windows, airtight wall-to-wall closets of clothes that sighed when prised open.

Heaven Has Eyes always held its audience's interest by building up to a miniature crisis at the end of every episode; there would always be some new secret yet to unfold or a discovery whose terrible consequences might yet be avoided by prompt action. Viewers would be left with an image of a couple in a passionate embrace, shot through a furtive telephoto lens, or a character's frozen face crumpling in response to an unexpected discovery. If the crisis was solved in the next episode, another one would arise. The title of the series promised a final judgment, but it was a judgement infinitely deferred.

"It's starting," Adelyn said.

They settled further into the sofa, a wall of cushions between them.

The first scene was in the family home. A young Indian woman, smartly dressed, nervously sipped tea and made small talk with Yee Siong and his wife.

"Who's that?"

"Shakuntala," Adelyn said. "You know, David's new girlfriend. David is Yee Siong's nephew. The one you said was gay."

"Look at the wife. What's she wearing? Some sort of pyjama suit? Doesn't she have any dress sense?"

"She's not so bad. Quiet. I want to listen to what they're saying."

The days to nomination day passed quickly. The university wasn't in session, and Zi Qiang worked mostly from home, trawling the internet and online databases for next semester's readings for his students, building a website for his next course brick by virtual brick. After breakfast, he'd retreat to the third bedroom they used as an office, the taste of coffee still lingering in his mouth, and turn up the air-con until the cold was almost unbearable in order to concentrate. He'd emerge for lunch, rubbing warmth back into his joints. He'd pass his neighbours' padlocked grille gates in the corridor and enter the empty lift that chanted out the descending floors in a crisp British voice, like a nagging schoolmistress. The estate would be clean and bare in the morning sunlight, the province of the very young and the very old. Retirees sat companionably in the shade of the void decks; old men in singlets and polyester shirts clustered over newspapers and cigarettes in the coffee shop where he bought a packet of bee hoon for lunch. On the way back, he returned by the same path, the brown paper wrapper comfortingly hot in his hand.

After lunch, it was difficult to concentrate. If he wasn't careful, his fingers on the mouse took him elsewhere, checking news websites for updates on the elections. Although he didn't expect to find anything new, there was something compulsive in his actions, as though time might slow down and finally become solid if he returned to the sites often enough. The governing party's candidates had been introduced in batches over the past week, four or five at a time. They were always amiable, well-groomed, well-dressed, and well-fed: they had studied and played hard at school, been sent abroad on scholarships, and returned to take up challenging positions in the public or private sectors. Most eagerly displayed how happily married they were, with designer spouses and beaming children who seemed to have wandered off the set for powdered milk advertisements; all had long résumés packed with voluntary work. Reporters dug deep to find something unusual: one of them was a marathon runner, while another could play the saxophone. But it was difficult to find anything interesting to say. They stood as obediently as trained seals at press conferences, picking the questions that were gently lobbed their way through the air like fish.

Occasionally, a young reporter or a recalcitrant member of the public came up with something unanticipated, then the candidates' heads would anxiously turn towards the senior Member of Parliament who stood next to them, who would stare back pointedly as if to say, *Get on with it.* The boldest of them might venture a direct reply, thanking the questioner for a very interesting comment, something that of course would be given due consideration when they were elected. Of course, balance was needed, no decision should be rushed. Then the others would smile in unison, showing perfect teeth. One would mention that his experience in the recent Bukit Kechil town council oral hygiene campaign made him able to truly empathise with the problem discussed. Standing there on the stage, dressed in white, they seemed less like politicians than a newly formed sports team, perfectly prepared for an upcoming tournament, planed and honed into splendid inhumanity.

Zi Qiang also liked to browse the opposition candidates' profiles, though not without a certain sadness. The photographs here were less posed: hairs were out of place, a jacket crumpled, or a face slightly out of focus. The résumés were shorter and grittier. At press conferences, they would answer questions straightforwardly, even unguardedly. Reporters for the established press would lay out a trail of questions like a row of chocolates, and a candidate would munch her way through it, taking bigger and bigger bites until all caution was left behind. Then the reporter would spring the trap that he had prepared. "So," he'd say sweetly, "you're saying that our country is a Third World Country?" Or "Let me get this straight: you are alleging that the minister is corrupt and incompetent?" The ruling party would threaten a defamation suit, and the candidate would issue a carefully worded apology and perhaps disappear from view for a few days.

As campaigning began, the newspapers and television highlighted the eccentricities of opposition candidates: the one who campaigned in a torn singlet, shorts, and slippers, or the man who seemed more interested in promoting his taxi company than running for office. For those who seemed less eccentric, questions of "character" were asked. Why had Candidate X underpaid his income tax by $15 ten years ago? Could such a person govern the country? Or why had Candidate Y attended the premiere of the movie *Spider Lilies*, which featured a lesbian love affair? Was she part of an LGBT conspiracy to take over the government? The last few days of campaigning reminded Zi Qiang of the dying seconds of the video games his nephews coerced him into playing at Chinese New Year; like his chosen avatar, the opposition candidates stood backed into corners, fending off projectiles hurled at them with increasing speed from all directions.

In the late afternoon, he went to buy dinner: economy rice from the eating house opposite his block. If you went early, you could get the food at its freshest before it was selected by the waves of commuters returning home or dried up under the lights. He ordered two packets of rice, then pointed out the dishes they wanted. For Adelyn, bitter gourd with black beans, salted fish with bean sprouts, steamed egg so soft it could be sliced with a spoon; for himself, steamed fish, white in the dark sauce dotted with red chillies, buttery pumpkin, green-black sweet potato leaves. The young men serving him liked to joke with customers. He remembered that Adelyn was particularly good with them. She'd ask what was best to eat. They'd say the fish, very good-looking, and she'd reply, "Not as good-looking as you," and they'd look at her in surprise, at a thirty-something woman with a wedding ring, and relish a harmless flirtation.

Now Zi Qiang asked, "Busy or not?"

The young man grimaced.

"We're like animals in a zoo," said his friend. The counter was, indeed, like one of those modern enclosures you saw at the Night Safari; they were separated from him not by bars but by a chest-high glass wall and a moat of food in which flat dishes of each item floated upwards, as round as water lily leaves. The two of them put down their spoons and mimed a struggle against imaginary bars.

"You're from Malaysia," Zi Qiang said. "How do you find it here?"

"The money's good," said the first young man. "But . . ."

"You can tell me. I won't be offended."

The young man paused while his friend served another customer. "Did you see the news about the orangutan in Australia? The one that escaped."

"Yes, I did. He went back to the cage after half an hour. I guess he didn't like it too much outside. The cage was too comfortable."

"It's like that here. Don't think I'm trying to offend you."

He passed Zi Qiang the two Styrofoam boxes stacked in a thin pink plastic bag; they rubbed together and squeaked as he walked home. He thought Adelyn would be working late, but around seven o'clock he heard the rattle of the grille as she swung it aside, the grunt of the key in the front-door lock that he needed to oil.

They held each other.

"You're early," he said.

"I wanted to catch the show," she replied, shedding bags, jewellery, and jacket on the way to the bedroom. In the ten minutes before *Heaven Has*

Eyes began, she washed her hair and reappeared in her sloppy T-shirt and oversized slippers. She sat down next to him, the food before them, as the theme song was playing.

"It's like an addiction."

"What to do?"

In the opening scene, Yee Siong's daughter Ting Ting was with her new boyfriend at a restaurant. She was as perfect as ever, skin luminous, ears studded with two tiny pearls like stars, baby-pink sweater thrown over her shoulders against the cold. She skimmed the menu, making suggestions. Her companion was less at ease, eyes edging past the tables to the open door. The camera moved closer. He was honest, fresh-faced, but not quite comfortable in his immaculately pressed shirt or the expensive watch that circled his wrist. Ting Ting's mother arrived. Small and her suit made her seem smaller, but you couldn't deny her presence; as she bustled between the tables, one or two diners nodded to her deferentially. Ting Ting stood to greet her. *Mother, this is someone I've been wanting you to meet for so long. Jing Wei, my mother.*

Conversation was formal but not overly frosty, and she insisted on ordering for the young man. Then, her questions: Where did he work? Where did his parents live? Where had he studied? Of course, she insisted, it was admirable that he'd gone so far with such—she paused and plucked a word out of the air—disadvantages. He'd done so well to win the government scholarship, to go to . . . Where was it? Oh yes, Berkeley. A public university, wasn't it? But there were more things to life than studying, weren't there? She cut a small piece of fish with her knife, pierced it with her fork, and conveyed it slowly to full, wine-red lips.

"Seems to be going well," Zi Qiang said. "I think she likes him."

Adelyn reached up to pull back her hair. "She's got her knife ready. She'll fillet him."

The mother ordered wine with the main course, and Jing Wei grew more voluble, waving his arms excitedly. His aspirations now seemed slightly vulgar and superficial; traces of long-forgotten "disadvantages" of speech returned. A sliver of arugula from the salad the mother had insisted on ordering for him had stuck to his cheek; it wobbled as he talked but did not fall. Ting Ting gestured to him impatiently, rubbing her cheek, but he failed to notice.

After dinner, Ting Ting vanished behind the smoked glass partition of the restroom.

"It's so good to get to know you," the young man said when she was out of sight. "You know, I was afraid you wouldn't approve of me."

The mother reached out and gripped his elbow, her face hardening.

"We've invested a lot in Ting Ting," she said. "It's important she doesn't make mistakes now that will ruin her future."

He looked at her in silence.

"How much do you want?"

"Mrs Tan," he protested. "This isn't to do with money. I love Ting Ting. What we feel is real."

She released her hold and looked out over the restaurant terrace to the river. His eyes followed hers across the reflections flickering on the sun-dappled water, the bumboats full of tourists scuttling backwards and forwards.

"Nonsense," she said as the music swelled and the camera returned to her face, immobile as a mask. "Everyone has his price."

About a week later, Zi Qiang received his polling card in the mail. The design had not changed in years: a simple black-and-white piece of paper with a government crest and his personal details printed in a simulated typewriter font. It seemed out of place on the table among the glossy, brightly-coloured flyers advertising tuition services or real estate, like the fossil of some magnificent long-extinct species, a snake with vestigial limbs or a ponderous, flightless bird.

Only the address of the polling station was unfamiliar, and he checked the election website. His block and its neighbours, he noted, had been moved to a new constituency, named after a coastal residential district some miles away and now linked to it by a thin loop of territory. He traced the constituency on the screen with his finger as it curved inland, his hand rising and falling in a gentle wave.

The accompanying brochure was more difficult to locate; he'd put it aside and could not find it again. After some searching, he found it in the wastepaper basket, where he'd thrown it together with a glossy booklet advertising Citifarm, the new preschool chain. The mistake was understandable; both brochures were printed in bright primary colours, with similar logos and cartoon strips that curved from page to page.

He began reading. Democracy was not simple, the booklet told him. It needed fine-tuning, like a car, to keep running smoothly. In life there were big people and little people, successful and unsuccessful ones. The electoral system had evolved to reflect this reality. Thus there were big constituencies which could elect several members from one party who stood on a common slate and small constituencies for one member only. A unique solution for a unique country with a unique history. When Members of Parliament were elected, they came in several flavours. First Class MPs, represented by a purple gummy-bear like figure, were elected through the old and now admittedly rather antiquated process. Second Class MPs, coloured yellow, were a new innovation, made up of the ten best losers. Third Class MPs were coloured bottle green; they would be chosen by a parliamentary committee from a group of concerned citizens who had put their names forward. In a final diagram, they were clustered together in segments of a circle, like festive treats laid out at Chinese New Year; he idly wondered which would taste best.

In the evening, he and Adelyn went to his parents' house for dinner, their weekly routine, although tonight the two of them were going to an opposition rally afterwards. His parents lived in the house where he'd grown up. In recent years, it had seemed as if the earth itself was trying to shake the old couple off. The road outside had been dug up for the new Mass Rapid Transit line and then again for a new highway; the old line of houses vanished behind steel hoardings while traffic snaked this way and that, clattering over a roadbed of metal plates. When things eventually returned to order, the house seemed much smaller, crouched near the up-ramp of a new flyover of asphalt, concrete, and steel.

Entering the house was like working your way into a fortress. First, the heavy wrought-iron gate with its paint-gummed padlocked hasp that you had to nudge open from the outside. Then, the yellow herringbone tiles of the car porch, slippery with fallen leaves and flowers after rain, and the swollen wooden door, always jammed half open, its frosted glass panels lit up like jewels from inside. Finally, the heavy security grille that creaked as you pulled it aside. Sometimes, this would cause his father, sitting in a chair in the living room, eyes glued to the new LCD television, to turn to his visitors with an expression of surprise that quickly melted into recognition. At other times, he would not notice, and, if they were feeling playful, they'd creep up beside him and stand still. Wait a moment, and he'd look up in a slow smile of exaggerated astonishment, belatedly acknowledging their presence.

His mother would come in from the kitchen to greet them. Recently she had taken to embracing him when they met. As his arms encircled her body, he could feel her thinness, skin and bones like the tortured, dusty Christ that hung on the crucifix above the sideboard. At these moments, he felt as if she were trying to pull him down, far back, into a secret, private place from which he had struggled to escape.

Adelyn chattered brightly as she helped bring out the dinner; for her, the house had nothing to hide, no burden of memories. For Zi Qiang, it wasn't so easy. Rub hard on any surface or chip off the new gloss paint on the window frames, and you'd descend layer on layer into the past. Behind the glass doors of the cabinets by the stairwell, he knew, were family albums, arranged neatly year by year. As you moved further back in time, he grew smaller and the colours of the photographs less distinct; finally there were only the monochrome pictures of his parents' wedding, his father sparkling in a cream suit, his mother's stomach rounded into a hint of a curve. Upstairs, crammed into the sagging bookcases in half-forgotten bedrooms were his schoolbooks, yellowed and shrunken, a prayer book, foxed with brown spots, and sheets of Chinese writing paper, gridded with pale blue lines, in which he'd written long-forgotten characters in a neat, obedient hand. Once, he lay down on the bed he used to sleep in every night, looking out the open window at the long branches of the rain tree, its leaves as small as fish scales. He could hear his parents whispering somewhere in the house, but he could not understand what they were saying. At that moment, he felt unmoored, floating and not sure whether he was rising or falling.

They gathered round the table in the living room for chicken curry swamped in yellow gravy, sweet potato leaves, gailan fried with translucent half-moons of garlic, and steamed pomfret so tender it smelled of apples. Adelyn served his mother first, selecting the choicest pieces, peeling the white flesh of the fish from bone as easily as if she were opening an orange. Conscience-stricken, he took the pomfret cheek and placed it carefully on his father's plate.

The television flickered and muttered; his mother had turned it down. The news with its bold subtitles: another policy announcement and preparations for election rallies throughout the island that evening. The size of the opposition meetings had been unprecedented, and, with changes in technology, this could not be hidden. Bloggers, exploiting a grey area in the restrictions on political coverage, had posted pictures of huge crowds. A few days later the print and television media had reluctantly followed suit, no longer cropping out the huge crowds from their coverage of opposition candidates. Tonight there were images from a rally by the ruling party: the journalist at the scene, hair blown about by the wind, opened lips so wide he seemed in danger of swallowing his microphone. Even strategic camera shots could not disguise the thinness of the crowd; a few hundred at most, Zi Qiang guessed, clumped awkwardly under umbrellas in the pouring rain.

He caught his father's eye. "Would you like to come to the opposition rally, Ba? Adelyn and I are going later."

A half-smile. "You are?"

"Look at the sizes of the rallies. Do you think things are different this time?"

His father shook his head. "Always like this. Everyone likes to watch a good show. But see how they vote."

The news anchor was crisp in her white jacket. Then advertisements for shampoo or skin-whitening cream, in which ethereal pan-Asian women emerged from water like dolphins. Zi Qiang was turning back to the table, feeling his way back into conversation with Adelyn and his mother, when the familiar theme tune started up faintly. Over the next few minutes they fell away from the conversation one by one, eyes glued to the television set. Finally, his mother reached for the remote and turned up the volume.

"Don't know why we watch this programme," his father said. "Useless people. Waste of time."

"Maybe we love to hate them," Adelyn said.

They grunted, their eyes already on the screen.

They hadn't, Zi Qiang reflected, missed too much of the serial in the last week; most of the action seemed to have been devoted to a sinuous sub-plot that had now reached temporary resolution. Ting Ting's young boyfriend had marked time, showing remarkable resilience. Her mother had, after her stratagems failed, finally called on Yee Siong to intervene, but he'd been uncertain how to approach his daughter. Finally it was decided: the patriarch, the old man, would give her a talking-to. He cornered her one Saturday morning; they drank tea, and he expressed concern. How was she adjusting to being back in the country after studying abroad at that top liberal arts college? At first, she sat stiffly on the sofa, pulling a powder-blue cardigan around her, pearl buttons catching the light. He drew her out by talking of his own college days in England over half a century ago. She talked about how difficult it was to come back. How much smaller everything seemed—even the buildings, which had seemed so tall to her before she left, now seemed shrunken, like toys or models. This was her home, she was sure, but she no longer knew how to inhabit it.

On the sideboard behind them, the family photographs stood to attention. He moved on the offensive. It was easy in this modern world to forget who you were or your duties to your father and your mother, to your society. The first drops of rain gathered on the window outside. He sketched out the path the family had mapped out for her. She needed to have courage now to walk forward, upwards, not to look around too much, not to be distracted by alternatives that seemed easier for now.

Here she sighed and ran her fingers through a waterfall of dark hair. She seemed on the point of saying something, then thought better of it.

He knew what she was thinking, he said. He knew the word that had been forming on her lips. *Love.* She was young. It was natural for young people to feel this; as a young person, he too had been attracted to things that were new. But it was best to be with your own kind. Best not to be governed by emotion. She shook her head almost imperceptibly, and he smiled, his face pale in the gathering darkness of the house. He wasn't saying that emotion wasn't important, or ideals. But these were things to be guarded, to be locked away and treasured. Somewhere very secure, very safe. She needed to go on living in the world. She needed to give the young man up.

While he talked, she sipped her tea, eyes downcast. Outside the rain was stronger, curtaining the garden.

The camera cut to her face, showing what the father did not see; in the corner of one eye, a teardrop swelled, then broke and fell, trickling down the flawless cream arc of a cheek. She took a tissue and wiped it away.

"You're right," she said.

"You'll give him up? You'll tell your mother?"

She nodded, struggling to hold back the tears. "You'll have to excuse me. I need to go out soon."

She fled upstairs to her room, locked the door, flung herself on the bed, weeping, pulling the covers to her. But only for a minute. Something had crashed to the floor. She searched for it and held it up: the photograph of Jing Wei she kept by her bedside, covered with a spider's web of cracks. Music swelled in the background. She reached into her bag and drew out a tiny red handphone that perched on her hand like a brilliant wingless insect. She paused for a moment in thought, then sent a text, her fingers a blur of motion on the keypad. The music faded; she changed, pulling off the cardigan and designer T-shirt to reveal a tattoo that licked the top of her shoulder. Later that evening, Ting Ting met Jing Wei for dinner in a restaurant by the river. She told him what had happened; they embraced and swore they would never give each other up. Then the camera moved back so that they were framed by other diners at tables on the wharf, the stone embankment, and the black water beneath. The scene softened, and a face swam into focus in close up on the bridge across the river. Her uncle. Watching.

During the commercial break, his mother brought them translucent fingers of fragrant pear, wedges of dragon fruit that tasted very faintly of lemon, and slices of overripe mango that slid off the tiny, two-pronged forks they were using.

Zi Qiang looked at Adelyn. "Ting Ting's in trouble now."

She smiled and slowly shook her head.

She was right again. Yee Siong met the young man for high tea in a discreet corner of a huge tourist hotel. As the older man waited, the camera picked out Jing Wei walking cautiously across the marble floor, the thirty dizzy storeys of atrium opening up above him. His body was hunched in defiance; when he entered the lounge, he stumbled on the thick pile of the carpet. Yee Siong was all charm. He rose to shake Jing Wei's hand and indicated a plush chair next to his own. They made small talk as the crisply dressed waiter took their orders. The young man perched warily on the edge of his seat. Yee Siong kept the conversation bubbling along, with none of the underlying malice his wife had shown. The food came: open sandwiches and small scones with condiments arranged on a pyramid of silver platters. They ate and sipped tea, and the young man grew impatient.

"Mr Tan," he said finally. "I'm really grateful for you meeting me like this. But I'm sure you didn't invite me just to talk like this over tea."

Yee Siong held his gaze for a few seconds and smiled. Jing Wei was right, of course. And courageous and tactful to raise this point without seeming rude. He had to confess that the Tan family had been concerned when they'd heard Ting Ting was dating someone of whom they knew nothing; the young man should understand that they were concerned about their eldest daughter and about the family's future. Possibly that might make them overreact. So they'd run some background checks. They'd been impressed with Jing Wei's record. Yee Siong and his wife were modern people; it would be wrong for them to stand in the way of Ting Ting and her choice of a partner. They thought they might offer Jing Wei a position in the family business. Something modest at first, but with good prospects if things went well, both personally and professionally.

Tea slopped into Jing Wei's saucer. Yee Siong touched him affectionately on the arm. "You don't have to give me an answer now. Think about it, and let me know."

He passed Jing Wei a business card. Just at that moment, his mobile phone rang. He answered and barked an order. "I'm afraid I have to go. Urgent business. But make yourself at home here."

He spread his hands wide, as if to embrace the plush carpet, the tables inlaid with mother-of-pearl, the solitary, silent, grand piano, and the soaring emptiness of the hotel interior. The young man leaned forward and reached for his wallet, but Yee Siong waved him away. "It's already taken care of."

The camera drew back as the music gathered again; the young man sat with his head in his hands, marooned in the vast lobby, his lonely chair woven into the gorgeous expanse of carpet as the credits began to roll.

Adelyn nudged him, pointing to the clock on the wall. "We need to get going. The rally's starting soon."

"Ba?" Zi Qiang asked. "Do you want to come?"

The old man shook his head, reaching for the last slice of pear.

The MRT station was cold, gleaming steel and polished granite. Before they took the escalator upwards, Adelyn stopped and reached for his hand.

"Something wrong?" he asked.

"Feels funny. Just one minute."

Their fingers sought each other like small, frightened animals. Then he felt it too; a sense that the floor and walls, even the escalator railings, were no longer quite solid. A tremor, perhaps, deep underground, then everything was still again. Knots of people passed them and ascended, not the smooth flow of rush hour but a slow, persistent trickle against gravity, falling upwards into the heat of the night. Outside, they were surprised to find darkness had already fallen, the last pink of the sun still showing through a scratch in the clouds. They walked towards the stage that rose in the distance, looking for all the world like a boat waiting to be lifted by a rising sea—like one of those pictures of the ark in children's storybooks, slowly filled up by a patient line of paired animals. There was something similarly elemental here; the crowd flooded inwards, like insects sucked upwards to a light. They flowed around a green metal railing, then a line of carts selling cooked food or water, trimmed with yellow bulbs like squid boats staking out a line in the darkness. The coarse grass of the field itself was softened by the rain. He stumbled, and Adelyn passed him a torch from her bag. His sandals and feet were slicked over with thin brown mud.

Nearer the stage, the crowd thickened, and they came to a standstill. Above them, dull orange clouds reflected light from the street lamps; on each side, the empty, echoing faces of housing blocks. He peered over the shoulders of the man in front of him towards the fluorescent lights and banners on the stage. A rustling in the crowd. Someone was shouting on a megaphone, *Sit down.* The wall of bodies in front of them folded like a curtain; he reached into his backpack for the beach mat and unrolled it. The people standing behind them did not sit. Later, when they looked at pictures of the rally in the newspapers, Adelyn would say they must have been just there—in the last seated row, that bay, lit up by light from the stage, just before the cliff of standing figures that stretched far off into the darkness.

The time the rally was due to start came and went. Zi Qiang found himself in conversation with an older man on his right, a retired schoolteacher, his hair thin, his face etched with shadows. He'd been to many opposition rallies over the years, he said, but this one seemed different. Not simply bigger. The feeling wasn't the same. How so? Difficult to say exactly. He shrugged and sipped water from a bottle.

Time crawled. Someone nudged Zi Qiang's toe, softly stroking the skin on the top of his foot between the sandal straps. He looked down in surprise. A frog, its body no bigger than his thumb. He placed it on his palm and cupped his other hand over it, not quite sure whether he was protecting or capturing the animal. He could feel it settle there, the skin of the throat fluttering against his skin in either breath or heartbeat. Then the music started, and the lights came on. He placed it carefully on the mat by his feet.

The speeches began. First, an older man, in awkward English, then switching to passionate Tamil; the crowd roared approval, though few understood what he was saying. They looked around for an Indian face. *He's saying we're not children,* a voice told them from the darkness behind, *saying there's more to life than family and food.* A second speaker, a younger woman, nervous, her Mandarin fired out like bullets from a machine gun. *My country is not a business,* Zi Qiang translated for the retired schoolteacher. *I won't be bought.* He looked down. The frog had hopped away. Then the third speaker, taller, more remote. Adelyn nudged him. "The chairwoman." He'd seen her on television, but she seemed different here, less self-assured. She spoke first in fractured, bookish Mandarin before switching to English.

"Like she's a nun come down from Emei Shan," Adelyn said.

She talked about stories, how often we believed in them, how we think they will never end. But stories were made by people; they had the power to end one chapter, however well told it had been, and begin another. The crowd warmed to her as the speech progressed, and she stepped down from the podium to thunderous applause.

At last, the Secretary-General came forward, a stocky man garlanded in purple flowers. As he stepped up to the microphone, a thin rain began to fall, just enough to cool the crowd before it passed over. He waited for a moment, as if puzzled, then spread out his arms, looking skywards. "Ti wu mak."

"What did he say?" Adelyn asked.

Zi Qiang shrugged. "It's Teochew. I don't understand."

The old schoolteacher turned to them. "Heaven," he said. "Heaven has eyes."

Penguins on the Perimeter

Spheniscus Orientalis, the Asiatic Penguin. Order: Sphenisciformes. Family: Spheniscidae. A small bird with white plumage that inhabits water margins. Historically endemic to much of Southeast Asia. Hunted almost to extinction in the colonial period; now apparently returning to much of its former range. The only member of its order with the capacity for flight.

1987

He used to see them as a child, the old man tells him, at Tanjong Rhu when the light was fading. A flock of birds like a long low cloud, each standing upright, lining the beach right up to the edge of the water, as if they were taking part in a ritual. Waiting, clad in white, to slip into water that had become briefly molten, as brilliant as a mirror. Sunset would smudge them golden. A shiver would go through the crowd. It would crumble at the edges and begin to peel. The birds would take flight, wheeling east to roost. They would pass over his boat, and the sky would darken further, under the whir and hiss of stubby wings.

David aka Da Wei, twelve, squatting next to his grandfather on his weekly visit, knows that's not possible.

"Gong Gong, what kind of birds?" He stumbles in his textbook Mandarin.

The reply is incomprehensible. A word in dialect that David can't reduce to Hanyu Pinyin to look up in his dictionary.

"Gong Gong, can you write it down?"

The old man takes up pen and paper eagerly but pauses, his forehead bunched up in thought. He begins, then stops. David watches. 鸟字旁: the radical for bird. And then? The old man can't seem to work it out. He rehearses the stroke, groping with his pen in empty air. He begins again. 鱼字旁. Perhaps a fish? He pauses once more.

"David!"

His mother is calling from the kitchen. It's his cue to set the table and help bring out the dishes his mother and Ani have cooked. He stands up, flexing calves that have gone to sleep. His body's changing, with a new heavy strength that can easily tip over into clumsiness. His grandfather puts the paper down, and the moment passes, submerged in the depths of Ani's chicken soup, hidden in the rice bowl, forgotten beneath the tangles of sambal kangkong and the flat red-scaled body of the steamed fish whose white flesh he loves yet whose name he also does not know.

During the next week, David can't let the idea of the birds go. He thinks of Tanjong Rhu the last time he saw it. From the Sheares Bridge, with its battered shipyards, its jetties crumbling into the river among the green of trees. He remembers a sky darkened by thunder, not by birds.

The following Saturday, he makes one addition to the comics he borrows from the library at Stamford Road. He wanders into an unfamiliar section of the building, searching for a call number he has noted down on a scrap of paper. Less crowded than the fiction shelves, this area is cool and quiet, like a church. He finds the book easily enough: *Birds of Malaysia and Singapore: A Field Guide.* He thumbs through the plates, looking for the species his grandfather described, marking up the most likely candidates with carefully placed Post-it notes.

He wants to linger here. His life is filling up with noise. In his new school there are only boys, with hard fists and harder tongues. "Your father," they mock. "Where is he? When did he run away?" Girls from primary school have become suddenly remote, just when he wants their softness in his life. He checks his watch. On his way out, he stops at the children's section and borrows two books for his cousin Shuyun: books about animals with bright pictures and large text. Make sure they're age-appropriate, his mother has said. He likes that phrase; he turns it over on his tongue, whispering it to himself on the bus to his grandfather's flat. He finds a place to sit at the back, over the rumble and bump of the rear axle. He repeats it like a mantra and forgets where he is, returning to awareness only when the small sliver of a ticket falls from his unclutched hand.

When he arrives, his grandfather is listless. Women's whispers scuttle into the corners of the room. His mother reviews the medication and asks Ani whether the hospital appointments have been made. In the kitchen, the two women check the pill box with its rows of compartments, counting out capsules and tablets in red, white, and pale pink. David retreats into the living room, where his grandfather is adjusting the lens on his camera.

"Gong Gong, can I show you something?"

The old man gives the lens a last twist and looks up. "Da Wei?"

"The birds you talked about at Tanjong Rhu? Can you show me?"

Again his grandfather says that unknown word. But when David thumbs through the pages, pointing out the pictures he has marked, the old man shakes his head repeatedly. Not that one. Bigger than that. White colour, not grey.

"David! The plates!"

He leaves the old man to browse the book. Useless to carry on the conversation. Back from the kitchen, bowls in hand, he sees that his grandfather has given up on *Birds of Malaysia and Singapore* and picked up the books he borrowed for Shuyun. His grandfather is excited, more animated than he has seen him for a long time. He smiles, beckoning his grandson over with his little finger.

In the taxi, returning home from the flat, David tells his mother what happened. Those birds at Tanjong Rhu. Gong Gong insists they were . . . penguins. Impossible, David had argued, with the help of his dictionary. Penguins were a 南极洲的种类. An Antarctic species, confined to the chill of the southern hemisphere. But the old man grew truculent, brushing away any arguments to the contrary.

His mother laughs. "So that's what they teach you in school?" Then, perhaps thinking she's dismissed him too readily, she asks him how school is going.

He shrugs. It's okay. When they leave him alone. When they don't mention Father.

The taxi is cold. When they turn into the road leading to their home, he slithers across the plastic of the back seat, squeezing his mother against the door. It's dark outside. He can see traffic cones and bollards next to a hole in the road; behind it, the wooden Malay house that persists on its bare plot. Then he notices that his mother is crying. He will never forget this.

"Ma," he says. "I was right, about the penguins."

Look, she tells him. At the roadworks. The longkang, with an elephant's trunk of a hose stretching downwards. If you go deep enough, what do you get? Sai. That is a dialect word he knows. Shit, it means. That is what you find if you spend too much time digging into the past.

2001

David, now studying abroad, returns on a holiday visit to Singapore. At Changi Airport, walking out of the air conditioning to the taxi rank, what envelops you, embraces you a little too hard, is something more than the warm, humid air. On Sunday, sleeping in after that long intercontinental flight, he wakes to the sounds of car horns and raised voices in the street outside. The churchgoers are here, his mother tells him when he stumbles downstairs. Parking is so difficult now. After ten minutes, the noise subsides. He sits with her in the front room, drinking barley. Too sweet, he thinks, but there's something in the texture of the drink. He stirs it with the teaspoon, sips and sips again, feeling the grains bump up against his teeth. He's a child once more, playing games with food: do you tilt your head back and let the last barley grains go down in a single, explosive clump, or use the teaspoon, as your mother prefers, to spoon them gently into your mouth?

In the morning light, his mother seems older, more careworn. *You haven't changed,* he tells her. *Not one bit. Not a single grey hair on your head. What's your secret?* She smiles girlishly, gap-toothed. This strong, clean-limbed young man is so charmingly convincing that what he says might just be true. But during this visit, after all the news has been updated, the gossip told, the relatives visited, they find that they have less to talk about than they expected. At times they sit together in silence. Ida, the new helper, bustles in and out. He reads, but his mother simply sits, without distractions. Sometimes she glances at him. He wonders if in these moments she is searching for the son she once knew.

Part of this, of course, is inevitable. Children grow and become themselves, and they leave their parents behind. There's a photo she still keeps of a thunderstorm, when David and the Malay neighbour—what was his name?—from the house opposite carried on playing football, even with the rain pouring down. She came out to tell them to go inside, picked up the ball, and then, laughing, threw it back to them, water streaming through her hair, down her face, her long hair and blouse soaked through. Gong Gong had captured them through his telephoto lens looking into each other's eyes, wet through and absolutely happy. But they grew apart year by year: he entered worlds of his own and closed doors behind him. He still loved her but from a distance.

What he remembers most now is the tension of those Saturday rides back from his grandfather's flat: how they would sit, awkwardly separate, in the back of the taxi. Then the visits had stopped. Instead, a brief efflorescence, in which the lane outside the walk-up flats where his grandfather had lived grew a canopy and bloomed with pale flowers. A flood of relatives and friends, many of whom he had never met. Conversations, some forced and others surprisingly deep, momentarily breaking through the surface of everyday life. Peanut shells and packet drinks to be cleaned up, and the slow procession to the crematorium. Then the door of the flat was shuttered and barred. No more taxi rides. A year later, suddenly an empty space, and finally a new en-bloc development where the walk-up flats had been.

Last year, after his most recent flight home, a final separation between them when he told her he would no longer go to Mass. *I just don't believe in it anymore,* he'd said. When tears began to gather in her eyes, he added, *You know, you can stop believing in God and still be a good person.* He had thought this emotional release might have brought them closer, but it has driven them further apart. She has not spoken about it again.

He notices how she complains to him now. She is a good person, she tells him, but no one returns goodness to her. His father was a selfish man; he left when David was very young. She helps the neighbours, but they never help her. Her friends shop and shop and eat and eat and talk and talk.

She follows and grows tired of listening. She would care for others if they would let her, if they would care for her.

Despite these claims of goodness, he senses a slow hardening of her heart. As early retirees do, she has thrown herself into a round of activities and good works. She tutors for CDAC; she volunteers at the community centre; in the morning, long before he stumbles downstairs, she has already returned from her exercise class. Yet as this part of her life has opened, something about her has closed off. One incident in particular surprises him. She tells him that she would like to go on some of the trips that the community centre organises, but she has no one to go with.

Go with Ida, he says. You get on well together now, after those difficult first few months. What she says next shocks him.

I am not happy. I cannot bear it that she should be happy.

David finds himself clinging to her words, repeating them to himself, as he did with other words as a child. But this is different. It is as if you were out walking in the midday heat and came across something inexplicable: a hole, perhaps, in the centre of the road, cold, infinitely dark and deep. An emptiness in a heart that you thought was full.

A week later, in the afternoon, he walks out to a silent street. The church-goers are long gone. The open drain has been covered over: the street is neat and orderly, its pavements enclosed by concrete kerbs. There are orange signs telling you where you can or cannot park and little parking bays marked with bright white lines. If he listens carefully, he can still hear the sound of water, flowing beneath a metal grid set into the pavement.

Children no longer play in the road. He struggles to remember what it was like for him as a boy. Purposeless activity with friends; riding your bike here or there; improvised football games; scissors paper stone; guppies;

spiders in the long grass by the drain; once, a dragonfly. The street is bare now and seems hotter. Perhaps there used to be trees that have now been cut down, but he cannot remember them, and there are no visible stumps. As he wanders through the neighbourhood, he sees a helper putting out the laundry or washing the car, exchanging quiet glances with the postman; the work crew with hard hats digging up the road; early in the morning, on future strolls, a group of seniors practising tai chi in a small sliver of park. Yet the owners of the houses stay behind locked doors.

After a few days, he realises the Malay house is no longer there. It was wooden, on stilts, brightly painted, with a set of worn stairs at the front, leading up to a door that was always open. The compound surrounding it had been quite bare, perhaps with a tall red sealing wax palm in one corner or fruit trees behind the house. In Malaysia he has seen similar houses with new wire mesh fences, coated in green plastic, so he remembers the house opposite as having such a fence, although he cannot really be sure. It has, like his grandfather's flat, disappeared without leaving a trace behind; he is uncertain which of the new dwellings has superseded it.

His mother points the replacement house out to him, almost directly across the street. By current standards, at least, it is still modest: two storeys, with the rough stucco walls and terracotta tiled roofs that are fashionable at this time. She tells him she has seen its occupants only infrequently. She does not know their names. They have built a wall next to the street, broken only by small peepholes covered with wrought-iron bars that curve outwards. In the week before he flies away again, when he loiters, solitary, on the street, he sometimes catches hints of life through these gaps in the wall: clothes flapping on a drying rack, a potted plant, a plump brown arm, raised, and, once, an eye that looks back at him, winks, and quickly vanishes.

In the week David stays with his mother, something about the house begins to bother him. If he goes near the house in the daytime or in the evening when its inhabitants are not about, he hears something cry out. *Something*, he says to himself because it is not quite human. At times, he hears a low, drawn-out syllable, repeated ten or twenty times, rising in volume, then falling again. If it is a word, it is not quite comprehensible, although he feels it should be. Perhaps it is in a language he does not speak; if so that language is raw and elemental, uncivilised. At other times it is more musical, like a tuba or a French horn, a snatch of the music you hear at a wake that is too short to settle into a melody. As he approaches the wall, the sound dies away, replaced by a scratching and shuffling and the sound of beating wings. It is as if something is aware of him, through the layers of stucco and plaster, waiting.

He mentions this to his mother. She's noticed it too. A bird, she tells him, that they keep in a tiny cage, suspended from the eaves. A parrot, she thinks, or maybe a cockatoo. He should try talking to it, see if it will repeat what he says. One afternoon, he sidles up to an opening in the wall, hearing the rustling, a creak of metal as the cage sways back and forward, out of sight. He starts talking, self-consciously, too fast, introducing himself. A pause. In return, he receives that same old drawn-out syllable, rising in intensity and falling away.

"It's cruel," he tells his mother in the evening. "You should call the SPCA."

She shrugs. The bird is clearly mad, after its long confinement. If the door of the cage opened, would it really fly out? And where would it go? You cannot reason with a bird.

On the night he is to leave, he takes a last walk through the neighbourhood. The sun has just set, and the houses are, for once, full of life. Lights have been switched on in ground-floor rooms; he can smell curry and fried chicken, hear the clatter of chopsticks, a Taiwanese soap opera blaring on television, and, in one bungalow, a piano, played hesitantly. A few of the houses are lit up in silence, odourless, marked only by the quiet hum of an air-con compressor. He turns into the road to their house. Frogs croak and fall silent as he passes. He feels an overwhelming sense that he is being followed. Something behind him steps on the cover over the storm drain, making it clatter and vibrate. He quickens his pace. There is a patter on the concrete, on the tarmac, like falling rain or the imprint of tiny webbed feet. He turns around. Nothing. An empty lane, with only the sound of a bird's voice that cannot possibly be human, rising and falling.

2015

On the cusp of middle age, settled back in Singapore, he returns to the street again. When he comes to visit his mother, he crosses the street to the site of the old Malay house and its dumpy successor. A developer bought up a few adjacent lots and is building a condominium there. David has booked a unit for his family, and the building is now nearly finished. A long steel gate, not yet operational, will roll open at a touch on his handphone. The Bangladeshi workers know him from previous visits, and he enters, shoes crunching on the grains of sand scattered on the granite of the parking bay. The workers, who have been putting finishing touches to the garden, are asleep in the shade of the porch, their bodies in dirty blue overalls, scattered like discarded laundry. One, he notices, has a smile on his face, sleeping as effortlessly as he once slept as a child.

He enters the building doorway to the marble entrance hall, its chandelier still encased in plastic. There are flats upon flats up there, reached by twin lifts. In his new apartment, a room for his mother if she wants it. In her early seventies, she is still spry but easily tired. Best to be prepared. All she has to do is move across the road. Rooms for his two children, cool, safe, full of the things he never had in his childhood. The girl's room, he imagines, will be a parlour for a princess, a bed scattered with pink cushions and plump, stuffed hearts. The boy, a year younger, will choose something more austere: posters of footballers, a gaming laptop. In the lounge, a home theatre with padded seats: this is where the family will gather in the evening or on slow weekends. For the master bedroom, he and his wife have already chosen the furniture: a baroque dressing table, a four-poster bed, and white, billowing curtains for the long, wall-length window that looks out over the city.

The lifts are not yet working, but it should be easy enough to climb the staircase to the apartment. As David steps forward, he's conscious of a tightness in his back at the base of the spine. He pauses to stretch. This is when he becomes aware of a smell. It's very faint: sweat, perhaps, or a touch of mould? Of course the air is trapped here, unable to circulate through the development; things will be very different when the air conditioning is installed. Then he remembers what the foreman said to him in confidence: something about drainage in the basement car park being a problem, how water gathers there after storms. He walks to the door at the top of the car park stairs. When he opens it, the smell is stronger, like an uncovered drain in sunlight. He descends, leaving the door open for light, cupping his hand over his nose, nauseated. Two flights of stairs, and another door to open. The air is rancid, as if something has died in there, far below ground. With his free hand, he fumbles for the switch for the temporary lighting the workers have rigged up. Light floods the parking garage. It is worse than he feared: a ramp slopes into a surface of dark, brackish water. He takes a step downwards, then another, trying to figure out how serious this is, how deeply the garage is flooded. Disgust turns to anger; he should never have trusted the agent, with his proffered cigarettes and easy smile.

A splashing in the water. There's something in here with him. A fish, perhaps, washed in from a storm drain. But it seems to be bigger than that. Out of the corner of his eye, in the darkness he sees a flash of white, a flicker of what might be a fin or even a wing. Then a call, a single repeated syllable from the darkness of one corner, which is answered by voices from other recesses of the room, and a flutter, as if wings are being outstretched. He turns, scrabbles up the stairs, and bolts the door after him.

Make sure you clean it out, he tells the agent on the phone. *Fix the drainage, or there'll be trouble. And bring in pest control.* When he finishes talking, he is sweating. The Bangladeshi workers stir, look at him in puzzlement, then turn their eyes quickly down. He realises he has been shouting. The agent, of course, deserves this. But he still feels ashamed. Where, he wonders, does this sudden anger that floods the body come from? Where does it hide, and what brings it so quickly to the surface these days?

When he returns home, he is calmer. He swims laps in his condominium pool, one after another, and cancels an afternoon meeting. Then a shower, and the steel and glass of the lift, carrying him upwards. Home. The apartment is empty in the early afternoon. He looks out across the basin to the new National Stadium, glistening in the sunlight.

He still feels uneasy here at this moment; time has stopped, snatched out of everyday routine. He walks the long corridor to the master bedroom, slippers on tile, trying the doors of his children's rooms. The girl's is open: the bed neatly made, a notebook computer perched, almost decoratively, on an overly tidy desk. Pictures in heart-shaped frames. In one, the girl blows a kiss to her schoolmate, Nadia, the tomboyish one with the shorter hair, the one she listed as being "married" to on Facebook. Perhaps they should talk to her about whether this is appropriate? He closes the door, pads further down the corridor. The boy's room is locked, and he rattles the handle, feeling the anger rise. What does the boy have to hide?

We are a happy family, he pictures himself telling his son in the evening. *So we should have no secrets from each other. Correct or not?* Life has a rhythm now. On weekdays, work, then tuition for the children. On Sunday, Mass, not at the church of his childhood but a new building, as luxurious as a cinema. He is buoyed by his newly rediscovered faith: his family accompanies him, and the girl sings in the choir. He returns home, refreshed. Yet he has an uneasy sense that something is missing in this apartment that is so full of things. Or perhaps there is something that should not be here: loneliness, persistent, like the echoes of a distant bell. Later in the day, his wife and his children return, one by one, and the house fills up with noise again. He tries to talk to his son about the locked door, but the boy looks at him and turns his eyes down, just as the workers did. David swallows his anger and forces a smile.

At night, he dreams of birds. Not sparrows or mynahs or bulbuls. These are heavy birds with stubby wings and sharp beaks. They crowd around him, shuffling on tiny feet in an elaborate tango. One of them pushes him; he falls, and the birds collapse on him like dominoes. They rub against him, slobbering and slithering, he is drowning in a basement of wet, bloated, fishy bodies. He wrestles himself to the surface, to the bottom of the stairs. But he cannot move: the birds are waiting for him, lined up on the higher treads, looking at him with cruel, hard eyes. Every now and then, one reaches forward and pecks at him experimentally. Strangely, this tickles him more than it hurts, and he has the urge to laugh.

At two o'clock, he wakes, his mouth dry. He exits the bed quietly, pads to the kitchen, and pours himself water. The apartment is flooded with moonlight. In the living room, he looks out over the city, gleaming silver. Then he checks email and social media on his handphone, scrolling down and down, looking for distractions. An hour later, his wife comes in search of him and leads him back to bed.

The birds again. They have escaped from the basement, but they seem to have showered and been blow-dried. They ambush him in the carport, on the flattened boxes left by the Bangladeshi workers. They are huge and fluffy; one lumbers over and presses him against the wall. He is frightened that he might suffocate, but just as the feathers reach his lips, he feels them dissolve into something sweet and dry, like kueh bangkit in the mouth. He bites, involuntarily, and something sticky oozes over his tongue. He sucks and nibbles away, gnawing his way back into memory. And then, finally, snatches a few hours of dreamless sleep.

He wakes again a little after six, tired out but his mind active. It's Sunday, and the apartment will be quiet for hours. He gets up, feeling in the wardrobe for a T-shirt and shorts. A short walk, to see the sunrise.

Outside the condo gates, he moves quickly along the road, flexing his shoulders but unable to shake off a stiffness that tightens around him. As a young man, he never realised how middle age would ambush him, not so much physically but emotionally. Here you are at the prime of your life, a career of solid achievement behind you, loving and being loved. Yet you feel fears that you never felt before. Let's say you are asked to speak in front of a crowd. You used to enjoy this: to build rapport through a few jokes, some easy self-deprecation, and then to inspire. This has always been second nature to you, even though in conversation you are often tongue-tied: speaking is a talent, people say, and one that you have made full use of. But when you get on the stage now to applause, you feel a trace, somewhere, of panic. You push it back, hide it, start to speak. The moment passes. Despite this, five minutes later, you find that a word or a memory overwhelms you with emotion. Your voice breaks, you tear up: you cover your confusion by coughing, taking a sip of water.

How do you respond to this, in speaking but also in life? Mark out those boundaries around yourself and the ones you love. Live inside them. Do not think of the past or of what might lie outside the wall. Seal up the basement: comfort yourself with what you know. You may not be entirely happy, you may not be happy at all, but you will be safe. It does not matter if you hurt yourself. Insecurity is a scab that you pick at, a wound that you always, deliciously, want to keep open.

Something is hiding inside him. There's a memory there, on the tip of his tongue. He turns the corner of the road and walks out onto the embankment by the water, with its railings and slender bridge. Across the Kallang Basin the city is growing lighter, although the sun has not quite risen. What was it his mother said, of Ida, all those years ago?

I am not happy. I cannot bear it that she might be happy.

He shivers. There's a faint breeze, and the light is growing. For a moment, land and water merge. As the sun rises, the sound of wings overhead. A single bird first, then another, then many more. As he looks up, the sky darkens but not with the threat of rain.

Two Among Many

Then Raffles said, 'O Sultan, hear what is enacted by English law. The murderer according to it shall be hung; and if not alive, the corpse is hung, notwithstanding. Such is the custom of the white people.' Then at the same time he ordered the corpse to be brought and put in a buffalo cart, which was thereupon sent round the town of Singapore to the beat of the gong, informing all the European and native gentlemen to look at this man who had drawn blood from his Raja or Governor; and that the law was that he should not live, but in death even he should be hung. When they had sufficiently published thus, then they carried the corpse to Tanjong Maling, at the point of Telok Ayer, where they erected a mast on which they hung it, in an iron basket, and there it remained for ten or fifteen days, till the bones only remained. After this the Sultan asked the body from Mr Raffles, which was granted; not till then was it washed and buried.

—Abdullah bin Abdul Kadir, *Hikayat Abdullah*, 1849

She will not meet him for two years. But when she steps forward, when the alarm sounds under the lintel of the metal detector, when the brisk woman in her crisp blue uniform comes forward with hands extended to pat her down, it's decided. The date remains to be fixed, but it is certain that they will meet.

She has waited in Changi Airport for hours, after the crowded flight from Phnom Penh, bumping through turbulence over the Gulf of Thailand. Her connecting flight delayed, she walked the pastel corridors with their low lighting, taking in the purple orchids, the koi pond bridged by a narrow arch. It's cool here. Quiet. The heat outside must be just like the heat of the cities she's visited before—Hanoi, Ho Chi Minh City, Bangkok—but she's insulated behind glass, like the flickering silver fish in the tank in the waiting lounge. Outside, the planes bake on the concrete, gleaming white, wings sharp as knives.

She's passed through the airport once before to change planes, just as she is doing now. Today's different, though: she's much less certain of herself. More time to think things over. As much as she would like to forget, she cannot quite avoid her purpose here. She's calm, but it's a willed calm, carefully maintained, like the pruned beauty of the palms in the light well. This submerged nervousness leads her to seek familiarity. She finds a Starbucks, marooned like an island in a vast expanse of purple carpet. She orders a latte; they take American dollars and return change in an unfamiliar currency. When she sits down, she sorts the coins idly with her spare hand. Different colours, different sizes, all mirroring each other: on one side, a crest; on the other, flowers.

His housing estate has corridors too, lined by planter boxes of purple bougainvillea and trim palms, maintained by an invisible army of workers who vanish each morning. It's in the north of the island, connected to its fellows, to the city centre, and to the airport by the arteries of the MRT and highways. He likes the fresh paint, the well-scrubbed tiles of the estate, the bus that always comes on schedule, the solid pillars of the Light Rail Transit system. Everything is cared for. When the LRT passes blocks of flats, its windows mist over automatically, shielding balconies lined with washing and potted plants from the prying eyes of passengers. Yet when he goes to the kopitiam each morning, he's looking for a sanctuary from this overwhelming newness. Not that the coffee shop's so old, but in the twenty years or so since it was built, it has already acquired reassuring layers of grime. In one of the angles where a pillar meets the ceiling, a pair of swiftlets have made a nest, a small pocket of feathers and twigs glued to the walls. Today he pauses to watch one of the birds return with food, noticing the high-pitched chirping of the young birds in the nest, the way the yellow rims of their unformed beaks open and close. He's glad that no one's thought to clear the nest away. Then he sits down gratefully at a Formica table worn white by the scraping of plates, finds that his hands tremble when he unfolds the newspaper. He's gestured for coffee; they know him here, and the kopi O arrives promptly.

He has counted out the change for the coffee vendor carefully in preparation, but he still fumbles when he picks it up. His palms are sweaty, and the silver and gold coins cling together, eluding his fingers. More haste, less speed. Then he pulls them free. Next the roti prata arrives, a pillow of folded, crisped dough, and he repeats the performance with greater success.

He arranges everything on the table precisely, like a surgeon preparing for an operation. To his left, the newspaper, unfolded to the letters page, weighed down in one corner with a bottle of chilli sauce so that the overhead fans will not turn the pages prematurely. Nearer to him, the kopi in a heavy china cup printed with English flowers, a fading colonial memory caught beneath the glaze, mismatched with an orange plastic saucer. He stirs it so that the sugar will dissolve, takes an experimental sip. The handle is tiny and difficult to grip; he pinches it between two swollen fingers. Finally, he reaches to his right. He eats the prata with spoon and fork, pulling the layers apart along hidden seams, dipping a small piece into the curry sauce, feeling its soapy texture on the tongue followed, after a moment, by an explosion of taste.

At Starbucks, she drinks her coffee, reassured at how it tastes the same as in any airport. It will also taste the same in Sydney when she arrives late in the evening or now—in all probability—early the next day. The accompanying croissant is dry in her mouth; she chews with deliberate slowness. Later, in the interview room, she will tell them everything about her that they want to know. Who she met in Australia before she left. Who paid for her trip to Cambodia. Where she went. Who she met there. Eventually, her whole life, from the beginning. She was born in a refugee camp on the Thai border; her mother had fled from Laos, but she's not Laotian, she's ethnic Chinese. Teochew. She never knew her father. They—her mother, herself, a younger brother—migrated to Australia when she was four. She cannot remember much about her childhood. But later life was hard: she couldn't afford to go to university. She did sales and marketing, but her brother got into debt. Into trouble. He needed money. And so . . .

Now she returns the tall glass with its plastic stirrer, the empty plate speckled with crumbs, to the barista. Not the woman who first served her, but a young man with a mullet and a tattoo that curves down from his neck until it's hidden by the collar of his shirt. He nods but doesn't speak. He can't place me, she thinks, he doesn't know what language to use. And I won't help him. Here, I am one among many. In Australia, every now and then, a stranger can burst open my sense of belonging: the man in the shop who tells me I speak English very well; the immaculately dressed old lady who asks me if I am an "Oriental", and, when I nod, speechless, continues, "Oh well, dear, never mind." In the few days I spent in Vietnam, the taxi drivers knew from the way I dress that I was from somewhere else; once or twice they thought I might be Viêt Kiêu, overseas Vietnamese, and gave an experimental greeting, only for me to answer them conclusively in my mangled phrasebook pronunciation, my broken tones. It is just here, at this airport, that I fit in, in transit between lives.

When she shoulders her pack, she feels the tug of the packages taped to her lower and upper back.

He is also one among many. She's flotsam, moved across continents by the currents of the world. He's like a limpet. He has stayed here, stubbornly, while the world has changed around him. First the British, under whom he started working. Mr Grouse, the superintendent, taught him well. In his teens, in his twenties, in the late 1950s, everything that was solid began to melt: colonial retreat, insurgencies, elections, merger with Malaysia, and then, in 1965, unlooked-for independence. He remembers the press conference on a flickering television screen, the prime minister who paused to wipe away tears at the failure of a life's work. And then, when he was still married to his first wife, a reverse process: the sudden solidifying of the nation-state, the deep freeze of post-independence politics. Through all this, he's kept his job, kept up his standards. Some things never change. He still uses, in his work, the 1913 tables that the British devised but have long since abandoned. He's tried unsuccessfully to pass on his skills, trained two successors who each left the service when the time came to shoulder responsibility. Even if he's supposed to be retired now, the government still calls on him when he's needed.

He sips his coffee. They are both Catholics. She went to church every Sunday, for as far back as she can remember. At ten, she took her first communion. Even when as an adult she returned home to visit, she would accompany her mother to church, performing the masquerade of a double life. But she, like her brother, has long since ceased to believe. Forget other worlds: the business of living in this one is more than enough. She remembers. Money to help her brother? She could go to Cambodia, pick up a package through to Sydney. Through Singapore? She laughed in incredulity. You don't understand, the man had told her. They don't mind if you take stuff through, in transit. They just don't want it coming into their country. Here's the name, the phone number, when you're in Phnom Penh.

In Cambodia, even on Tonlé Sap, they have churches: boats with a high-pitched roof and a wooden cross that float across the lake. In two years' time, before the meeting in the prison, they will ask if she would like to see a priest; she'll acquiesce, and they'll talk, separated by glass. Even in prison, she'll play this masquerade again: on the surface she'll be numbly calm; on the inside something will move restlessly within her, like a bird beating itself against glass. She will allow the priest to think he has comforted her.

He goes to mass faithfully, every Sunday. He likes the grandeur, the ceremony, the statue of the Virgin Mary garlanded with flowers as he climbs the steps in the morning heat up to the church that has no walls, the nave supported by pillars only. His first wife said to him, haven't you read the Ten Commandments? How can you carry on doing the job you do? But for him, it has never been like that. Your life is a series of compartments, like the segments of the oranges his Chinese neighbours give him at New Year. When government service calls him, he will leave his flat in the cool of the night, go to the prison, spend hours checking that everything is in working order.

After it's all over, he'll return in the midday heat, sink into the soft leather of the couch beneath the ceiling fan, pour himself a single glass of brandy. When she walks towards her waiting flight, the corridor narrows. She tries not to think too deeply, to drink in sensations of the present: the purple carpet, the potted palms, the advertisements for credit cards and frequent flier miles. On either side, the gates in orderly rows, dimly lit, like empty glass tanks. Or cells, she thinks. As she reaches the brushed silver walkway it sighs suddenly into life. As she's propelled forward, she becomes conscious of the soft music. Lennon's "Imagine," without the vocals. She smiles: a protest song become Muzak, oiling the smooth flow of money through the airport. For a moment, she remembers again: the packages on her body, the white crystals reduced to powder in the cheap hotel room, the door locked, the fan switched off in the gathering heat. Keep walking. Don't think. By the gate ahead, the early crowd is gathering. When she steps off the walkway, she feels calmer, as if she's entered a ritual, like one of the masses she attended as a young woman. Her body moves forward—it does not disrupt the ceremony—yet she is propelled towards her destination by habit only. She joins the line at the gate.

When he stands up, he's wearied by the sudden weight of his body. It's hotter now, and he can taste acid in his mouth; his right knee creaks in protest on the first few flexes. Strange, he muses, how he can control all bodies other than his own, weigh each one, subtract the weight of the head, calculate the exact length of rope for the clean, momentary fall into darkness. What he does is not the most difficult thing to do. Think of the doctor who is always waiting. If the organs need to be harvested, Dr Yeh will wait two minutes, then go up a free-standing ladder next to the corpse that is still not quite yet a corpse. He'll lean forward, hold the body still, put stethoscope against the heart, and listen; only then will the doctor give the signal to lower the body down. Compared to this, what he does is nothing. There's a mirror on one of the pillars in the coffee shop, and he catches sight of his reflection: still a full head of hair, a fuller belly. He doesn't look his age. When he comes out from the shade of the awning, the space between the buildings seems less like a corridor than a conduit, a storm drain filled to the brim with a surge of light.

Before they meet, there'll be a process. First the court case, then the failed appeal, then letters to the press, fruitless representations from politicians and celebrities for clemency. A war of images: her old passport photo, her mother in tears, lawyers at the prison gates, the prime minister with his awkward smile. A war of terminology, also: barbarism, colonialism, sovereignty, rights. Her face slowly becoming invisible, written over with layer upon layer of words.

He keeps his mind active. His grandson taught him how to use the internet. He likes those sites where you can find an address on a map, then zoom out from a block of flats to the town and then to the whole island of Singapore caught in an indentation at the tip of Asia, snagged like a corpuscle on the wall of a capillary. Reclamation has long ago softened the island's shape. It's rounder, fatter: Tanjong Maling has been swallowed up by the wharves and gantries of a container port. But he's still struck by an uncanny symmetry here: how blood in the body flows like water in the straits, how the impossibly large resembles the impossibly small. The lines of silt that trail out into the Strait of Malacca are viscous, like venous fluids under a microscope.

In public life, too, he's haunted by unacknowledged symmetry. This is something that he senses but can't articulate, why he celebrates the new but seeks out the old. In this gleaming, brilliant city, he always feels unclean, something that persists beyond the daily rhythms of showers, clean tissues, or the careful soaping of hands. The memory of something else swells beneath the skin of the present, something before, when he was younger, when a nation was coming into being. There were words he and his friends heard often and were not ashamed to speak: equality, rights, socialism, democracy, justice. If he searches hard, he can still detect traces of them in the present, but they are almost erased, written over by the crisp new language of social order, economic imperatives, retribution, discipline, punishment. He's not sure how to picture this change. You think the city is perfect; visitors love its shining schools, hospitals, factories, and shopping malls. Then you look more closely, and you see scar tissue, like the keloids that grow on your arm after an immunisation jab. Imagine a scarified body, its skin like armour, memories and desires sealed up within it, their retrieval an impossible effort. In time, you come to think these perfect scars are also not without their beauty; they are hard enough to resist the storms of the world.

In this particular storm, they will both be in places of calm. She behind reinforced glass, thick concrete walls. Even her mother will not be allowed to touch her hand. He, and so many others, behind other walls: routine, the soft intimacies of family or of friends, the weary, forgetful business of living.

At the end of the island, next to the airport, there is a prison. It is clean, modern, and well planned; its corridors meet at perfect angles. Like the airport. Like the estate. They will meet there, in two years. Two among many.

AWAY

When Pierre Met Harry

10 August 2015

Dear Madam Chin,

Thank you very much for your recent correspondence.

We are pleased to accept your donation of the papers of your late husband, Dr Chin Boo Geok, to the National Archives. As per our prior discussion, given the sensitive nature of the documents, particularly those from the period of Dr Chin's residence in London, we will not list them in our online catalogue. However, they will be available for consultation at the Archives, subject to application by individual researchers.

There is one item that we regretfully cannot accept. We found among Dr Chin's letters a short typescript that purports to describe, from Mr Lee's point of view, a meeting between Mr Lee Kuan Yew and future Canadian Prime Minister Mr Pierre Trudeau at the London School of Economics in 1947. While the meeting is historically possible and we have determined that the document has been typed on an Oliver portable typewriter of an appropriate vintage, the pages must be either an elaborate fictional joke or a forgery. They do not correspond to any notion of history that I am aware of and surely represent muddled thinking on Dr Chin's part. We are certain you will agree that to include them in Dr Chin's papers might confuse readers, especially younger Singaporeans who frequently use our facilities for their National Education project work. This is particularly true given the public mourning in Singapore on the passing of Mr Lee in March this year and the current SG50 celebrations of the fiftieth anniversary of our nation's independence. The document is thus returned to you with this letter.

You may wish to approach the National Archives of Canada in Ottawa to see whether they would accept the document for inclusion in the Pierre Trudeau fonds. I understand that they have a more liberal approach to these matters.

I would like to once again thank you for your contribution to nation-building.

Yours sincerely
Chia Lixin (Miss)
Assistant Archivist

Archives Reading Room: +65 6332 7909 DID: +65 6718 3004 Fax: +65 6332 3238 National Archives of Singapore, 1 Canning Rise, S179868

We make knowledge come alive, spark imagination and create possibilities.

PRIVILEGED/CONFIDENTIAL INFORMATION MAY BE CONTAINED IN THIS MESSAGE. IF YOU ARE NOT THE INTENDED RECIPIENT, PLEASE NOTIFY THE SENDER IMMEDIATELY AND DELETE THE MESSAGE.

—

Does he think I'm invisible? He pushes past me, without as much as a by-your-leave and takes the seat on my right, resting his long arms on the desk in front of him. He doesn't even take off his trench coat. He just sits there, thin wet hair plastered on his head, a notepad produced miraculously from the folds of his coat.

"Professor Laski's lecture? I'm in the right place?" he asks me.

"In a minute. He's not started yet."

The lecture theatre is only half full. No need for him to have rushed. As he relaxes, he seems to notice me for the first time.

"Pierre." He thrusts out a hand. It's bony, as I expected, of a piece with those deep eye sockets, that Roman nose. His accent isn't quite properly English.

"American?"

He laughs. "No, Canadian. And you?"

"Harry."

"Chinese." It's not a question.

"No, from Malaya, from Singapore." But I remember how, on the *Britannic*, on that long voyage to Liverpool last year, they fobbed me off onto the Aliens Manifest as a deemed citizen of China, in the company of the Argentinian doctor, the Italian teacher, and the students from Hong Kong. Only later did they cross my name out and put me at the bottom of the list of British subjects. I am only Malayan on sufferance, when they want me to be.

"You're a student here, in London?"

"I used to be. Now I'm at Cambridge. I didn't like having to dash about on the Tube or bus from lecture to lecture."

"You should have bought a motorbike."

Now that he says this, I can smell petrol on him, mixed with the scent of Woodbines. The cuff of his coat, I notice, is finely hemmed with a thin, barely visible thread. He drums his fingers on the desk in front of him.

"You don't have a pencil?"

I fumble for one, conscious of the shabbiness of my jacket. He takes it cautiously, as if it might not be quite clean.

"We must talk more, afterwards," he says. "I have plans for a tour of the Orient. Your perspective would be very useful."

I put my finger to my lips and point. Laski's here at last, doffing his black, shapeless hat and hanging up his old blue overcoat. The auditorium is full now. He smooths back his hair from a centre parting, marshals his notes, and looks up at us over the rims of tiny wire-rimmed glasses. An insignificant man; you might pass him without noticing in the street. He is only remarkable when he begins to speak.

He will talk today, he says, of something dear to the hearts of many of his audience: the end of colonialism. There are students here from India and Pakistan, flushed with the excitement of independence, and also students from nations in waiting: Burma, Ceylon, the Gold Coast, or Malaya. He extends his arms as if to embrace them. He has talked in recent weeks about the programmes of the Labour Government in Britain, of how it will transform society, yet how much more difficult this process has been than he and others had first thought. Part of this, no doubt, is class interest. Doctors, fearful their incomes may be cut, are resisting the funding of a National Health Service. There is also a larger structural problem. We have nationalised industries, but they still run as if they were private corporations. The old foremen and managers are still there. Walk out onto the street, to Houghton Street and the Aldwych, into the grey fog of a London day. 1947. Rationing remains in place; people's faces are pinched in poverty. But walk further up into Bloomsbury. Look at how the wrought-iron railings have vanished from the gardens; notice the bombed-out sections of the terraces, their retaining walls shored up in timber, grey-green with damp. Signs of the times, gentlemen. There are no barriers now: any one of us can walk into a viscount's garden or a duchess's drawing room. Pathways to a New Jerusalem.

Pierre pushes his pad in front of me. *Brilliant,* he has written, in a spidery hand. I nod and turn away. I want to listen.

Laski continues. Names fly through the air: John Stuart Mill, Jeremy Bentham, and Thomas Babington Macaulay. Statistics, too, spat out like bullets. For me the details blur. I can see the structure he is building but not quite the details, the individual bricks. I look around. Some students are like me, listening open-mouthed. Others, like Pierre to my left, take copious notes, nodding periodically or scratching their heads. It is warm in here, out of the rain. Smells of chalk, Brylcreem, stale cigarettes, and, underneath it all, unwashed humanity.

He is coming to an end. The War taught us or should have taught us this. The age of colonialism is over, despite the European powers' efforts to return to Indonesia or Viet Nam. But as colonies become nations, so the search for real democratic freedoms will become ever more difficult. He looks around, pauses, and waits until the faces of the note-takers turn up again, towards him. Those of us here from colonies and new nations comprise two classes of people. Government scholars, possibly from humble or modest backgrounds, who will go back to employment in the civil service, and rich men's sons, who will return to oil the cogs of commerce, to help family businesses reach out to the world. In each case, you must reflect and work to make change. There will be a change of flags, and the managers and foremen will change too, over time. It will be very easy to carry on within the same basic structures, to become new copies of those who went before. Much more difficult to search out those absent railings, those gaps in the terraces, those pathways to the future.

Pierre is pointing to a single capitalised word in the margins of his notes: *LUNCH?*

I nod. He pockets my pencil, and as the lecture ends, we make our way out, down the stairs. The queue for the canteen has already started.

"Not here." He tugs at my arm. "I know a place."

We go outside, into Houghton Street and then into the bustle of the Aldwych, with the columns of Bush House looming over us like a cliff. As we wait to cross, he offers me a Woodbine, lights his cigarette, then mine, with one of those metal lighters that American servicemen use, sleek as an aeroplane, nestled like a bird in his hand.

It's warm and airless in the pub. Pierre chooses the lounge bar, with its lumpy cushions and stained flock wallpaper, and settles us at a corner table, leaving me to guard his hat, coat, and satchel. A minute later, he's back from the bar, two glasses in hand.

"I'm sorry," he says. "The food doesn't look very appetising, after Paris."

"Nor after Singapore."

He shrugs and raises his glass to mine.

"Cheers!" I sip. The beer is soapy, bitter, and flat: even after almost a year in England, I still cannot get used to it.

"The worst thing?" he remarks. "You can't get fresh oysters."

Food, it emerges, is one of the few things on which we can agree. I take another sip.

"Laski's lecture," he says. "What did you think?"

I try to explain. I left London for the quiet, so that I can focus on reading Law and spend time with my newly arrived fiancée (at this he raises his eyebrows). But when I come down to London, I still go to Harold Laski's lectures. I am impressed, of course. I would like to believe.

"But you don't? You find some contradictions?"

He leans closer, puts his glass down on the table, waves his hands.

"You're sceptical? You find the fact that an Englishman is telling colonials how to go about decolonisation laughable?"

I open my mouth to reply, but he won't stop.

"Then again, you might say Laski is a different sort of Englishman. Jewish. He knows what it is to be different. Just as my heritage"—and here he spreads his hands out, perfectly pressed cuffs peeping out of the rich wool of his sweater—"is both English and French. This gives him a way in, that pathway that he spoke of. And I, like you, have studied Law. This offers us a further way in: the courtroom, maybe, can be that place where the new society will be built."

He pauses, and I get the chance to speak at last. I would like to believe. But I think sometimes that human beings are not, as Laski seems to think, naturally good. What I saw in the War, with the Japanese in Singapore, convinced me of that. We retreat, ultimately, into tribal allegiances: we speak fine words, but ultimately self-interest wins out.

He leans closer. "But surely . . ."

Does he remember just now, when we came out of Houghton Street into the Aldwych? Look up, to the two great statues high up on Bush House, their ridiculous togas just covering the groin. The inscription: To the Friendship of English-Speaking Peoples. Does he think this includes me?

"Neither does it include me."

But it's different, I tell him. He can pass as English in this city, if he does not open his mouth. And even if he does, if he is seen as American, he will be taken as a younger brother, the second of those two statues, vigorous, reaching out to help its aged companion hold the torch aloft.

He smiles. "So the world cannot change?"

I do not answer, and the buzz of conversation in the pub returns. Pipe smoke, thickly scented, like the interior of a Cambridge tutor's office.

He is discomfited, I can see, and changes topics. He has a dream, he tells me, of travelling across Europe and into Asia. On his Harley Davidson, possibly. He traces out a route with his hands. Avignon, Rome, across the Adriatic to the Acropolis, then the Bosphorus, Tehran, Bokhara, Samarkand, Kashgar, and the Silk Road to Shanghai, Pearl of the Orient. He wants to see the world.

Better to go by sea, I tell him. Pass Aden, then Bombay, Colombo, Singapore, Hong Kong. The Beautiful Bay, the Lion City, and the Fragrant Harbour: their names are just as romantic. What he will find there will not be so very different from London, Paris, or Montreal. I have found nothing here, nor in Cambridge, that I had not seen in Singapore.

I can see I am a disappointment to him. He likes his Orientals as he likes his oysters: raw, not cooked. He drums his fingers again, finishes his pint, and leans forward to speak. At the last second, he turns away: he is looking at the clock.

"Goodness. Is that the time? I have an appointment." He looks at my half-full glass. "Harry, don't leave now on my account. Stay and finish your drink."

He snatches up his coat and hat, then ducks and weaves his way to the door. A last backward glance. "See you at Laski's lectures sometime?"

I raise my glass in response as the door swings shut.

I'm more conscious of patrons' stares now that I am alone and finish my drink quickly. It is not until I gather my things that I notice the satchel he has left behind. I would normally not pry, but there is no other way to return it to him. I undo the strap carefully. Slim pickings: the notepad he was using in class, my pencil, which I take back, and a loosely folded letter, its envelope missing. I find myself blushing when I read it, but I have the afternoon free, and it does suggest to me a plan:

Pierre,

> *Yours is a strange kind of love. You talk of freedom, but you do not practise it. Sometimes I think how easy it is, for men especially, to become that very thing that they think they oppose. Love me with respect—or not at all.*
>
> *At the Lion House, then, in Regent's Park Zoo. Half past three, today. Don't be late.*

Hélène

The zoo is crowded, with chattering schoolchildren in long lines and dour men in grey coats and pork pie hats. The sky is overcast but blank; umbrellas are carried but furled. I look at my watch. I've made good time to get here, rumbling up the Tube to Camden Town, striding briskly up Parkway, Pierre's satchel over my shoulder, then along Prince Albert Road to the canal. I can loiter.

The first section of the zoo is unremarkable: a few cages of dozy owls, high on their perches, doing their best to ignore hooting noises made by two grubby boys. Some sleek, well-fed pheasants peck repetitively at scattered corn and give way to an aviary full of miserable, hunched birds, clearly accustomed to warmer climates. Across the footbridge that spans the canal, prospects improve: zebras, a giraffe, and a hippopotamus wallowing happily in mud. Outside a larger enclosure, a movie camera has been set up. Two baby elephants await, and two tiny, violently blonde girls are being encouraged to climb onto their backs. One elephant is still; the other turns away, then rolls over on the ground. The keepers come with a hose and towels; these are kindly meant but somehow have the appearance of instruments of torture. The elephant is washed, dried, and readied once more. The little girl prepares to mount again, then quite unexpectedly bursts into tears.

The British are organised; you have to give them that. Each animal has its own separate place. Some thought has clearly been given to arrangements: animals that might disturb each other are kept separate, and the order of the cages, one suspects, is also arranged with a visitor's pleasure in mind. I know from my reading that they work hard behind the scenes to keep the zoo's inhabitants in their apparent state of nature. The beavers, for instance, try every night to dam up their pond; early in the morning, before the zoo opens, the keepers remove the structure their little guests have made, twig by twig. The orangutan, newly brought from Malaya by a returning colonial official, is not yet on display. I have seen photographs of him nestling into a tweed jacket very similar to mine, splaying fingers towards his minders. For the moment, they seem to want to kill him with kindness.

I stop at a kiosk and buy a cup of weak tea and a doughnut filled with virulently red jam that squirts out and sticks obstinately to my fingers. A crowd of children has gathered in one of the open spaces, chattering with excitement. I stand on a bench and crane forward to see. The chimpanzee tea party is starting, each ape led into the arena by an attentive staff member. These are not the cuddly keepers with lab coats and sweaters you see in the Pathé News reels; they have crisp, dark uniforms, shiny boots, and peaked hats, and move with the determination of soldiers. Some of the chimps, if you look carefully, are anchored to their guardians by thin, slack leashes attached to collars around their necks. They climb up steps to a platform, shamble hesitantly, then sit around a table, each in his own chair. The children in the crowd cheer hungrily. A keeper brings lunch on a tray: a jug of milk and plates of food. One chimp is cautious, studiously feeding himself with a correctly held spoon. Another grabs his spoon by its bowl and shovels: soon he is upending his plate, tipping its contents into his mouth and onto his fur. The children go wild. They point with glee and turn their heads to their parents in curiosity, wondering why they do not disapprove. After this, fruit is served, and the boldest chimp crawls on the table, helping himself to the contents of other plates. The others eat on, apparently oblivious. Then one takes the jug of cream and pours it into his mouth. Later, their bellies distended, they are brought to the railings. Their guardians hold their hands firmly and let laughing and screaming children reach out to touch, but they keep those thin leashes loose, waiting.

I wonder if those leashes are something more than a sensible precaution. They are almost invisible; a few brushstrokes on a negative, and they would cease to exist. Yet possibly they are a sign of something else, of an order that prevails behind the facades of the animal houses, where training involves beatings as well as kindness.

At the aquarium, the king penguins stand forlorn without fish, still as statues. Cigarette smoke. A chance remark, in a thick Northern accent: "They might as well be dead, mightn't they, for all the action we get to see?" Then on to the lion house. I check my watch again: quarter past three. Ideally, he would be here early. I could return the bag and take my leave, without the embarrassment of new introductions.

The lion house is beautiful. I walk through the gallery at the rear, peering over a parapet through the bars, as one looks over a bank counter, into the lions' den. Straw, fur, and sweet-scented darkness. Outside, at the front of the house, the enclosures extend into the crowd like fingers, elongated birdcages with slender, barely visible bars. I work my way to the front. Two lionesses prowl, pacing towards me and then retreating into the warmth behind. A further round, then another. They seem ghost-like, caught in a trance, far more impressive than that lazy tiger brought in from Whipsnade and its fractious, hyperactive cubs. They pace again. A keeper pushes a lump of meat, impaled on a long handle, between the bars. There is a growl, a flurry of teeth and claws. The crowd thickens.

I move away. In one of the other fingers, I find a solitary lion. He stands still, looking out, his mane stroked by a hint of breeze. I move closer. He turns to look at me, and the black pupils in his sandy eyes dilate. He seems to plead with me. Of course the keepers are right. I cannot trust him, I cannot let him out. At the very best, I might be able to build a cage without bars, one that he might not even realise he was inside.

The satchel slips on my shoulder, and I snatch at it before it falls into the mud. It's strange how memory works, how those very things you want to forget stick obstinately in your mind. That sentence from the letter I should not have read: *Sometimes, I think how easy it is, for men especially, to become that very thing that they think they oppose.*

I look at the lion again. He stares back without moving. In each other's eyes, we see our respective futures. A long-anticipated moment of escape, only to find we have entered a new enclosure.

I feel a sudden impatience. Time is pressing. History cannot wait. I cannot wait for Pierre, for the explanations, the introspection, the long theoretical disquisitions on the nature of humanity. I have a train to Cambridge to catch. The satchel can go in the lost property at Liverpool Street. I turn back to the lion one more time, but he has slunk away into the darkness. I shift the satchel onto my shoulder, feeling its love letter and its pages of scribbled notes shift and settle. I work my way as quickly as I can towards the exit, without a further backward glance.

Letters from London

3 March 1994

Dear Raja,

It was good to hear from you. We haven't written to each other for years. So imagine my surprise when I found that fat envelope with its Singapore stamps in my hallway, mixed up with the phone bills and flyers. It did take me back to our days in London during the War. It got me thinking, too, about how we fell out. You went back to Singapore, and you had a stellar career. Cal and I would read about you in the newspapers, and we'd be cheering you on in those early years in journalism and politics. First Minister of Culture, and then, after independence, Singapore's Foreign Minister. You stood up for your country and for others in Asia; you spoke back to the Americans and the European powers. I stayed on here, like a mouse or some other nocturnal animal, following a well-worn path. I've never left Belsize Park.

Of course I did retrain. I did grow in other ways. It was after Cal and I saw that lovely psychiatrist, not pathologising but accepting, that I trained as a psychologist, as you know. It's been a good career, although I'm winding down, like you. I only see a handful of clients nowadays. And, yes, your letter came to the right address: I still live here, only two streets away from our old boarding house on Steele's Road. You're supposed to get more conservative as you age, but my ideals haven't changed. I wonder sometimes about this: have I kept the faith, or am I just an old fool, an ancient fossil left over from a previous age? As I write to you, I'm sitting at my desk, looking out over the road through a lattice of bare plane trees. This house is too cold, and my fingers ache.

About your request. Let me think about it. As I've grown older I've learned to wait, to let thoughts and feelings settle. Of course I forgive you. That's easy to say. Yet I think you know from your own readings of psychology in the War years how powerful the unconscious is, how wounded feelings and their poisons can bubble up. I don't want these to influence my response to you. I'll just pop this card in the post for now. I'll write soon as I've had time to think.

Yours with memories, mostly fond,
Charly

10 March 1994

Dear Raja,

I'm replying at greater length to you, now that I've had that pause to think. After sending the previous card, I thought I'd just walk past the house in Steele's Road. It was a brisk spring day, and the leaves were budding but had not quite yet come on the trees. I remember how you always complained about those long dark winters and the even longer wait for spring: the procession of snowdrops, then crocuses, then daffodils on the Heath. I took a photograph of the house, which I developed and am enclosing here.

I don't have your skill in photography, but I thought it might spark some memories in you.

Raja, I can't treat you as a psychologist, nor can I diagnose what's wrong. Do you have a doctor in Singapore that you can approach? Might your brother or your nephew—if I remember right—help you? But I think I can promise, as a friend, to "listen" through the letters we exchange. What I often do in my work is simply to bear witness to the experiences of the people who sit in front of me, to listen and then to reflect back what I have heard, so that they see themselves from the outside, in a new light.

I'd like to be a clear, true mirror for you, but of course I'm not. Given the story of my life and our own history of friendship and conflict, it'll be more like looking into those mirrors on the fairground up at the Heath. Do you remember the one that made us all look awfully fat? And then the other that made us so very thin? My replies to you will be like this. Some things in the past will loom large, and others will vanish. I'll watch myself, of course, but it can't be helped.

Let me repeat back what you wrote to me, then, in my own words, to make sure that I've understood. You had a dream that still haunts you. You were in the Steele's Road boarding house. Piri had crept in to see you, quietly. I remember that Mrs Churchill in those early days didn't approve of lady visitors, so you cut her an extra copy of your key. She'd wait until after dark, until you signalled the all-clear by waving a handkerchief from your window. She'd climb the stairs to the porch, let herself in noiselessly, then climb the curved staircase, treading softly over the worn carpet. There was a place on the landing where the floorboards creaked, and she'd learned to avoid it, walking around it as if circumventing a hidden trap. Your door would be open, and you'd close it once she came in and take her in your arms. I'd see nothing more on those visits, but I do remember visiting your room at other times. The old wardrobe with its foxed mirror, the bookcase heaped untidily with paperbacks, pamphlets, and magazines, the tiny desk by the window that looked out on the road. The room was always stale with the smell of cigarette smoke, and sometimes you'd pull up the sash window, even in the middle of winter, to let it dissipate. Piri didn't seem to mind, of course: you both smoked, and she was in love. And then, of course, the bed. Narrow, uncomfortable, with a coil spring mattress that squeaked even with the slightest movement. A contraceptive bed, she said to me once. Any rhythmic movement would summon up that dragon of a landlady from the depths of the house.

But in your dream something was different. You had not been expecting Piri to come. You were writing, smoking, looking out into the darkness, to the plane trees in the road kneaded by the wind. She suddenly reached out and touched your hair in the lamplight. You turned, startled, about to cry out, but she put an impish finger to her lips and closed the door behind her. When you kissed, her lips were very soft. You were both very young. Yet something was not quite right. Some sixth sense told you that this was impossible: the woman you loved could not be here, at this moment. So you stood up and pulled her to you, so that your face nestled into her hair, so that you could feel the softness of her body against yours, but you did not have to look into her face.

Just at that moment the air raid sirens sounded. There were footsteps on the stairs. You knew the drill. You should go down to the kitchen at the bottom of the house, crouch with Mrs Churchill and the other boarders under that great wooden dining table. But you couldn't leave her. You sat on your bed and held hands. First, silence. Then the crump of a falling bomb somewhere to the north. Searchlights in the sky. The crackle of the ack-ack guns. A little later, the bleating sounds of incendiaries falling nearby. A sudden, brilliant blue-white light. You both rushed to the window, but the bomb had fallen on the next street. You were safe. And then silence again, as you waited for the next wave of bombers or the all-clear.

The building began to fall away. No bomb had fallen nearby, but the house began to crumble, from the bottom up. The walls softened: they ran downwards like sand in an hourglass. You stood on a section of flooring that fell smoothly, as if you had been in a descending lift, down to the first floor, then the ground floor and further, into a deep hole that had opened up in the earth. Piri did not move. Somehow she was suspended there, even though everything around her had dissolved. She dwindled away until she was a tiny point of light. Then you woke up.

Did I hear you correctly, not just the substance of the dream but also the feelings of confusion and loss that accompanied it?

You asked me how I would interpret your dream. As you know, I'm not a great fan of Freud, less so his followers. It took me a long time to get away from those efforts to "treat" me, to realise that my homosexuality wasn't the cause of my anxiety and depression, but that it was social attitudes to gay men that were the problem. And I don't think, as Freud suggested, that dreams are the royal road to the unconscious. They're a way we piece together the fragments of our waking life, making sense through greater madness.

I did notice two things that may help you. The first of these is grief. You are still grieving Piri's death, and this is natural. It's a process that cannot be hurried. In our dreams, the dead return and seek a new relationship to us. We should be open to this: we should make space for them. I've read about how in Singapore cemeteries have been cleared to open up land for housing. The same thing happened in London a century or more ago. We push the dead away; we want to forget them. So it is natural that she should come in a dream and seek you out again. Don't push her away.

The second thing I thought of was the building itself. Of course this is the moment that I enter your dream, when I hold up the distorting mirror of my life to yours. Let me hide behind questions for now. What structures have you helped build during the course of your life? What made you think that they were so solid? Did you ever have doubts about them, about the voids and silences they were built over? And in what way now, in old age, do those voids and silences return—in what way are those so very solid structures undermined?

Yours ever,
Charly

10 August 1994

Dear Raja,

You're right about ageing. No one ever prepares you for it. In my late forties, my eyes began to go, after a lifetime of never wearing glasses. Now my hearing is getting a bit fuzzy. If I go out to the pub with Cal, I can't hear what he's saying unless he leans very close. He also can't hear me. Yesterday we were talking at cross purposes for a couple of minutes, gossiping about a friend, surprised at each other's revelations, until we realised we were discussing two completely different people! And words too. Sometimes they get stuck in my throat. I can see someone's face or the cover of a book, but the name or the title just won't come. Cal's frustrated with me. Name things, he tells me. Don't expect me to guess what you're talking about. And then those aches and pains in the body, knuckle joints gumming up in the morning, creaking knees. When you're young, your body silently does everything you ask it. You never notice it. Now, as we age, it nudges us, tells us that it's here, lets us know its power over us.

But some of what you describe seems more severe than the normal process of growing old. Those holes in memory; those times when you forget something that happened very recently. That struggle you experience to read a novel now, to keep all the characters and events in your head even from chapter to chapter. And that loss of a sense of smell. It's not a weakness to reach out and ask for help.

Raja, I think I should also get something off my chest. I'd always thought of you as principled. In government, you began to change. We read of those restrictions you placed on the free press. And then, the Singapore government's stance on homosexuality. What you said about the boat people, too, about them being short-sighted and only interested in making money. Before, you were always open. You found out about Cal and me early on, soon after we met. You were so accepting that I thought you might be that way yourself. Do you remember your friend Subra's story about sleeping in the same bed as a naked Cypriot and being poked in the back by what seemed to be a stick of butter but ended up being bread? How you winked and told me it was surely a metaphor? And like the boat people, weren't we all refugees in London during the War, brought by ideals, by the need for shelter, not money? I've worked with Vietnamese refugees here who have been touched by trauma. A few years ago I treated a young man who'd lost his legs in an explosion as a child searching for scrap metal the Americans had left behind. Talk to individuals, open yourself, and your heart fills up with compassion. There. Now I've said it, I already feel lighter.

Raja, do make sure you schedule that appointment with the doctor to run some tests.

Best wishes,
Charly

2 February 1995

Dear Raja,

Today I walked up Haverstock Hill, then down Pond Street towards the Heath. Do you remember the bookstore there that Mr Westrope used to run? Where we'd meet monthly for our book club discussions? I've forgotten its name, but I do remember how fuggy with smoke the back room where we gathered was. And that insufferable clergyman, who insisted on lecturing you on how grateful you should be as a colonial subject.

I'm glad you saw a doctor, even though, as you say, the diagnosis is troubling. "Mild cognitive impairment" could be many things. You're courageous to write to me of your fears of where it might lead. Dementia is, of course, a possibility. For people like you and me, who exist through reading and writing, through lives and memories that crystallise into words, it's particularly terrifying. Yet there is hope, as you say. At the moment the condition has touched you, but it has not changed you. Further developments may come slowly or not at all.

Thank you for the book of your articles and speeches you enclosed for me. It seems to have cost you a pretty penny to send it as an air parcel. I do realise that Singapore's achieved so much, of course, under the stewardship of your party. And you're right that the Western press hasn't given you a fair hearing at all. Singapore's trajectory has been upwards, whereas Britain has declined. Perhaps, as you write, people want stability and peace in their lives, above abstract ideals. Yet I'm not quite sure if you yourself fully believe this.

I don't want to criticise here without knowing the full story. But I was curious about how much forgetting comes into your writing. You write of how forgetting for a new nation can be blissful, how we can let go of the trauma of the past. But can we really forget? Don't the bones of the dead, the stories of those who have suffered rise up again, even as we try to bury them? In no way do I want to make light of your present struggles, but in the new forgetfulness that has come into your life, does unfinished business return, unbidden, as it does for all of us? It's as if the ground around you is clearer now and quieter. If you listen, is there a voice? What does it say?

Yours warmly,
Charly

3 July 1995

Dear Raja,

It was good to get your letter. Your plan seems an excellent one. Since you find it increasingly difficult to write, you'll dictate these letters to your secretary, Andrew, and he'll type them out and send them to me. It was wonderful to hear your news and also look at the photograph that you—or was it Andrew?—enclosed. You look well, and that's certainly an impressive study behind you, with its bookshelves that go on and on and up and up. A marked improvement on that untidy little bookcase in Steele's Road! Isn't that your old copy of *Capital* from your student days on your study's second shelf, the one you liked to thumb through and underline?

You wanted to ask me about this second dream of yours. Let me reflect it back to you. You woke up in the night, or at least you thought you had woken up. But you were not in Singapore, in Chancery Lane, in that bungalow that you've lived in for so long. You were back in your room in Steele's Road, in that narrow bed, the wardrobe looming over you. You were cold;

you were wearing flannel pyjamas and had wrapped the woollen blanket round your body like a shroud in your sleep, but you still weren't close to being warm. You got up, put on your dressing gown and slippers, and looked out over the street. An inch or so of snow had fallen, covering the surface of the road. It was very early in the morning. No one was up yet, and the snowfall was undisturbed, sparkling with new frost under the street lights.

You could sense that the cold wasn't normal, despite Mrs Churchill's careful rationing of fuel that made the kitchen the only warm place in the house. So you tied up your dressing gown cord, passed my room, and descended the stairs, past the first floor, where Mrs Churchill and Silloo, the Indian girl who studied music, slept, down into the kitchen and the dining room with that big oak table of which our landlady was so proud. The cold persisted here. The boiler had gone out. You shivered. You searched for the coal scuttle, but it was empty, and the door to the cellar was locked.

The temperature dropped further. You needed to set a fire, but there was nothing to light it or kindle it with. You patted your breast pocket but realised your cigarettes and matches were still in your jacket in your room. You searched again and found a half-empty matchbox in the dressing table drawer. Then the frozen air clutched hold of you. It was so cold that you thought you might die here, here at the bottom of the house. Your landlady would find you in the morning, stiff as a board, eyes staring out in fear.

So you reached up to the shelf where Mrs Churchill kept that old coffee tin full of her household money. You felt guilty even to touch it, and before you opened it, you glanced up through the open door, half expecting the dragon lady to come slithering down the stairs. Nothing. When you opened it, it was full of notes and coins. The coins, you noticed, were very big. Of course coins *were* big then: do you remember those worn copper pennies, as fat as a watch face, that would weigh our pockets down? But these were larger than that and thicker, glistening. They were swollen, wrapped in golden foil but made of a waxy material, like firelighters. The notes, too, seemed much bigger than the notes we have now. There was enough to light a fire.

Anticipation made you less cold. You took your time. You crinkled up the notes and arranged the coins in a little circle, in the middle of the tiled floor. Then you lit the match. You could see yourself in the mirror in the dining room, kneeling down, like a supplicant to a strange new god. You paused, uncertain. Then you dropped the match. There was instant warmth. The coins and notes burned merrily, evenly. You had been worried that the fire would soon burn through all the materials you had provided, but it seemed to be self-sustaining, even to grow a little. You felt comforted, and above all you were now warm. You moved to a nearby chair. The warmth made you drowsy, and you nodded off.

You were woken by a hissing sound. The fire was hotter. It had advanced across the tiles and begun to climb the flock wallpaper under the mantelpiece. There was a low table on which Mrs Churchill kept photographs of her family (although we never dared ask if the gentleman in the photographs was Mr Churchill) and former lodgers. These were beginning to burn, twist, and turn black. You turned and noticed that the table behind you was covered in more framed portraits. There were pictures of your family at the plantation house in Seremban, of you and your classmates at King's College, and several of your friends here, gathered in the garden at the back of the house. There was that one you took of Piri in a mirror, looking back at you, her face floating in the darkness. The flames crackled. The photographs began to blacken and disintegrate. On the floor the pile of burning coins was growing and growing, like lava welling up from the earth. You realised you had to get out. But the door to the stairs was now shut. You tried to cry out, to warn those others sleeping on the floors above you, but try as you might, no sound came. Then you woke up. You really woke this time, in your bed in

Chancery Lane with the fan turning above you. You went to the window, and the sky was tinted with the first hint of dawn, but you could not shake off the smell of smoke, the sense of being trapped.

Raja, I don't think dreams have any single meaning. But I do have some questions for you to think through, as always, some reflections in the mirror I'll hold up. I'm curious about this strange god whom you felt uneasy in bowing down to. How did you light the spark? What did you hope to achieve? And how did the fire that gave warmth for a time come to burn out of control? What did it destroy? What can we retrieve from the ashes? The fire you started is still burning, all over the world. Can we find a way of containing it, of bringing warmth but not destruction? Or should we put it out?

I do hope my "listening" has been helpful. You wrote to me some time ago that this was a very lonely journey for you, and I hope at least I have been able to walk a little way by your side.

Thinking of you,
Charly

2 January 1996

Dear Andrew,

I hope it's all right for me to write to you directly. I was a little concerned that I hadn't heard from Raja for a time. And then yesterday, quite out of the blue, a letter from him. It seemed suspiciously thin, but Cal and I were in a hurry to go out to the cinema, and so I put it aside. I've just opened it now, and there's only this list, which I'll enclose with this reply. It looks like a shopping list that Raja's maid—Cecelia, is it?—has prepared. Did you—or more likely Raja himself—intend to send me a letter instead? Has it gone missing? If you do find it, be sure to send it on. We do think very fondly of Raja and wonder how he is progressing.

Yours,
Charly

20 January 1996

Dear Andrew,

Thank you for writing to me and explaining the situation. You're very calm and matter-of-fact when you write, but I can sense your frustration and anxiety.

Please do not take some of those things that Mr Rajaratnam has said to you too much to heart. From my experience, patients who are suffering from dementia often go through stages in which they struggle with the condition. At first they try to cover it up, and I've found professionals and educated people are particularly good at this. They'll joke with you when you ask them the standard diagnostic questions and try to weasel the correct answers out of you from your gestures or your hesitations. Later there's another stage. The lapses in memory are greater, yet the patient cannot quite believe what is happening. At this stage there is often anger, and it is often directed at those they work closely with, care about, or even love. Accusing others of stealing mislaid items is, unfortunately, very common. It's hurtful, I know, especially if your relationship has been based on absolute trust. You also describe finding Raja outside on the road at the traffic circle, watching the passing cars in the heat of the afternoon. Wandering and associated confusion are also markers of this stage. However, there's often a third stage—of acceptance. Here the patient is able to accept forgetting and even to laugh at himself and with others.

Let's hope that you'll come through the current tempests to calmer waters. In the meantime, let me think what I can do. I'll search for some old photographs from Raja's time in London. Cal also made a very good suggestion: we can make a mix tape with some of the songs he used to hear and with both of us talking, sending him a message of care. I know Raja once told me how magnetic tape gets mouldy in the humid tropical air. Would it be all right for me to send him a cassette tape for you to play to him? We could also call him, of course, although we wouldn't want to startle him. I'll let you be the judge of this.

Keep your spirits up!

Looking forward to hearing from you,
Charly

13 June 1996

Dear Andrew,

What a pleasant surprise! I had thought that I might not hear from my old friend again. That moment of lucidity, as you tell it to me, must have been startling. I must confess I laughed out loud when you told me how Raja pouted when he heard Cal's voice on the tape. Truth be told, they never really got along. Thank you for telling me of the smile when he heard me speaking. That's very precious to me. You mention that sudden mad urgency that came over him. He wanted you to tell me about a recent dream he'd had. I appreciate that what you've sent me is fragmentary. You were taking notes, and of course he wasn't fully coherent. I can picture him now, cajoling you to type it up and send it to me. My reply is perhaps more of an interpretation, more of an imagined reconstruction, than my previous letters. But I'll still write it up in the way that I've done before. And since the recording seems to work, I'll also record my reply and pop the cassette in the mail with the letter.

Dear Raja,

Thank you for finding a way of recounting your dream to me. I hope that you don't mind that I now enter it, in trying to piece it together. I move through the mirror, so that your dream also becomes mine. Here goes.

Piri came to visit you again, in your sleep. This time it was towards the end of the War. The Blitz was long over, and the doodlebugs and V2 rockets had stopped coming. You were living together as man and wife at that ground-floor flat in Priory Road, with its kitchen, living room, and much more capacious bed. This must have been some time in that long spring and summer in 1945 when the world changed. First the victory in Germany, then news from the Far East, although still little from Singapore. You had a map of Asia on the living room wall, and together you'd plot the Allied advances on it. Iwo Jima. Okinawa. Balikpapan. In early July, in England, the general election. Churchill ousted in a landslide, and the world turned upside down. A new Labour government that would surely let its colonies go. In August, the atomic bombs on Hiroshima and Nagasaki. And then the Japanese surrender and your frantic efforts to contact your relatives and friends in Malaya. This was the time when you began to prepare to return.

All that long summer, I did not see much of you in those weekends I could get away from the Non-Combatant Corps. Other friends said the same thing. You'd vanished into that flat together, wrapped up in each other. I do remember meeting you once, though, at the Railway Pub near West Hampstead Tube. Piri must have had to stay late at work, because you came to the pub alone. I remember it was 1945 because you talked about Japanese militarism and your hopes for democracy there after the end of the War. You always stood outside popular hysteria. You hated those propaganda photographs of buck-toothed Japanese soldiers with bayonets dripping in blood. It was fascism we were fighting, not a people, not a race.

But you didn't want to talk to me about this. As we stood outside and drank our pints of bitter, you started to tell me about photography. You'd recently acquired a new camera—goodness knows how, during the War, when everything was so scarce. You told me you'd been taking photographs, mostly of interiors. Portraits, too, of Piri and yourself. So, with that delicious floating feeling that comes after a couple of beers, we walked down Priory Road to the flat. It was hot, I remember, and the leaves on the trees were very full, with that lush beauty that comes in high summer, after the initial freshness has gone. You showed me in, and we went down to the cool of the cellar, where you'd set up a darkroom, lit only by a dull amber lamp. You started talking to me about the principles of photography.

Taking photographs, you told me, showed the world in a new light. Or rather, showed the world *as* light and as nothing else. Think of what it would mean, you said, if we could see the world not as forms, not as substance, but simply through the play of light and shadow. Then you laid your hand on mine. *Look at our skin,* you said. In the outside world, we were branded with difference. Here, under the amber light, nothing.

You began to do some work on a sheet of paper in a shallow tank of chemicals. You placed it there with tongs, and on it an image slowly began to take shape. It was formless at first, an abstraction. Then, like Narcissus look-ing into his pond, I could see a face. I could place the image, give it a name. You said to me, *I can take it out now, while it is still light. Or let it darken slowly. What shall I do?*

There. I've framed your dream for you, haven't I? Now let me recount it to you. You were working in the living room in the Priory Road flat. It was late, and it was dark outside. The room was hot and a little stuffy, because you'd kept the windows closed to stop the moths from gathering. There was downlight from your Anglepoise lamp, falling on the desk and onto the car-pet. The dresser and the bookcases reached up into the darkness of the ceil-ing where the heavy mouldings were only just visible. Just then Piri came to you. She was wearing an ivory slip made of silk, with thin ribbon straps over her shoulders. She would wear this garment later, sometimes, in old age, when both of your bodies had changed. She carried a camera, and she smiled as she offered it to you. You took it from her, its metal casing cold, its weight settling into your hands. As you did, a thought came to you: it was much too dark in the flat for photography. Your hands couldn't hold the camera steady enough for the long exposure needed, and the image would be blurred. You'd need a tripod, and you did not have one at hand.

Despite this, you held the camera up and looked at Piri through the viewfinder. The map on the wall of the room behind her had vanished, replaced by a clear mirror that stretched up and up into the dark. You saw yourself next to her, reflected, both your faces lit by the same light. Behind you, strangely, was another mirror, so that image reflected image, so that your faces repeated in an infinite sequence, growing smaller and smaller, as if leading the way down a tunnel into darkness. You were struck by the beauty of the scene, but you could not quite frame it in a single shot. You moved back. You crouched down. You tilted your head. She smiled calmly at you all this while. Finally, you managed it. You just needed to adjust the aperture. The camera was unfamiliar, so you looked down, twisted a little silver knob on the top of the case. When you looked up, Piri had vanished. You wondered whether she had gone into the adjoining room. You thought you could hear her voice there, her laughter. Then you began to feel that sensation that accompanies waking, that tug, that feeling of being plucked upwards by a strong, relentless hand. You fought to stay in the dream. Try as you might, you couldn't hold on. You woke, bereft, in your bed at Chancery Lane. You lay there, hoping that you could fall asleep again and join her, and sleep refused to come.

Of course, this dream is part of your process of grieving, of developing a new relationship with Piri now that she is no longer with you. But I wonder if there isn't also another dimension. Raja, I've been re-reading those speeches and articles in the book you sent me and those articles you published recently, after you stepped down from government. I wonder if what you write can help us understand your dream. In London, in those years we spent together, we dreamed that racism would wither away. Not just racism, but race itself. If we removed power and coercion, we would no longer need to remember our differences. Yet in Singapore, when you and your comrades cast out your net of governance, you could not haul in things that were infinitely small. Categories had to be fixed, like those pictures in your basement darkroom; each of us had to be placed within a frame of birth certificates and identity cards. These frames became real, part of the furniture, so to speak: even you, the marginal man as you loved to call yourself, couldn't escape. So that dream, "regardless of race," as you so elegantly put it, fell further and further away from you, just like those images grew smaller and smaller until you could no longer see them. Is this what worries you now?

Or perhaps I'm being too fanciful. As Dr Freud is supposed to have said, sometimes a cigar is only a cigar. A dream is only a dream, but remembering through your dream has made me think again of you and those times in London, with warmth and also with longing.

I hope hearing my voice will give you joy.

Yours,
Charly

12 March 1997

Dear Raja,

Charly here again. I haven't heard from you for a time. Andrew has kept me up to date, and of course he's willing to forward any correspondence to you. I thought, however, I'd send this package directly to your house in Chancery Lane. Cecelia will know what to do.

There's the tape enclosed, as usual. I thought, however, you might be most interested in the photograph. Do you recognise it? It's taken in the garden of the Steele's Road house. You can see the brickwork on the wall and the ivy and that heavy roller that Mrs Churchill used to get us to pull after we'd mowed the lawn. Got *me* to pull, I should say. You would usually make yourself scarce for a smoke on the front porch! There's a garden rake too, leaning against the wall, next to a pile of leaves. It must have been autumn, then, in the late thirties, before the War.

Do you recognise the people in the photograph? There's George Padmore in that elegant suit, with Dorothy. They left for Ghana, soon after Nkrumah came to power there. Then there's you and Piri. You do look fetching in that grey smoking jacket. And then there's me and Cal. Sorry about that face he's pulling: it does rather ruin the picture. And then, next to us, the final couple. That's your friend Subra, isn't it? The writer from Ceylon. And his English girlfriend. He went back in the end, I'm told, and left her here. He was miserable in Jaffna. He married again, but he still missed her. What was her name again?

We are old now. Memories rustle and float up like leaves, too many to gather up. The wind scatters them: I put up my hands to grasp them, but they slip away. Raja, what does it mean to remember, and be misremembered by others? And what will it take to truly forget?

Yours,
Charly

Forbidden Cities

早晨 — *tsao3 ch'en2 — early morning*
複習 — *fu4 hsi 2 — review, revise*
流亡 — *liu2 wang2 — to go into exile*
自由 — *tzu4 yu2 — freedom*
自愛 — *tsu4 ai4 — self respect*

"You're learning Chinese."

I fumble with my flash cards of Chinese characters, upsetting the little pile I've built for myself on the café counter. The man who just sat down apologises; he didn't mean to startle me. He, like me, is waiting for the waitress with her beehive hair, polyester apron, and bright early morning smile.

Coffee first. We turn our cups right side up in expectation. As he talks, he rebuilds my pile of cards, pushing away my hands. He was just impressed, he says, to see someone like me studying Chinese, the language of the future.

The coffee comes. He stares in puzzlement at the Creamo, so I pick it up, look at him with raised eyebrows, and, when he nods, stir it into his coffee.

I order my usual bagel and cream cheese. After a quick scan of the menu, he chooses an English cooked breakfast.

He reaches out his hand to me. "Lee."

"Tessa Marshall. I'm a student here at UBC. In Asian Studies."

He has finished reassembling my cards: they are stacked up in the neatest pile I have ever seen, so perfect that I feel I never want to touch them again.

"I add five cards each day," I say. "Sometimes twice a day, if I can. Things I come across and look up in the dictionary. Then I put aside the five cards I know best."

Mr Lee nods approvingly. He tells me he's just arrived in Vancouver. He didn't realise Asian Studies was offered at UBC. His hosts on campus are from the Business School. He looks away, over the clatter of cutlery, through the glass windows to the trees on Main Mall, still clinging to their leaves. A sky grey with high cloud, and the dark finger of the clock tower raised towards us.

I cannot place his accent. Not English, not American, but fully at ease with the language. If I closed my eyes and listened, I would say that he was from India. Look at him without listening, and I might think that he was an affluent uncle visiting my host family in Taiwan. There is something solid about him. I push back my hair and resolve to tie it back before attending this morning's lecture.

"You've come here on sabbatical?"

He smiles. "You might say that."

"You're a professor?"

"No, no, no."

Something about the way he says this makes me feel rebuked, as though I am a small child who cannot possibly understand these things. Our food arrives, and we could not be more different in the way we eat. I chew on the bagel, wiping away surplus cream cheese from the corners of my mouth with a napkin. He cuts his cooked breakfast into small, perfectly formed parcels that are conveyed with astonishing regularity to his mouth, wielding his knife and fork like surgical instruments. Eating, perhaps, mollifies him. When he has finished, he is more conciliatory.

"I'm a politician," he offers. "From Singapore."

I do my best to look intelligent.

"I'm here to rest for a little. To stand back, to think."

He is staying in the Faculty Club, with its tired menus, its fuggy bar with Bass Ale and liquors, its half-baked pastiche of a Cambridge senior common room. He has been dining there, but for breakfast today he thought he would escape, leave his secretary behind, and explore the campus. It's good, he tells me, to meet young Canadians like myself, rather than a parade of officials, dignitaries, and hangers-on. What I say takes him back to his own undergraduate days in England, after the War. Only twenty years previous, but the 1960s seem very different from the late 1940s. He, too, has changed. It now seems to him a lifetime ago.

When the bills come, he pays mine, brushing my protests aside. As we get up to leave the café, he puts on a hat and an immaculately tailored coat. I'm conscious of my shabbiness, slipping on the baggy army surplus trench coat with fraying waistband that I borrowed at Sean's house this morning. Lee gestures that I've missed a loop in the belt and waits as I re-thread it. As he opens the door, there's a sigh of cold air.

We walk together up the Mall. The trees are dark, branches bare and beautiful, fallen leaves in brown heaps, the pavement wet, the mountains invisible under cloud. At this time of year, I tell him, you might visit Vancouver and never realise there were mountains at all. Has he seen them?

He saw them from the plane on Saturday, he tells me, descending to the tiny white hut they call an airport here. He's not used to nature like this, massive, in the raw, in contrast to a second-rate city and this campus cowering in the inlet.

Isn't it liberating, I ask him? A contrast to the stuffiness he remembers from Europe. I've been to Taiwan, seen the restless possibilities of a new world. In Asia, politics dams it up. But in this city, on the west of this continent, it can flow out. Young people like me are demanding freedom, an end to war and the capitalist system. A social revolution.

He looks at me in exasperation. I should think carefully about what I am saying. Think of the ravages of the Cultural Revolution in China, the teachers bludgeoned to death at struggle sessions. Those Czechoslovaks who lined up to cheer Dubček, where are they now that Soviet tanks have come into Prague? And what about the demonstrations at the recent Democratic Convention in Chicago, those hippies, is that what you call them, and their leader, that man Jerry Rubin? Leftist riots will mean the right can appeal to law and order. They will hand Nixon the election on a platter.

"Yippies. They're against violence." I correct him, but I'm conscious of how light my explanations sound against the weight of his common sense. "And Jerry is coming to UBC in a couple of days' time."

He shrugs. He has a way of making me feel like a petulant little girl. He looks out over Burrard Inlet at the white mass of cloud. A ship's foghorn sounds.

"You know," he says. "There was a time when I thought as you do now."

He pauses, and I wait for a "but" that never comes. His face twitches, his expression changing. I can't quite read it. Pain, perhaps, or more precisely that moment of anticipation of pain when you stub your toe, in that second before the sensation comes. Or the sudden apprehension of a smell, pleasant in itself but connected by a long, inescapable thread of memory to something long forgotten, long hidden away. He recomposes himself.

"I have a funeral to attend," he says suddenly. "A friend who died. I am to be a pallbearer."

At the entrance to the Faculty Club, he shakes my hand. "Miss Marshall. A pleasure to have met you."

"Mr Lee. Perhaps I'll see you on campus again?"

"Keep learning Chinese."

After that morning's lecture, before lunch, I make my way to the Main Library stacks, click my way through the turnstile and clamber downwards on the narrow metal stairs. The building always surprises me: the original grey stone Gothic library from fifty years ago, little bigger than a Shaughnessy house, now nestles between puce-coloured extensions that stretch away on either side like enormous wings. The heating is on, and the stacks are dry and airless. I find what I am looking for: the *Singapore Yearbook* from 1967. There are pictures of cranes, of a harbour full of ships, of land stripped raw and levelled for new factories just as land is levelled on our campus for new buildings. When I was in Taiwan for my year abroad, I was not so far from Singapore, yet I never thought to visit. I read on: the economy is booming since the separation from Malaysia. Soon enough I come across a picture of my breakfast companion. Mr Lee Kuan Yew, the prime minister, touring new housing estates, a garland of flowers round his neck. *Socialism that works*, the book tells me.

Statistics bore me. I replace the handbook and work my way back along a seam of bookshelves to the high, cool ceilings of the reference room and its rows of encyclopaedias. Lee studied Law at Cambridge, I discover, and returned to Singapore to enter politics. He has been in office since 1959. A different story from the yearbook: his party is centrist and a strong anti-Communist ally of the United States. He has been so successful in his struggle for power that there is now not a single opposition member of parliament.

I go to the newspapers next, taking them down from their racks and spreading them out on the table in front of me. He arrived three days ago. At a press conference, he refused to answer most questions about politics, about Malaysia, about Vietnam. He was here for a sabbatical, he said, for a time to step back after ten years in power; he was searching for new energy and fresh ideas. He would be giving two lectures while in Vancouver but would not speak further to the press. This satisfied no one.

A note to myself: contact Albie from the *Ubyssey*. I've written for the student newspaper before, and perhaps I have an opening here, the chance of an interview with Mr Lee, a way of unravelling these contradictions. A scoop.

Sure enough, splashing my way under an umbrella from the library steps to the Buchanan Building, I run into Albie scuttling in the opposite direction. "Sure," he says to my suggestion, pausing to wipe the raindrops from his glasses. "Get the copy in by Friday evening, though. Jerry Rubin's coming to campus, with that pig they've nominated for president. You'll be fighting with them for column inches."

In the afternoon, I write out a new set of cards:

解放— *chieh3 fang4 — liberation*
社會主義— *she4 hui4 chu3 i4 — socialism*
新加坡— *hsin1 chia1 po1 — Singapore*
李光耀 — *Li3 Kuang1 Yao4 — Lee Kuan Yew*
服喪 — *fu2 sang1 — to be in mourning*

It's five o'clock when I get to Sean's place. I leave my bike outside, take the salmon I've bought, climb up the peeling wooden steps that flex, creak, but never quite give way. The doorknob's solid brass, cold to the touch now, a rare reminder of how magnificent this house must have been half a century ago. The door's unlocked, as it always is, and I push my way in, along the long corridor lined with heavy coats that tug at me on either side. The salmon's awkward to hold onto in its paper wrapper, and I find myself cradling it like a child. Past the coats, I pause at the foot of the stairs. This place, I have discovered, is the still centre of the house. To the side, the stairs clamber up to bedrooms in the roof. At my feet, an iron grille, installed for some long-forgotten purpose, gives a glimpse of the basement floor. Stand here and you can hear everything: lovers' whispers on the futon downstairs; the rattle of plates in the kitchen; pages, even, crinkling as they turn over at a study desk in a room above. I listen. A radio is playing. Someone's been smoking grass, and the smell still lingers. There's something else too: a vibration that runs through the house, almost undetectable, below the threshold of the senses.

In our family home, when I was growing up, we had a lodger in the basement suite, Mr Hsieh, a physicist, a refugee from China. My parents helped him, and often he'd come up from the basement to the living room, eat with us, and tell us stories of the past. So it's natural that I would major in Asian Studies and begin to study Chinese, chanting out the four tones in class, twisting and pressing my lips and tongue into unfamiliar shapes to say *jen*, to distinguish between *chi, ch'i,* and *hsi*. After a year I flew to Taipei, to the university off Roosevelt Road, to the heat and bicycles and buses. I studied hard. I wrote pages of characters on notepaper grids, again and again until my hand ached. During the vacation, I flew via Hong Kong to Bali, to the breakers and sunset at Kuta Beach. That's where I met Sean, on the hippie trail through Asia, his lean body browned by the sun, blond stubble on his jaw, a Canadian flag sewn onto his backpack. From the same city as me. I fell for him. After my year abroad was over, I fell again, back to him, across islands and an ocean and mountains.

When Sean comes up behind me and puts his hand around my waist, I'm startled, then fold into him, as if he were another of those old coats in the hallway. He pulls me into his room. I lock the door after us, hook into eye. His hook into my nether eye. From where I lie, on the mattress, I can look up, into the branches of the horse chestnut tree outside the windows. Fading light. The leaves have not yet all fallen; those that remain stretch out towards me like splayed hands. Soon the ground will be thick with them, clogging, wet. I might burrow into them, just as Sean burrows into me, for warmth as much as for pleasure now.

By the time he wakes up and comes to find me in the kitchen, it's dark. I'm scaling and cleaning the fish with a blunt knife. The stove is hissing with warmth. He touches my shoulder and sits down at the table, next to the books I've taken out of my bag, which sit in a haphazard pile on the table under the downlight. He picks them up one by one. The *Singapore Yearbook 1967* is quickly discarded. *The Tasks Ahead*, the first manifesto of Lee Kuan Yew's party, interests him more. He thumbs through it, nodding along with its plans for a socialist society as if keeping time to music. I wrap the salmon in tinfoil and place it in the oven.

Sean's face is earnest, shadowed by the light. He is like a bear, I think, although a thin and still elegant bear, before the fattening up of fall. He likes to hibernate. When he emerges, he is hungry. He lumbers into politics as he's lumbered into my life, as if it were like a berry patch, pulling at every-thing in sight, stuffing himself full of sweetness, moving with a brute heft he does not quite understand.

I tell him about my breakfast conversation and my discoveries in the library. While I check the salmon, he looks at the Singapore books with renewed interest.

"This Lee," he says. "Is he a revolutionary or a reactionary?"

"Maybe I'll ask him."

He shrugs and returns to the books on the table. I find, miraculously, some clean plates on the shelf and trawl for cutlery among the mismatched knives and forks jumbled in a lower drawer. I look at Sean again. Something discomforts me about his ease, his quiet inevitable confidence. In Taiwan, in the classroom, every now and then, the building would shift under our feet. The chain on the ceiling fan would suddenly wriggle. We'd look at our teacher, and she'd smile. Only a tremor. Nothing to worry about. Tectonic plates shifting in the earth, many miles away.

In my life, in my body, other things shifted in Taiwan. You take off your shoes before you enter a house. You cannot wear sandals without back-straps outside the house. You must never stick your chopsticks upright in rice. You learn to make yourself small. You leave a world you have known and enter a world of strangers, and in that moment a loneliness comes that never quite leaves you, even when the strangers become your best friends. Sean has never known this. He has travelled far more widely than me, but nothing in his sense of self has changed. Underneath this city the plates are locked together: there has not been an earthquake for hundreds of years.

He looks up from his reading, his forehead furrowed in concentration, his finger tapping on the page, and smiles.

"Have you thought about it? You'll move in with me?"

The room is full of the smell of salmon. Move into the house, and the future is clear, despite what he says about equality. A career for him. A skillet in one hand for me, a baby on my hip. Perhaps a Craftsman house of our own in Kits when we tire of too alternative a lifestyle. A lifelong struggle not to forget the new language I have learned.

"Hmm."

His mouth opens, he's going to ask another question but thinks better of it and returns to the book.

The salmon's ready. I serve it, with vegetables from the stove. He sits there. I sometimes wonder whether the world has really changed. I cook for him, just as my mother cooked for my father. In bed, I am solely responsible for precautions. I realise I am changing. I am on a different path. I am falling out of love.

"Jerry Rubin's holding a rally on Thursday," he says, his mouth half full of food. "With that pig that they put up for presidential candidate. Are you going to be there?"

Of course, I tell him. But first I have to try to get an interview with Mr Lee.

In the morning, I write out more cards:

地震 — *ti4 chen4* — *earthquake*
灰熊 — *hui1 hsiung2* — *a grizzly bear*
矛盾 — *mao2 tun4* — *contradiction*
男女平等 — *nan2-nü3 ping2 teng 3* —*sexual equality*
大男人主義 — *ta4 nan2 jen2 chu3 i4* — *male chauvinism*

It's not till the afternoon that I can get away from classes. A grey day, umbrellas sprouting like mushrooms on the Mall. The Bus Stop Café windows are steamed up; as I walk past, I notice that someone has drawn a peace sign on the glass with an unsteady finger. The oak trees are darker now, shedding the last of their leaves. No piles to kick on the sidewalks, only a black mulch that clings to the soles of my new boots. The boots themselves are too tight; they pinch at my calves on the steps up to the Faculty Club.

It's warm in the lobby, with the sweet scent of pipe tobacco. I hear the clink of glasses in the distance and the murmur of conversation. A man's voice laughs, suddenly loud.

"Excuse me!" The Suit at reception looks at me sceptically over steel-rimmed glasses.

I struggle to fasten my umbrella closed.

"You do know this is a members-only club?"

"I'm a journalist. I'm here to see Mr Lee Kuan Yew."

He picks up a pen and looks down. "From which newspaper?"

"*The Ubyssey.*"

He raises his eyes. "The student newspaper? Do you have an appointment with Mr Lee?"

No, I tell him. But I met Mr Lee yesterday. We talked. It seemed that we had many things in common. I'm sure he would want to share his experiences with students here. I stop talking, but I can still hear my voice bouncing around, too shrill among the leather chairs, beechwood tables, and bright steel banisters.

The club has a policy, he replies, of not disturbing guests. Perhaps I might like to leave my name and contact number?

"Can't you just check?"

"It's against our policies."

I look sideways, up the stairs to the guest suites. I think, if I could just run up there and knock on his door. His eyes follow mine, and he shakes his head, slowly. He offers me pen and paper. "Just write your details here."

He passes the pen to me but is already looking over my shoulder to the staircase, his expression softening. There's a Chinese man descending slowly in a suit as crisp as Mr Lee's coat.

"Mr Yeoh," says the Suit, as if I don't exist. "I hope everything is now to Mr Lee's satisfaction."

Mr Yeoh nods. "Just a couple more questions, Mr Gardiner." That accent again, those full vowels.

"Of course. The dinner arrangements?"

The man is next to me. I am expected, I know, to stand back. But I remain at the counter, ignoring the Suit's glares.

"Mr Yeoh," I find myself saying. "I'm so glad I've managed to meet you." I tell him, in something of a hurry, about the breakfast yesterday.

He shakes his head. "Mr Lee has come here to rest and to study. He's already said all that he wanted to the press."

"拜托, 拜托您," I say. *Please.* He looks surprised. Then he reaches for the phone and dials an extension. He gives an elegant summary of my case and waits for instructions. After a pause, he turns back to me.

"Mr Lee would be delighted to see you tomorrow at four. Do make sure you are punctual."

"Thanks," I say. "I'll be there."

"Make sure you sign in as a guest when you come," the Suit says as I take up my umbrella. "We can't just have anyone roaming around in here."

There's a sudden lightness to my feet on the steps down. I've dared, and I succeeded.

In the evening, I sit at my desk in my Dunbar basement suite. I write out more flash cards, now that I'm on a roll:

> 光臨 — *kuang1 lin2 — honour someone with yr. presence*
> 總理 — *tsung3 li3 — prime minister*
> 游行 — *yu2 hsing2 — demonstration*
> 敢作敢為 — *kan3 tso4 kan3 wei2 — to dare to take action*
> 禁城 — *chin4 ch'eng2 — the Forbidden City*

It's already dark outside, turning the glass of the window into a mirror. My face among the rustling, fallen leaves. I told Sean I wanted this night to myself, to think. There was a time when I felt the same as him. Freedom was simply a door we opened into a new life. I didn't realise then how deeply conventions write themselves into the body, into the lips, the palate, the fingertips. How difficult they are to unwrite or erase. What, then, might liberation be? To always be in motion, to never rest? I shiver. Behind me the single bed is swallowed up in shadows.

By the time Sean and I get to the Hebb Theatre the next day, the crowd is spilling out onto East Mall. We stand on the fringes in the thin winter light, yet after five minutes, we're hemmed in. I can see nothing apart from the branches of trees above. In the nearest tree is a young man, blond, startlingly beautiful, the hairs on the back of his neck lit up by the sun. Sean squeezes my hand, but I pull it away.

"The SUB," the boy is shouting. "The theatre's too small. Jerry'll talk to us from the stairs." The crowd flows across the road to the Student Union Building, through the rows of saplings to that new, raw concrete concourse. Sean and I are close to the front, and, when Jerry Rubin appears at the top of the steps, we can see him clearly.

Jerry knows his theatre. I saw his picture once in a newspaper, appearing before the House Un-American Activities Committee wearing the costume of an American Revolutionary War soldier. Today he wraps himself in a red and blue flag, a caped crusader.

"What's he wearing?" Sean's voice, and stubble, in my ear.

"The NLF flag. National Liberation Front. From Vietnam. Shhh."

Jerry starts slowly to a mixture of boos and cheers, shouting through his megaphone. He stops, waits until the crowd falls quiet. We're about now, he tells us. This is our time. Society wants to turn all of us into policemen, policemen of ourselves. There's no need to obey those rules. We shouldn't be the spare parts that keep someone else's automobile running. Universities like UBC? They're babysitting agencies when they could be so much more.

He tells us about the Democratic Convention in Chicago. November 5th will be election day in the United States. The tragedy is that Americans are choosing a world government, a government for whom no one else in the world can vote, not even here, in Canada.

The woman next to me takes a long toke from a rollie. She passes it to me, and I send it on without sampling. There's feedback on the megaphone, and I lose track of what Jerry is saying for a minute. He's talking about Pigasus, the porker they nominated for President. Why have half-pigs like Hubert Humphrey, Governor Wallace, or Richard Nixon, when you can go the whole hog? I've seen the Chicago protests on TV, a drove of police officers hustling Pigasus off into custody. But he's here before us now, squirming in a yippie's arms. They were going to roast him after the election, Rubin tells us, but that pissed off the vegetarian members of the movement, so he's been reprieved. Cheers from the crowd, even from the engineers.

We need to stop talking, he tells us. We need to act. We've got all these people together: we need to do something. Is there anywhere on this campus that needs liberating?

"The Faculty Club," I say, more to myself than anyone else. Someone nearby picks up my words and shouts them out. Others echo them, nearer the stairs.

"What was that?" he says. "The Faculty Club? The Faculty Club! Lead the way."

The crowd oozes past the library, gathering onlookers and activists alike. Sean and I are at the back again. When I get to Main Mall, there's a little rise, and I can look ahead to the Rose Garden and the sea. The Mall is full of bodies. Students in their thousands, surely: our own little march on Washington.

At the club, the mass slows, coagulates. "Should we wait?" Sean tugs at my hand.

"I'm not standing around."

I leave him behind. These are the bystanders, I see, crowding the parking lot, not daring to enter. The atmosphere's festive. But the real action is inside. I push my way through them to the entrance.

Reception's deserted. In the dining room and lounge, a few faculty members remain, hunkered down in their easy chairs or staring mournfully into their consommés, sunken islands in a sea of students. Squeezing my way into the bar, I meet Albie, passing out cigarettes. A friend of his has found the key to the liquor cabinet and lined up bottles of spirits and liqueurs on the bar counter. Mix your own cocktail, he tells me, thrusting a drinks menu into my hand. I look at the names: Mai Tai, Tom Collins, Doctor's Special, Stinger, Screwdriver, Singapore Sling. This makes me think of Mr Lee and our appointment.

After climbing the stairs, I find the doors on the guest suites corridor locked. Outside one, a bearded man in a tweed jacket fiddles with his tie.

"What do you think you're doing?" he demands.

I push past him and carry on as if I know where I'm going. At the corridor's end, there's a glass door, then a balcony running back along the length of the club to the guest suites. As I pass through the door, I look down to the courtyard with its pool. Two students, with what looks like a Zippo lighter, are trying to set fire to an American flag that refuses to catch alight. Splashing in the water. It's the golden-haired boy, swimming naked. He stands up, nipples pinched with cold, and shakes his upper torso dry. Behind him, dark green cedars and the mountains of Bowen Island and the North Shore.

There are French windows at the far end of the balcony. The first room I go past is empty, and in the second, I find what I am looking for. Mr Lee and his secretary sit in armchairs. Mr Lee is nearer the window, a coffee table piled with papers and books in front of him. He is reading one of the books, paying no attention to the commotion below.

I knock on the glass. Mr Yeoh looks up and comes forward reluctantly. He can't see my face, I realise; I'm just a silhouette against the sky. Recognising me, he shakes his head and points to his watch. Too early.

"I'm afraid we'll have to ask you to leave."

It's Tweed Jacket at the end of the balcony, accompanied by the Suit from reception yesterday.

I'm here for an interview, I tell him. His friend should remember me.

They come closer. Why don't I go downstairs, he suggests. Join the fun and games. I have to understand that the club isn't a zoo. I can't just wander round, looking at the big game. They have a guest staying here, a very important guest whose care is of paramount importance.

"And my interview?"

"Regrettably postponed. If you don't leave, we will call the police."

"Why don't we let Mr Lee be the judge of that?"

We turn to the window again. Mr Lee is beckoning Tweed Jacket with his little finger. He hesitates, then draws a circle with his hands: he'll enter by the corridor. When he enters the suite from the back, we're treated to a silent movie. Mr Lee listens, then points with his fingers; Tweed Jacket replies, speaks, and finally shrugs. Mr Yeoh opens the balcony door.

"Sit down, Miss Marshall."

I take the offered chair.

"Professor Huberman here," Mr Lee says, "has been concerned to protect me. But this doesn't bother me at all. It would take something of much greater seriousness than a student protest to get me excited."

The chair is small and hard, quite unlike Mr Lee's plush armchair. Mr Yeoh has placed it in such a way that I am looking into the light and see Mr Lee in his armchair in profile, like one of those silhouette miniatures at the art gallery. The French windows are still open a crack, and I hear music starting up from below.

"Now," he says, settling back in his chair. "You have some questions for me?"

I pull out my notebook and clear my throat. I have so much to ask.

Downstairs, afterwards, I sip Scotch beneath a sign that reads PEOPLE'S BAR: FREE FOR EVERYONE. In the corner, a bearded professor explains Freudian repression to two women in Afghan jackets. Or rather, to their breasts. No Sean; I've left him behind. I find a place by the door where I can see the action. The golden-haired boy ambles up, smiling. At first I think he's hitting on me, but he's tripping; he's somewhere else. This new, liberated world feels very much like the one it has replaced.

I want to nurse my disappointment with the interview. All those questions that Mr Lee would not answer, that he turned away with disdain or laughter. Only forty-five, he told me, yet he seemed in our conversation so unutterably old.

I look through the smoke to the dancers by the pool. They've brought in an amplifier, and the floor shakes. A girl with long hair plays the mouth organ, holding it closely, nervously, as though she is biting her nails. What now? Storm the walls, enter the Forbidden City, then you realise that power is not here. Habits grow back again like mould. How do you persist when you have overcome? How does real newness come into the world?

When I look up, Mr Lee is descending the staircase, two policemen in front of him, one behind, while Mr Yeoh scurries along at the rear. Mr Lee looks down into the foyer with something like contempt. For a moment our eyes meet, and I think he nods to acknowledge me, but he flinches and looks away. Perhaps he no longer recognises me; he is catching, clutching at a memory only so that he can crush it. The university authorities will come for him, he told me at the end of the interview. They will take him to a place where he can read in quiet and prepare his speech. At that moment, as now, he looked infinitely weary. You have to understand, he told me. We are the masters now, in our own house. We are on our own. We will not follow anyone. But as the policemen part the crowd, I wonder. I have seen how he commands, but at the moment, flanked by his guards, he might just as easily be a captive, led off to imprisonment.

My notebook is still with me. How will I write up the interview? How will I tell this story? How will I live now, and what new doors will open for me?

The last I see of Mr Lee is his back, tightly encased in that tailored coat. Mr Yeoh opens an umbrella. The door closes after them. In the Faculty Club, the party continues all night.

自新 — *tzu4 hsin1* — *make a fresh start*
自作主張 — *tzu4 tso4 chu3 chang1* — *to decide for oneself*
自作自受 — *tzu4 tso4 tzu4 shou4* — *to suffer for what you've done; to get what you deserve*
實用主義 — *shih2 yung3 chu3 i4* — *pragmatism*
大志 — *ta4 shih4* — *high ideals*

Pigeons and Doves

The day she meets her new client, Eileen is nervous. She is still training as a psychotherapist. Her office is cold and bare, its sash window leading onto a tiny courtyard lined with sooty bricks. Pigeons' wings flutter against glass in the leaden London air. Her new navy jacket weighs her down like armour. She looks at her hands, trim nails held out, the little finger that she bites hiding itself underneath the others. When the client shuffles in, she is for a moment lost for words. She must compose herself to speak. Wait for the lumps of the accent she thought she had suppressed forever to dissolve in her mouth. For that new, calm therapist's voice to come.

"Mr Lim."

He has taken the seat opposite her. He's on the edge of his chair, looking at her through thick, round framed glasses. Hunched up, as if he might startle and take flight.

"I'm Eileen Tay. Was it difficult to make your way here?"

He shakes his head. He speaks slowly, with a noticeable accent. Flat, she notes mentally. Expressionless. He took the Tube to Tavistock Square and walked. Once he found the street, it was easy to count off the numbers and find his way.

"Mr Lim, tell me why you came to us."

He meets her eyes briefly, then looks down at his feet. She snatches a glance at the clock on the wall, the red second hand moving in the arc of a slow-motion somersault. Once. Twice. Breathe. Let the tightness go. You are here for the client, not for you. Do not rush to fill up silence with words.

He looks up. "You're very young."

Her cheeks burn. A thought like a sting, pricking and leaving no trace. Don't scratch. Let the irritation fade away. Reflect back his emotion and the thought behind it.

"You're sceptical," she says, "because you think I've not seen enough of the world to understand you."

His face scrunches in puzzlement. Then he starts to talk.

At the end of a long day of sessions, Eileen finds herself rehearsing what happened when she climbs the stairs to her flat at Lancaster Gate. The boiler's out, and the radiators are stone cold. She lights the stove, holds her hands near the kettle for warmth.

She sits down with her tea and begins to write up her notes. Most of the clients' stories are simple: depression or anxiety, driven by ingrained patterns of thought. A young man feels a sense of dread when he enters the office each day, as strong as a blow to the chest. A middle-aged woman finds that anger still flares whenever she talks to her mother, although each time she resolves to be calm. An old gentleman is insufferably lonely and finds himself unable to make new friends.

Such cases, her supervisor, Dr Harry Brightman, tells her, show the nature of human beings. They are like onions, taking patience and some tears to peel, layer by layer, to the core. Her clients are caught in an eternal moment: when the trigger event occurs, emotions overwhelm them. The trick is to help them notice the thoughts that flicker, that connect event to emotion, thoughts that have become so habitual that the client no longer notices them. Peel off the layers. Find that hidden thought. The young man is convinced that nothing he ever does works out right. The woman feels her mother's judgement stab, even without words. The older man knows that he is fundamentally unlovable. Unwrap the thought. Look at it carefully: is it really, completely true?

This is how we progress, Harry tells her. Intellect governs emotion. We expose these hidden thoughts to the clear light of reason. It's good to gain a client's trust, of course. To make them feel comfortable. But soon you need to discipline them, to make them, however recalcitrant, rule themselves.

She smiles and sips her tea. With Mr Lim, then, she surely shouldn't worry that in the first session she's simply let him talk and reflected back his feelings. She can introduce the process of change, the thought record, in the next session. She has saved his case notes for last. These should be clinical, Harry has told her, factual. But she finds that she remembers fragments of their conversation where words flew up beyond that familiar grid of behaviour, emotion, and thought.

A great wave broke and left me on the shore.

Islands are never apart from each other.

I see pigeons all around me, but I dream of doves.

She writes these words down, then crosses them out.

She did not think Mr. Lim would return for the second session, yet he is sitting in the waiting room. He carries a bag of apples that he wants to give to her, and she says, gently, no, we are not allowed to take gifts.

She asks, when he has settled in his chair, how his last week has been, and he tells her there has been little change. He falls asleep easily, in the double bed he shares with his wife, but two or three hours later he is wide awake again. His boys sleep blissfully through the night. So does his wife.

When he wakes up, sleep refuses to come again. Thoughts race through his head. He goes back over those things that happened, those stories that he has begun to share with her. Could he have acted differently? In agreeing to come here, in leaving Singapore, in writing that letter resigning from the party, did he betray his friends? Then there are the sounds of the street at night, even in the quiet of South London suburbia. Footsteps on paving stones, growing louder. The hiss of car tires on wet tarmac. Once, a police siren, in the distance, coming closer. He broke into a sweat. He was sure it was coming for him. Despite the stuffiness, he kept the windows closed. He lay and waited for the knock on the door, the voices outside.

"What do you do if you still can't sleep?"

There is a small desk and an uncomfortable chair in the living room where he can sit and read. Books and magazines bought from Gwanghwa in Soho. Echoes from Asia, from Singapore, from another, faraway life. Sometimes reading works. After two or three hours he can return to bed, doze, only to be awakened again by the light leaking in round the curtains, the new day slapping his face.

Mornings are the worst, he tells her. He and his wife get the boys ready for the day. He prepares for work. He feels as if all the air has been sucked out of the world and replaced by thick treacle, clogging any movement he makes. This feeling persists until lunchtime, when the weight suddenly vanishes from his temples and his shoulders. He sits on a bench in the park with a sandwich, dropping crumbs and watching a flock of pigeons peck and rise up into the air. They are like a kettle boiling. There is the memory of the arms of his youngest boy, soft and warm with sleep, wrapping around the pillar of his leg. At times he smiles at this. At others he cries, and the darkness returns.

"Let's slow down," she says. "You're there, in the park."

He nods, gazes at the floor, and breathes.

"You're sitting there, on the bench."

"It's cold. I'm alone. And then I think of the boy. He reaches out to me."

"What does he say to you?"

He looks up at her, takes off his glasses and wipes the corner of his eyes. "爸爸."

She knows the word well: *father*. "Can you stay there? In that moment."

He sighs. "It's very cold. And then I feel the warmth of my son's arms."

"What's the feeling inside you?"

His lips move, but no words come. For a moment, she thinks she should back off. Like a record player, Harry has told her. Lower the needle very carefully into the groove, so you don't scratch it. Raise it again with equal care.

"Sickness." He is trying out words, as if reading them from a hidden dictionary. "Fear. Disgust."

"What's the thought that goes through your head?"

"I'm not a good father. I let you down. The world is not right. I am powerless to change it."

"What is the deepest thought?"

"I let you down."

"Again."

"I let you down. I let you down."

She lifts the needle. She asks him how what has happened felt for him. They catch their breath. Then she asks him to find another moment at which he was most distressed. First the situation. Then the feeling. Finally, the buried thought.

At the end of the session, she gives him the Thought Record, a foolscap page with columns and pink, mimeographed headings. Homework. Just fill out the first three columns, she tells him. The situation when depression comes. The emotions. And then the buried thought. When she passes the paper to him, she thinks she sees the ghost of a smile on his face.

—

Winter deepens. In late November, a sudden cold arrives. Ice on the footpaths and the roads. At Lancaster Gate, Eileen totters to the Tube on unsteady feet; she exits at Holborn to the first flakes of snow. She calls her parents in Newcastle. It's much worse here in the North, they tell her, voices crackling with static. When she puts the phone down, she glances at the mantelpiece. Their wedding photograph. Father was caught in London, during the War. He thought he would go back to Malaya, to help make this new world out of the chaos. Then he met Mother. This slip of a Geordie girl who haunted the meetings of the Left Book Club. After the War he did not take the passage back; he followed her North. Marooned, he learned to fit in. Even the way he talked, he told her, changed. They had both wanted their only child, Eileen, this pale, serious girl, to keep something of him. Something more than her name, an infinite loop of translation: Eileen, Ai Ling, 愛玲. The long hours with Mrs Chiu on Saturday while her classmates played happily outside. Writing Chinese characters until her hand ached. Dictation. One day she had suddenly refused to go. Quite out of character: she was normally so compliant. She had cried: they had cajoled her, then bribed her, but she still refused. Now much later, she regretted her wilfulness. She tried to pick up the language again, attended evening classes after she came down to London to study. But it would not stick. Words would perch on her lips only to fly away when she opened her mouth.

In London, the deep freeze persists until January. Football matches are cancelled at the New Year: the Stamford Bridge and White Hart Lane pitches resemble Siberian permafrost. On Hampstead Heath, three men fall through ice into the ponds and drown. Prime Minister Callaghan suns himself in the Caribbean. *Crisis? What crisis?* he says at Heathrow Airport on his return. The train drivers strike, then the lorry drivers and the bin men.

Rubbish piles up. Ambulance drivers refuse to drive. In the North, even the gravediggers put down tools.

In this chaos, Eileen senses the sweet taste of success. Winter is the worst time for depression, Harry warns her. Less light and less time outside. Yet her clients continue to come each week. The young man has bought a new pair of boots to make his way through the snow. He does not fall. *Nothing I try ever works* becomes *If I put my mind to it, I can do it.* The middle-aged woman no longer tries to read her mother's mind. *I count to ten,* she tells Eileen. *I know it isn't me that's her target.* In the depths of winter, the older man says, neighbours have rallied round. *I'm not unworthy of love, but I am shy. If I reach out, others will care for me.*

Only Mr Lim, or George as she now calls him, doesn't respond. He comes every week with his thought record in a leather satchel. Each week, he tells her, he finds those moments of sadness, when the clouds descend and will not lift. He writes them down as she has instructed him. First the moment, then the emotion, then the fleeting thought, caught in her purple net of lines and words. So far, so good. But thoughts lead to memories. Singapore. A speech at a rally, when his words caught fire, so that he became part of something much bigger than himself. The first years in prison, waiting for a freedom that would not just be his but also a nation's, and then the prison gates opening and the assembled crowd. He and his comrades were released and carried on the shoulders of others. He remembers the garlands of scented flowers heavy round his neck, white doves rising like ashes into the sky. Several years later, the second detention, the arrest in the night, the same prison as before, some of the same jailers but under the new regime that had replaced the colonial order. Solitary confinement. Then optimism and the solidarity of comrades imprisoned with him. Over the years, gnawing despair. To be released he had been forced to write two letters. The first to the Prime Minister, his erstwhile comrade who had imprisoned him. The second to the Chairman of his Party, resigning from politics. The flight to England. The reply from the Party. *Do not think you have quit politics. What you have quit is anti-imperialist politics. You have become a willing and subservient tool.*

The other clients, she tells Harry, are shallow. History does not weigh them down. But for George there is no bottom to memory, no return from layer on layer of words.

Harry wipes a tiny speck of dust off the desk in front of him with a monogrammed handkerchief. Stop him, he tells her. Remember that we govern ourselves. It's difficult, of course, to whip flabby emotions into shape. But it becomes easier with practice. It's like making love: it's much easier the second time.

"But . . ."

"No buts. Do not indulge him, Eileen."

She covers her confusion and mounting anger by scribbling away in her notebook, eyes down.

"And the disputation? How has that been going?"

Her faces flushes, and she feels beads of sweat start on her temples. She hasn't been following Harry's template. The emotion is panic. The fleeting thought is, *You've found me out.*

"It's also been difficult."

"The proof of a therapist, Miss Tay, is how you handle the most difficult clients. I've seen so many of you fall at the last fence."

He resumes wiping imaginary dust off the white surface of the desk.

This is what disputation looks like. You've worked with the thought record to identify those buried thoughts. You've brought them out into the clear light of day. You've used the first three columns—the incident, the feeling, the thought—to haul in your catch. Now the clients must do a different kind of work: they must practise logic. They must dispute the thought, see how at the very most it is only a fraction of the truth. The young man realises that he does not always fail; often if he tries, he will succeed. *It's hard, but I can do it.* The middle-aged woman comes to understand that her mother's rage is not directed at her. *I am not the cause of her anger.* The older man comes to see that rejection is not automatic. *If I reach out, some people will respond.*

There's a trick to disputation, though. The buried thought is persistent. You've brought it to the surface, but you haven't pulled up all its roots. Hack at it, cover it over, and it'll grow again in the darkness. So you lure it out a little further. Imagine, you tell the client, that you're in a law court. The case is to prove that the thought is untrue. But let's allow the defence to speak first. List as many reasons you can think why the thought is reasonable. Only when you've exhausted this will we turn to the prosecution, to list all the reasons why the thought may not be totally correct. Then we'll have our trial.

With George, there's first the barrier of a word.

"What kind of court?" he asks her.

A bubble of irritation swells within her. She presses her index fingers together, a gesture she has taught herself for times like these. Acknowledge what's happening. Let the bubble grow and pop and dissipate. Observe. He's put on weight. His shoulders are stiff. Even after several sessions working together, he's still on his guard.

"Any kind of court."

He's silent again. His hands move, as if trying to sculpt words.

"What about a court that meets in secret, to which the defence has no access? Where the accused cannot speak? Or a court without a jury, in a country where juries have been abolished?"

"An ideal court. It's just a metaphor."

Justice, he tells her, is not a metaphor. Even though you cannot always find it in the world.

Spring hesitates to come. Her parents talk of communities in the North that are still cut off by snow. The strikers return to work, but something in the air has changed. An election approaches. She walks to the Tube past Conservative advertisements on hoardings, showing long lines of the unemployed. *Labour Isn't Working.* On television, Mrs Thatcher rails against the current order. We have become a flabby country. Like guppies in a fishbowl. Every human being is an island. Society does not exist. Competition will drive us forward.

Each weekend Eileen calls her parents, falling into that rich language of her childhood. We'll vote for Thatcher, her father says. She asks, what about those stories you told me about 1945? That vision of a just society for everyone? How you both voted Mr Churchill out, how one of the new Labour MPs in government said in Parliament, *We are the masters now*? It was a dream, he tells her. This is their reality now. The way the world works.

In session, they put the court metaphor aside but run into a further difficulty. George can effortlessly list all the reasons why those buried thoughts are reasonable. Yet he can find very few arguments against them. What she still calls the defence—although not to him, not aloud—speaks confidently, fluently. Switch to the prosecution, and silence descends.

They have worked through the thought record once more. They have excavated a thought. *The world is not right.*

It's easy to find support for this. The first weeks in solitary confinement in Singapore on his second arrest. In Outram Jail, an iron bed with a grass mattress, a beaker, a chamber pot, and the white, thick door. Heat and the stench of urine. Later, when they moved to Changi Prison, things got better and then worse. Liberal friends came, with kind, useless gestures: turkeys and puddings for Christmas. In the end he refused to see them. Finally he had a choice: to write a letter—or, more precisely, to sign a letter already written for him—or to go mad. Ten long years in exile in London, trying to study and failing, the drugs, treatments, the quest for work. Depression, always present, even when you turn your face away from it. A precipice next to you, a void into which you may at any time fall.

Eileen lets him talk until silence comes again. She waits for his words to settle within him, for the aftertaste that rises up.

"Do you remember what we said last time about black-and-white thinking? Catastrophizing?"

He's quiet again.

"Could there be anything of this in what you've just said?"

His face scrunches up again in that expression of puzzlement. His hands move. It isn't my thinking that is black-and-white, he tells her. It's the thinking of those who imprisoned me. And it *was* a catastrophe. A door to a new world opened, and very quickly it was jammed shut. We were all changed in a way that we do not yet know.

In her next supervision session, when Harry seems more relaxed, she asks him whether depression might not be a pathology but, in some circumstances, logical. A natural reaction to an unjust society. The only possible response to the cruelty of a world gone wrong.

He looks at her over the top of his reading glasses. What a strange idea. The world is not going wrong, surely. Every day we progress. Science lights up more dark corners. Development proceeds apace. Of course, there are obstacles on the road. Irrational moments. But in the end Reason will prevail.

He moves closer. "It's that resistant client of yours? The one who isn't willing to change?"

She nods.

"Miss Tay, it's the difficult case that makes the therapist. You've been too indulgent with him. Toughen up."

She opens her mouth to continue, but he interrupts her.

"I'll come to your session next week. And I expect to see the disputation working well."

She's fortunate that she sees George this week, before the session to which Harry insists on coming. She briefly contemplates begging her client to bail her out. Not to resist, as he always does, to fall away into silence in the disputation. For us not to go off from there into the world of the past.

Their session follows the pattern they've settled into over the last few weeks. They go over the thought record. They find that buried thought. She holds him to the disputation, but the defence is strong, and the prosecution fails to make its case. She pushes, but he grows weary and fractious. At these times she has learned to turn away, to work with a different part of him.

"Tell me," she says, "the moment when you felt most joyful."

A door opens. They enter the world of story.

At the end of the session, she summarises, as she always does, and says casually that her supervisor will join them next time. George shouldn't be alarmed: Harry is checking up on her, not on him. She is calm, but as she speaks something reaches up and catches at her words. Her voice breaks.

That hint of a smile in his face. "You're scared," George says, "because you think he doesn't value your work."

For the next session, she's aware how much is at stake. In the morning, she gets up early, just as the light comes. She reviews her notes, but she's easily distracted into a game she plays with herself, translating sentences from her notes into hesitant Mandarin.

I see pigeons all around me, but I dream of doves. 我看到周围都是鸽子, 可是我梦见鸽子.

In Chinese, in her limited Chinese at least, pigeons and doves are the same word.

When he came out of the prison, he released a dove. 他一出狱就放鸽子.

That also doesn't work. 放鸽子 literally means to "release a dove" but actually means to stand someone up. English is equally illogical. If you stand someone up, you also let them down.

It rains heavily, but she's still at the clinic early. George arrives as punctually as ever and plucks the completed thought record from his satchel.

In a third chair in the corner, Harry, with his clipboard. "Get started. Don't mind me."

She can feel her heart beating as she turns to her client. She breathes slowly, touches her fingers together again. She tries to forget she is being watched.

The first part of the session is like a dance. Eileen leads, George follows. They both know the moves. How has the last week been? Start with the weather, as the English always do. Go deeper. Hover and settle on a moment. Begin the thought record. First the incident.

On Thursday, George says. That's when it happened. I was reading the newspaper, and I saw his face. My former comrade, the one who imprisoned me. He's coming here for an official visit.

"What did you feel when you saw the picture?"

"Tired. Frustrated."

She waits, lets him shuffle through the feelings.

"Anger. Despair."

In the corner of her eye, just out of her direct vision, she senses a movement from Harry. A leaning forward.

"Anger," she repeats. "Despair. Take me further into that moment. Where were you?"

"In a newsagent's shop," he tells her. In Wimbledon. "While the man at the till goes out for a smoke, he lets you browse the newspapers. So I choose one. There's a smell of cigarette smoke from the door. The floor is wet; it's just been mopped. If I move my feet, my shoes squeak. The newspaper is difficult to fold and unfold. I don't want to spend so long here: I want to finish before the shopkeeper comes back. Then I see his picture. He's older now. Puffy cheeks. Bags under his eyes."

"How do you feel in your body?" she asks.

"Tight," he says. "In my shoulders. A pain in my head. A pounding. Just like those times in prison."

She leads him, gently, to the thoughts. Harry wriggles like a fish in her peripheral vision. An ache in her temples. This is where they always get derailed.

I hate this.

The world is not right.

The world is not fair to me.

The third thought is new. It's individualised, not social. A gift passed to her. He makes the case for the defence but with a little less certainty than he normally does. When the time for the prosecution comes, she is sure he winks at her, quickly, with the eye that Harry cannot see. Together, they dispute the thought, as easily as a knife through butter. They pare it back. They reach a final formulation: *The world is not always fair, but I can make my way.*

Harry beams. He's seen enough. The triumph of the human will! He makes his excuses and leaves.

She turns to George. "Thank you."

When George tells her he is going back to Singapore, Eileen feels something tug and snap inside her. Harry has summoned her and told her how impressed he is with her skills, even with the most recalcitrant of clients. She has enough client hours now to move to the examinations. She tells him no, she's abandoning her studies. Harry sputters. Now? At this late stage? But that's irrational. She should go back home and think about it, let her passions cool.

In these last sessions, she leaves what Harry has taught her behind. She and George no longer do the thought record. Instead they weave together past, present, and future. What does he remember? What values are most important to him? What most gives him joy? What might the future hold?

In the last few days before the general election, she hopes against hope. She goes to the polling station on election day, marking a firm cross next to the name of the Labour candidate. But on election night the swingometer needle moves decisively to the right. The next day Mrs Thatcher enters Downing Street. The world changes.

In their last session, she asks how it has been for him. He says he is not healed. But perhaps they have moved a little further away from that precipice. Far enough to wait for the next great wave to take him inland, into the interior of the island.

She drops Harry a note. Her decision is final. *I want to accompany others, not to oversee them. I will search for those things that thought alone cannot govern.*

He summons her to his office.

She stands him up.

Eileen has a secret. I can tell you now that Harry's no longer around. She saw George once, in London, outside a session, by accident. In Regent's Park, in the early spring, just when the crocuses had come. He was sitting on a bench with a woman about his age. His wife, surely? Eileen watched from a distance, careful that they did not see her. In front of them, on the grass in the thin sunlight, a small boy played, in a duffel coat so thick that he was as round as a ball. The couple watched over him. The boy came closer, but he was not looking at Eileen; he did not even register she was there. He was looking at the grey pigeons that hopped and pecked and cooed in the short grass by the path. He ran towards them and broke into a run. He flapped his arms. The birds moved away a little, just far enough, and carried on pecking. The boy ran forward again, faster, legs jerking, almost overbalancing. She smiled, thinking of what George had said to her, the weight of small soft arms clutching at the pillar of his leg. This time the boy succeeded. The pigeons took off, first one, then another, so that the air boiled with wings. The child stopped, amazed at what he had done.

Then a young man came up to her, in a cheap new trench coat, curling up his bitten nails into the cuffs. He asked for directions to Bedford College in a voice very like her own, a voice from which those short Northern vowels had not quite vanished. He was late for his admissions interview. She pointed him the way. That young man was me. This is also my story.

IN TRANSIT

Library

Michelle had never thought, she told her parents later, that she could fall. Late summer, and the banks of the river were thick with blackberries. She tasted some greedily on the way down to the water, trying to remember what her Canadian aunt had said. Pull gently, and if they come away in your hand, they're ripe. But she found herself fumbling, frustrated with herself, pulling here and pulling there, until her hands were purple with juice, a second's sweetness overwhelmed by bitterness in the mouth. When they pulled her out of the water later, they would find scratches on her bare forearms, made before the bruises from the river. The flesh around them had swelled, as though someone had gone over them with a marker pen, drawing a long trail down towards the stains on her hands.

At the water's edge, she could no longer hear her parents, aunt, and uncle, halted for lunch by the pile of tailings from the old mine. The water in the stream was too low to skim stones but low enough to tempt her to cross on the line of rocks that rose from the river. There was a slap of heat after she left the shade of the tree on the bank. She walked forward easily from rock to rock. *Don't stop.* Only when she reached the safety of a flat, midstream boulder did she rest, looking up at the V of the valley, the green-black layers of trees above her, an empty mountain face of bare stone, then the barer blue of the sky. She looked down. In front of her was a pool of calm water, protected from the river by a worn cedar log.

The next stage was more difficult. Another boulder, then another log, this one thinner, with stumpy branches and limp green foliage, wedged above a natural weir. She could cross it, she was sure, but she wondered if it might twist underfoot and slip over the lip of stone into the pool beneath. She looked back at the line of rocks she had crossed. Nothing much there: more unripe berries, a fussing mother, the heaviness of her own body, and the slow trudge home. No going back. The log gave slightly under her weight, then held. Its bark was grey, broken into long lozenge-shaped strips. Everything was new in this country: new textures and backgrounds, like entering a new level in a game on her phone. She tugged at a branch to pull it out of the way, but her foot slipped and her knee jarred against a knot in the trunk. She reached out again, hanging on to the branch, her legs spreading out in the water. She shouted for help. When she let go, she was surprised that the water was not very cold but it was heavy, pressing down on her as firmly as she had pressed the berries.

In the car, after her father's scolding, she was obstinately silent. When she cleared the WhatsApp messages on her phone, she opened the game with the alligators. Here you could burrow through sand and rock to make a channel for water. If you wiped out, there was no fuss, no pain. You simply began again.

At the clinic, she rolled her eyes in the waiting room but cooperated with the doctor when they were called in. She didn't have a headache; she didn't feel sick; of course she knew who and where she was. Michelle Tan Yi Ling, age 14, from Singapore, on holiday in Vancouver with family, visiting her Uncle Wei Ming and his wife Auntie Justine. Yes, she knew those mountain streams were dangerous. Luckily, the hiker had been there on the far bank. Yes, yes, *of course* she was lucky to be alive.

—

I told you, she muttered to her mother as they hunted for Dettol at the pharmacy. No concussion, just scratches. *No need to waste an afternoon at the clinic like that.* But in the evening she felt sapped of energy. She curled on the soft couch in her uncle and aunt's apartment, picking up and then discarding a magazine. The conversation at the dinner table was a buzz of noise. She did not listen, as she usually did, to see if they were talking about her.

"Michelle?" Auntie Justine had brought out cut fruit for her.

She took one and turned back to the magazine, but her aunt persisted. "How do you feel?"

"Okay."

"Pain?"

She shrugged, shook her head. *Go away.*

"What was it like, in the water?"

A strange question. She looked up at her aunt. Green eyes and a cloud of red hair. White arms dappled with freckles.

"Cold."

"What did you see?"

It was only now that she remembered. "Books. In the river."

"You mean garbage? Litter?"

She shook her head. Clear water. Her eyes open. A rock floor, with scratches of quartz leading downwards. Then a recess, a deeper pool, grey with sediment. For a moment she had been directly above it, floating, still waiting to kick out. The books were there. She could see only the spines. Jade-grey, peeling, like the dying salmon she'd seen below the hatchery, slowly merging back into the riverbed. A shaft of golden light made the quartz in the rocks fizz and sparkle, then it fingered the covers. One book was stamped, she thought, with letters in an indecipherable language. She thought she might dive down to it, pull it towards her just as you took a book down from a library shelf. Then her foot hit something hard; she gasped and took in water, not air. She coughed and realised where she was.

Wei Ming was glad when his sister's family left. He found these visits a strain, he told Justine after their guests had been shepherded to the airport, after they'd lingered awkwardly until the last possible moment to enter passport control, not quite able to say goodbye. Particularly after the accident with Michelle. Silly girl. He had never felt particularly close to his sister nor to the rest of his family. People in general bothered him; he much preferred libraries, the quieter and mustier the better. His sister, her silent husband, and their surly daughter had grazed the tourist attractions and shopping malls like a small herd of ruminants, chewing on low-hanging fruit and stubbornly refusing to be redirected towards the cultural and historical riches that he and Justine could have easily shown them. He tried to talk to them about what he was writing, but they found it difficult to grasp. *Why are you interested in old mines?* his sister had asked. *Why not new ones? Because there might still be gold, of course,* his brother-in-law said. Wei Ming had stumbled in reply. It wasn't the mines or the prospect of gold that drew him, only those old stories of discovery and what they told us about modern society. Michelle had nodded sympathetically, but he thought she was only agreeing with him to defy her parents.

With the visitors gone, his days fell back into their regular rhythm. He spent most of the day at the library or in the office at the university where he was spending his sabbatical. Justine would cycle downtown to the NGO where her part-time position in the resource centre threatened to grow into a full-time one. August evenings were still long and golden. They'd walk on the beach at Jericho, then come back to the apartment for a simple dinner:

fresh fish, lightly grilled, and greens from the farmers' market. After eating, they would drink wine and watch the sunset from the balcony. Sometimes he would return to his study for another few hours of reading or writing, to a messy desk enclosed by low walls of papers and books. She wanted him to linger with her, to take time out from work. Only a few more weeks, she reminded him, and she would fly back to Singapore to prepare for the next semester. He would be staying another four months; when the rains came in October, he wouldn't feel like doing anything but work. Now they had time for something more: for reconnection with themselves and with each other. This was what they had planned.

Yet each of them could not quite reach out to the other. They could talk, of course, but their conversation slipped into the same old comfortable patterns. When they had first met, fifteen years ago, she had wanted to know everything about him, to read every single book on his shelves, to be able to name every single relative in the old photo albums that he brought over, ever more reluctantly, from his mother's house. She had wanted to eat up all of his past and make it hers. At times she still felt that hunger, but she did not know where to start. They fit together perfectly, seamlessly, but like two fists held together, so tightly that no light could seep through.

On those long evenings, she found that the best way to draw him out was to talk about his family. They unpicked the visit, slipping from remembrance to criticism.

"Ee Kiong," he said, talking of his brother-in-law. "So cheap. Three of them with so much luggage and still don't want to hire a car."

She joined in. "It's Michelle that worries me. Always fiddling with the handphone: probably get trigger finger. They've forgotten how to play. Let her out into nature, and she falls into the river. And that story she told us about books in the river. Where did that come from?"

"Books?" He looked at her in surprise.

She told him what Michelle had said to her. Grey books, like salmon at the bottom of the river, with writing in an unknown script. Not Chinese, of course—the girl's Mandarin was better than either of theirs. *Where?* That day on the North Shore, where they'd rested for lunch, by the tailings pile from the old mine.

"Just a minute." He vanished into his study, wine glass still in hand. A minute or so of scuffling, and he emerged triumphantly with a photocopy.

"Here. The same place where Michelle fell." She took the sheet and spread it on the table before her. Blurred type with battered serifs, blown up from microfilm.

"Scott Watanabe's diary. Start from this column."

His finger at the first subtitle. She read, straining her eyes to make out the small letters.

June 18, 1952

*Last Saturday, a very strange incident, outside my understanding. I have hesitated to write it down until now. Indeed, I now wonder if it really happened or whether this is a final descent into madness. I have been recording my symptoms for months, this struggle with what my doctor calls the early onset of senility. Even now, writing this, I fish for words. I pause every few lines, my thesaurus open on the desk beside me. I know the shape of a word, and sometimes I can hear an echo of its sound. It is nearby. I can smell it. I approach it softly but find that it has gone, moved further into the undergrowth. There is a word, for example, for that place outside the bank on Georgia Street where I waited for the bus, sheltering from the rain. Not **awning**, because that is soft, made of fabric. This thing that projects from the building over my head is hard,* *made of steel and glass. The word has an architectural feel, like* **pilaster** *or* **architrave**. *Not* **foyer** *or* **vestibule**: *those are places inside the building. The thesaurus gives me* **canopy**, *which is better but not quite right.*

I took the bus to the end of the line. The rain had stopped, and I set off. A long June day stretched ahead, the woods green with promise. I crossed the creek near the mine tailings and followed what I took to be an old logging road. Hikers had beaten a path among the hemlock saplings. I climbed higher, and the undergrowth grew sparser underneath the forest canopy. Above me, the branches of spruce, cedar, and Douglas fir. The area had been logged perhaps fifty years ago. Huge cedar stumps still persisted, with little slots cut in them to support the platform for the saw. I stopped to drink water next to one of them. Something glinted on the forest floor, a little further down from me. An iron nail, thick, curved over on itself, like a fern frond. Two pieces of decaying wood that had been split and cut to size, laid next to each other. I looked left, then right. A straight line, a raised scar across the forest floor. The remains of a corduroy road, perhaps, or the bed of a railway, faint but still trace-able. I followed it uphill. There were two creeks, I remember, which must have originally been bridged by trestles: the line of what I now knew to be a railway broke up here, falling away into thin air. I was lucky that the morning rain had been a rare event that spring. The water in the creeks was low, and I crossed each of them, moving carefully from boulder to boulder. After a good hour's climb, I came to the entrance to the mine.

It wasn't much to look at. A flat space, covered in grass and stones, shaped like a baseball field. Where the infield should be, the clearing tapered to a wall of granite that stretched dizzyingly upwards. At its base was a concrete lintel, weathered, covered in green moss but on which I could easily read the raised capital letters of a warning: KEEP OUT. NO ADMITTANCE. *Below this, the dark mouth of a tunnel.*

I checked the flashlight in my pack. The beam was yellow and weak and gave me little confidence. But rummaging at the bottom of the knapsack uncovered a new set of batteries that I could not for the life of me recall buying. The light was stronger after the battery change and white enough to guide me. The mine was warmer than I expected. I thought there would be supports every few yards, but there were none, only the uneven arch of the roof above me, blasted directly out of the stone. The floor was dry. There was a small recess, and every now and then a frame of rusted steel beams, like another doorway. When I came to the first fork, I switched off the flashlight. Absolute darkness. I could not even see my hand when I waved it in front of my face.

I didn't feel afraid, but I did wonder how far in I should go. There would be more forks, making it more and more difficult to retrace my steps. There might be shafts too, straight down into the mountain, their guardrails rotten or even removed. Honestly, it was much less interesting than I'd hoped, fumbling around in the dark. The atmosphere grew humid, and I found myself sweating. The light picked out a seam of quartz every now and then, sparkling copper or gold, or blue-green stains on the walls. Once, an aban-doned drill, like an oversize piece of dental equipment, on which I bruised my shin. At the second junction, I turned right again, and the tunnel led, straighter this time, further into the mountain.

The flashlight had just picked out a third fork ahead when I heard something behind me: a thud, like a single, distant footstep, without an echo, and then silence. I waited. Nothing. I shone the light back down the tunnel. Just a cone of rock, bleached by the light, and then blackness. I wasn't yet afraid. The sound was too singular, too inexplicable. It might have come from anywhere in the mine or, indeed, from my imagination. Yet it served as a warning. I had found nothing of interest here. I should go back.

After a minute or two walking back up the tunnel, I found the cause of the sound. A flat, grey stone had fallen from the roof and lay in my path. I kicked at it with my foot. It was soft. I bent down, flashlight in hand. A book with a grey leather cover, or really, the cover only, its pages long gone, open like a discarded mussel shell. Where had it come from?

There was a side-turning, I noticed, hidden behind a flange of rock. There was a step up, with the remnants of another book balanced on it. The same grey leather cover. The pages were gone again; I was sure, this time, that they must have been removed. I held it up to the light. There were indentations on the spine where letters should be, but they were blurred. The script was not Roman, also not Japanese or Chinese. The passage led upwards. It was narrow but much more smoothly finished than the tunnel outside. I came to a metal door, something like stainless steel, much newer than anything I'd seen in the mine. Above it, a painted sign, faintly streaked with rust, its letters still decipherable:
LIBRARY.

She was at the bottom of the page. Wei Ming was scuffling in the study.

"Ming! The next page?"

"Just looking." He came out, thumbing through a sheet of papers. "You know, that's funny."

"What?"

"The entry ends there. The next page begins on the 20th, with his next visit to the psychiatrist." He showed her.

"He didn't go back?"

He shook his head. "He was pretty ill. He might have forgotten about it. He'd been exploring the North Shore since they let him come back from the interior in 1949."

"You think there's a connection with the books Michelle saw?"

"It doesn't make sense, of course. Books wouldn't last long in the river. They could never last fifty years."

Nevertheless they retreated to his study, sifting through the papers, spreading out stiff, unyielding maps over the worn carpet.

It took them longer than they expected to go back to the river. Wei Ming had wanted to do some cross-checking about the site's history. Then, on the Sunday they had planned to go, it started raining and continued for a week. Justine used the time to pack and get ready for the flight back to Singapore. She found herself checking blogs, news sites, Facebook posts, even the LTA expressway webcams near the university building she would return to. It was night over there: quiet and clear, jigsaws of light through the rain trees washed over by the headlights of an occasional car. A foot-bridge in the distance, thin and elegant, marked by a smudge that might be a human being. Each morning, she found new messages in her work email inbox:

Instructions on Reporting for Duty.

Important Notice to All Staff.

Ten Tips to Work Smarter.

Collection of Encrypted Flash Drives.

When there was a break in the weather, they waited another day or two before returning to the river. Not the path they had walked before, Wei Ming had shown her on the map, but a less well-used trail on the other side of the water. They soon reached the bank Michelle was trying to get to when she fell. He thought the river would be too high for them to explore and search for those books, but they could follow a trail along the bank into the woods and then, for the last few hundred metres, take the old railway bed, as Watanabe had done, to the entrance to the mine.

The river was even higher than they had thought, jade-grey, the silt-heavy water roiling noisily over stones. They turned into a narrow, gently curving gully. On either side were mounds of bleached stones where nothing grew. She prodded one with her walking pole. The regularity of the hillocks disturbed her: they were not natural, surely, but they had no purpose. They ran parallel to the water; when one finished, another began, each nestled inside the last like a plump segment of fruit. There were no straight lines. If you followed one of the little valleys between them, you would quickly lose sight of your companion: you would be close, so very close, yet out of sight. Then they left the mounds behind, crossing a creek clustered with aspen saplings whose leaves fluttered like tinsel, not yet quite ready to fall.

The trail climbed quickly. Once or twice there were gaps in the canopy, and they paused for water. They were making their way up the flank of the hill and could look back down over the river. She could see a hut, tiny as a toy, and those long, lobe-like mounds, like intestines or worm casts, she thought. Tailings, Wei Ming told her, left by the dredges of half a century ago, working over the river valley after the first wave of miners left empty-handed, wringing every last particle of gold out of the silt.

There were no tall trees here, only the thin aspens and small, whippy hemlocks. Every now and then they saw a cedar stump, big enough to lie down on, with a hemlock sapling growing out of it, its branches jutting out and then turning up at right angles like a piece of plumbing. He walked quickly, and she followed as best as she could, the chest strap of her backpack high and tight, almost choking her. Once or twice he looked back and asked if the pace was fine. She heard a challenge as much as concern in his tone. Then other voices, soft as water at first, soon growing louder. A bark, then another. Two trail runners passed them: smiling, young, in gym gear only, the girl with her hair tied back in a ponytail, a bottle of water clutched in the hand. Following them, a stumpy, panting dog.

Wei Ming quickened his pace. Justine wanted him to slow down, to listen to her and to the forest. To touch her. When they paused to rest, he fiddled with the GPS on his handphone. *Not far*, he said. *We turn off here*. He pointed to the screen, but she put a finger to her lips. *Quiet*, she wanted to tell him. *Listen to the beating of your heart. And the other sounds around us.* A rhythmic knocking, followed by the red, white, and black of a pileated woodpecker in flight. The boom sound of grouse, just on the edge of hearing.

When they started again, they moved more slowly. Mature second growth, the tall trees dark now, high branches and foliage shading out the plants on the forest floor. Yet the forest was not quite what it seemed. If you looked carefully, you could see traces of another life. A long, brown nail under your foot, wrapped round a tree root. In the undergrowth, pieces of what seemed to be wood or stone, perfectly formed yet unnatural, with the symmetry of sea stars or flowers. Cast iron machine parts, their surfaces smooth brown with rust, over which the new trees had grown. A pulley wheel was woven into the roots of a cedar, while a steel rope threaded its way through a tree trunk and emerged frayed but unblemished on the other side. Scarification become adornment, she thought. Yet this landscape, they both knew, had not fully healed. Minerals leached from old workings; embankments, their supporting timbers rotted through, threatened to collapse with each year's spring rains. Railway ties decayed, becoming part of the forest floors, but the metal spikes, loose from their baseplates, remained sharp forever, even if concealed in the trunks of trees.

They left the trail at the end of the railway line to the mine, where it curved up the side of the hill, barely visible. Sparse undergrowth under the darkness of the canopy, and a single creek to ford. After half an hour, the trees gave way to level ground, smothered in saplings and blackberry bushes, with a rock wall behind. She paused in the last few feet of shade and reached for sunblock, spreading it on her face, ears, and the back of the neck where her gathered hair did not fall, before working it into the loose skin of the back of her hands. A memory, somewhere, of a teacher at primary school telling her that you could know the age of a lady by pinching the skin on the back of her hands: see if the skin springs back quickly or if it remains puckered up in a ridge. Just as you tell the age of a horse by its teeth. So I am like that now, she thought, a dutiful daughter-in-law a little past her prime, traded and appraised. And that skin of hers, which burned easily and never browned. Care for it, and at best it would fill up with freckles, like crystals forming or stones at the bottom of a river coming ever more sharply into view.

She offered the sunblock to Wei Ming, but he waved her away and pointed ahead. "This is it."

In single file, they followed the faintest hint of a trail. The thorns tugged at them. She wanted to reach out and gather the fat, glistening berries, but he brushed the runners to the side and held them just long enough for her to follow closely behind. The rock face, when they reached it, was blank, but they shuffled along until they found an opening. He reached into his backpack for a flashlight.

"Look there." The edge of a concrete lintel, covered in moss. She reached up with a hiking pole and scratched at it, peeling the moss away like skin. Letters, weather-stained but legible: KEEP OUT. NO ADMITTANCE.

"Watanabe was right about this, at least."

She touched his shoulder. "And it looks as if someone else came later, to make sure."

A few feet into the tunnel, easily visible from the entrance, was a padlocked gate of metal slats. He rattled it, but it would not give.

"It's not just locked," he said. "Rusted shut or bolted, somehow, from behind."

She handed him a tissue. "Lunch?"

Her fingers, she noticed, were purple with blackberries. The back of one of his hands had been scratched, and blood was now beading, seeping through the skin.

"I'll figure it out," he said. "But you'll be gone before I can come here again."

"I know."

They put down the packs. She held up her hand and shivered, feeling a draught of cold air from the mine, a shallow, barely perceptible breath.

She found the return to Singapore easy at first. Two weeks, and she no longer noticed the heat, the sudden darkness in the evenings, the sweetness of Carnation milk in her morning coffee at the canteen. A frenetic series of lunches with friends, many of whom had not even known she had been away, gave way to a slower, persistent work routine. She might never have been absent. Without Wei Ming, too, she felt an immediate loss. In the morning, an undisturbed bed, which her body was not yet able to spread out into. Or those moments when, coming across something online or on television, she'd turn to share it with him and realise he wasn't there. After a week or so, this began to fade away.

She woke early. On some mornings, she worked from home, writing or preparing teaching for the new semester. At noon, she went out, locked the gate, and descended in the lift to the void deck. The estate had been upgraded a few years ago, and the lifts now had thin vertical slit windows in their doors, crisscrossed with embedded wires. She had not noticed them before, in her decade and a half in Singapore. Now she recalled the classroom doors in her school in Quesnel. A recorded voice chanted the numbers of the floors—*Floor Eleven: Going Down*—in American English. A woman's voice that had always irritated her and that she now realised reminded her of herself. If there were neighbours in the lift, she would talk to them: a mother with tiny twins clamouring to share a smartphone or the retired couple going marketing, with whom she spoke Mandarin. The speed of the lift gave her comfort, keeping conversations short, not deep. The doors would open in the void deck, and she'd say goodbye in relief. Not from the effort of another language, but from the growing effort of intimacy.

There were other rhythms to the day. An hour at the gym, carefully calibrated weights followed by a routine on the cross-trainer. She showered, weighed herself, dried her hair. Meetings. Teaching at the university would start in three weeks. She had a large lecture class, with graduate students taking the tutorials. She liked that. She could perform, hide in full sight in the lecture hall.

On those late mornings at home, she sometimes Skyped Wei Ming. It would be evening for him, still light and warm enough for him to sit on the veranda looking out over the North Shore. He told her he'd applied for permission to enter the mine. In the fading yellow light, her husband's face seemed suddenly distant: she was sure that in the course of their conversation it receded, as if he were falling away from her, imperceptibly slowly. Yet he seemed not to notice that anything was lacking; he chattered eagerly of his plans, and his conversation was peppered with new words drawn from this unexpectedly practical turn in research: *compaction, hoist, pillar,* and *bord.*

Once a week, she visited her parents-in-law and stayed for dinner at the round table in the kitchen, with its lazy Susan and stack of plastic stools. They would catch up on news, then retreat into a companionable silence. Her father-in-law would read the newspaper in the living room, while her mother-in-law would switch on the television and watch a Channel 8 soap opera. Below the flickering shadows of the ceiling fan was a cabinet of trophies Wei Ming and his sister had won at school, now corroded by age. On the wall, a brush painting of fish, graduation photographs, and a family portrait taken a year or so ago at a photographer's studio. Wei Ming's parents sat in the centre, surrounded by grandchildren: Michelle, eyes downward, and Wei Ming's elder brother's two sons on either side, stiff as the stone lions at a temple gate. Behind them were the middle generation: the elder brother and his stolid wife in the centre, sister-in-law and Ee Kiong to the right, smiling a little too brightly. On the left, Wei Ming and herself, her red hair dark, the pupils of her eyes underexposed, so that there was only blackness. She had always thought that she could belong. *Culturally Singaporean,* one of her students had said. Never easy, but possible. But in the photograph she stood awkwardly at the periphery of the group, as though she had been Photoshopped in as an afterthought.

On one occasion, her sister-in-law visited while she was at her in-laws'. They said grace before eating, then conversation meandered. Michelle's grades were not as good as they should be, Kiong's work was drawing him further and further from the family. After a couple of hours, Justine took her leave and returned to the silence of her flat, to the cool hiss of the air-con as its louvres opened.

At some point, the props you have built to hold up your life begin to fail. Lights flicker and go out. In this new world, which you know by touch alone, supports bulge, beams creak. Water enters, drop by drop. What was it Watanabe had written? She couldn't remember the words, but the sense came back to her. There is a world of feelings nearby. You know their shape; you can hear an echo of their sound. Yet you can no longer grasp them when you reach out.

Small things crumbled first. She found that she could not answer the phone: when it rang, she would mark time until it stopped and only then check for a voicemail. She had always switched her handphone to silent mode during class time; now she kept it on silent all the time. She checked the voicemail inbox religiously whenever there was a message but spent hours summoning the courage to call back. Her greatest fear was that a friend or colleague would not recognise her voice. She would stumble over her words, conscious of the tension in her voice, reaching out for recognition; when it was given, the anxiety would finally subside. Before lectures, too, she found herself short of breath. She would review her notes in her office but find it impossible to concentrate: five minutes would go by, then half an hour, her thoughts sliding away before she could catch hold of them. At the lecture, she would come to the podium, take a deep breath, cough nervously, and begin. As if in a dream, you let yourself fall from a cliff face, knowing at some level that you would not die but wake. Yet she could not wake: there was no way out of this world.

It was worse at nights. She found that, with some pampering of her body, she could fall asleep at ten o'clock or so in that high marriage bed. In the middle of the night, however, she would find herself awake, unable to slow an avalanche of thoughts. She would listen, in those first moments of waking, for the sound of the MRT, in the hope that it might be six o'clock, close to dawn. Nothing. After a few minutes, she would reach for the clock.

Midnight or just afterwards, with long hours of sleeplessness ahead. She tried getting up, reading, listening to music, or preparing hot milk with honey, in the hope that a memory of childhood might jog her back into sleep. Once or twice she went into the bathroom and switched on the light. The face she saw was familiar. A little older, perhaps, than she imagined: more streaks of white in the red of her hair, more lines in the corner of the eyes. The face was mottled but serene. *You age well,* her colleagues told her, *you have good bones. You are so happy,* she had been told only last week, *you always have such a positive attitude.* She ate well; she exercised. On the scales at the gym, she was only a little heavier than she had been at twenty-five. Yet something deep in the body refused to obey, stubbornly resisted this optimism. This woman in the mirror was not her.

The quick hiss of the air-con, then a slow sigh when the thermostat cut out again. Fingers of rain on her window, slick car tyres on the road by the playground. Silence, and then another sound, following each other in a slow procession. If silence returned for long, there was always the interruption of breath and, however much she tried to calm it, the too-fast beating of the heart. She might lose herself in a cycle of thought for ten minutes, but it would return her, exhausted, to the present, more wide awake than ever. At five or six o'clock, she would finally sleep, only for the alarm clock to sound after another hour, pulling her, worn out, into a new day.

She saw her doctor. She had noted down her symptoms, anticipating that she would be questioned and then dismissed with a wave of the hand, an earnest admonition to pull herself together. Instead, she found herself taken seriously. She emerged with a small plastic sachet of pale green pills—*take one at night, just before you sleep*—and the telephone number of a psychiatrist at the hospital. She called without her usual fluster and made an appointment in two weeks' time. Even the notion that she had done something gave her a faint flush of relief; in those first few days after the visit to the clinic, her sleep improved. And fell away again. Deeper in. Mornings were always dark, no matter the quality of the light outside. From her office, she looked out over the condominiums to Jurong, to the sea and the towers of petrochemical complexes hooped in red and white. She watched squalls building from miles away, slate-grey, eating up factories, trees, the containers stacked on the wharves at Pasir Panjang, until falling water beat against her window. In the bright sunshine that followed, the darkness inside did not lift. She took to locking her office door from the inside.

If she was brave enough, she might Skype Wei Ming, hunched in his study, his face underlit by the screen. The trip to the mine was on hold now, he told her. Something about permits and the deteriorating weather. She answered any questions he had with monosyllables, then shifted the subject. He did not seem to notice she had changed. She could not think of any way to raise her illness with him. It was not part of the bargain between them, this snapping in her soul. He did not look directly at her but to her left. She, too, looked into the camera, a tiny rupture the size of a sesame seed just above the screen, not into his eyes.

Around lunchtime, the darkness often lifted, as the doctor said it would. She would go out to the corridor, summon up the courage to ask a colleague out to lunch, and together they'd walk from the shade of the building into the sunshine of the car park, between the brilliant red stems of the sealing wax palms and up the crumbling brick stairs to the canteen. Returning, she was almost but not quite reassured. She wanted to be alone yet did not trust herself. As though the surface of the red brick path might open in front of her at any moment: there would be a tunnel or a dark shaft, down which she would be tempted to let herself fall.

In the cool of her office, she sat looking at the spines of books on her shelves, all read, barely remembered. She could plot each one onto the story of her life: when she had bought it and why, when she had first read it, when she had used it in her teaching. Yet she had mostly forgotten what was inside.

The psychiatric clinic at the hospital was full, mostly with elderly patients, their helpers or younger relatives in tow. She took a seat, one of four bolted together in a row. Its back rocked rhythmically: someone next to her or in the row behind was making a repetitive movement. She did not look up. In the corner of her vision, a limb twitched once, then again. A child's voice in sloppy Mandarin, asking how long the wait would be, then the parents' voices, soothing, precise, silencing.

She moved to an empty row, nearer to the television. She picked up a health magazine, the kind that seemed to have been written only for waiting rooms, skimmed it, and let it fall. Despite the bright lights, this too was a place of darkness. She held her hands out in front of her, as if groping for a way ahead. She had scraped the skin bare off a knuckle and couldn't remember doing it. No pain. She turned her hands, so that the fingers curled up towards her. They seemed distant: opening without conscious thought, like a chrysalis emerging or a fern frond unfurling. That half-moon scar on a second finger, where a balsa knife had slipped at school, and another indentation, in the swell of muscle between thumb and forefinger, made by an unruly potato peeler years ago. In some way these hands did not seem to be hers: this body was a skin she longed to shed yet which remained tightly wrapped around her.

"Mrs Koh?"

The psychiatrist's door was open. When she sat down on the seat by his desk, she noticed a flicker of surprise on his face, quickly suppressed. Her green eyes, freckled forearms, that red hair. Not your everyday Mrs Koh. She told him her symptoms, and he listened patiently, kind but tired eyes moving from her face to his folder of notes and back. His voice was plum-like, full, Received Pronunciation almost but with those full, Malayan vowels. When he reached out to take her pulse, she noticed that the skin was loose and speckled with liver spots. He was older than he seemed.

He paused, listened again to her worries, reassured her. There was nothing unusual here. He would give her something she could take when she felt panicked or uneasy and an antidepressant to correct imbalances of serotonin in her brain. This would act more slowly; it might be two or three weeks until she noticed any changes in the way she felt. With the time the medication bought her, she could work on other changes in her life. She could, in time, escape those cycles of thought.

She only half listened. Her eyes ran over the books on his shelves and the certificates on his wall. One from Singapore, from a university much smaller than the one she worked in now. Another from London. And then, finally, home to Singapore again.

He looked at her file again. She was from Canada? His daughter had studied in Vancouver: he and his wife had visited her a few times. Twice in summer, once in winter. They had taken a cable car up to the top of a mountain. Where would that be?

Grouse Mountain, she told him.

And a creek, he said, with rocks and a small suspension bridge? Not the commercial one.

Lynn Canyon.

They had gone there in December. They had not expected the snowfall; the shoes he wore, he remembered, had no grip, and they walked gingerly with short, firm steps through the parking lot. They did not try the bridge but descended a long flight of wooden stairs to the river, clinging to the railings at every turn. It was a weekday, and they were totally alone. The snow fell noiselessly; even the sound of the water seemed very far away.

The branches of the trees were layered in white: he had pulled on one in wonder, releasing a shower of powder over his hair and face. If she was worried, she should think of Canada.

In her meetings with him, it would always be like that. That desire he had for an outside, for her past. Perhaps he thought that this would give her comfort, but she felt strongly that it was really for him. She was obedient. If she burrowed back far enough in her past, she could find a trophy for him, a memory puffed up with light. So she told him stories about Quesnel, about the smell of the pulp mill that you could never get away from, seeing your breath on a winter's day, the first snow falling through your fingers, falling on your back and making snow angels on the field that, in summer, was the lawn.

But she wanted something different from him. Not to be pushed out of history but to be pulled in. I am here, she thought, now. I want to belong. It was his past she wanted: to read through those books, to pilfer the certificates. To be that unexceptional everyday Mrs Koh, to walk into a supermarket without anyone giving her a second glance. To speak Mandarin badly without anyone saying, *Oh your Mandarin is so good, so correct, with that Beijing accent, not like ours.* To talk in that effortless voice of his, with the ripe, over-precise vowels. To have a past here as long as his. Not to have privilege, not to have deference, not to be asked to speak for Canada, the West, not for anything but herself. For her partner to understand this.

And so, she had entered the mine. Easy enough when you try: the mind slips casually through all locked doors. Below the surface, it was always the same: dark, unchanging, in summer or winter, the temperature of the human body. You search there, scouring its arteries. You are searching for something. Someone is also trapped in here with you. Sometimes you find traces of him, flickering in your flashlight. A footprint. Litter, neatly bagged up, hanging from a jutting nail. A book, placed carefully on a stone, left just for you. But if you move closer, he retreats, moves further away.

When she left her psychiatrist's office, she felt she had entered a new world. She followed his instructions to the letter. Three times a day, she popped a chalky pill out of its blister pack, swallowed, and drank deeply from a glass of water. After two weeks, she thought the medication was having no effect. *I can't concentrate,* she wrote in an email to her doctor. *What can I do?* His reply was curiously unsympathetic: she could clearly concentrate enough to write so coherent a letter. They met again and then once more. Sitting next to him in his office, reaching forward, she fabulated her past for him.

After a month, she thought the medication was taking effect. She was calmer: some of the anxiety receded. She could think, could begin to research and read again with greater confidence. But the life she uncovered was still somehow abbreviated, a shallow imprint of its former self.

She woke to darkness, cold in the vast ocean of the bed. The air-con sighed, sputtered, and fell silent. She listened for the hiss of tyres or the rumble of the MRT. Nothing. Early, then, with long hours of sleeplessness stretching out before her. She lay still, struggling to quieten her mind, refusing to check the clock.

Something haunted her; a trace, a smell, or an echo. A thread that she held onto and followed back into the tunnel of a recent dream. She was in the mine with Wei Ming. She had led the way, her flashlight fingering the rough rock. They had decided to split up. It was only when they entirely lost contact with each other that she found what they had been looking for. The side-turning with its sign, just as Watanabe had written. Steps upwards, then a doorway. The flashlight flickered out. She shook it, and the light flared again. A marble floor, panelled walls, and above her the interior of a tower lined with books, shelves of grey spines climbing upwards into the darkness.

She was spellbound. She wanted to tell Wei Ming this secret she had discovered and that she would share only with him. She turned around but could no longer find the door she had entered through. Only panels of marble. Touch it, and it is cold. Push, and it resists you, indifferently. Scratch at the surface, and it reflects yourself back at you, unchanged save for your bleeding, juice-spattered hands. Shout at the top of your voice, as loudly as you can. There will be no sound.

In your waking life, you cannot escape the taste of this dream. On Skype to Wei Ming, the light from the screen creeping into the lines of his face. On the bare walls of the psychiatrist's office, which you paper over with those landscapes of the past. In the seminar room, where your students learn, haltingly, to speak a language you wish to forget.

But there is a way out, you know, if you can find it. If you can sleep, if you can retrace your steps in the mine, enter once again that chamber with its marble walls. Don't look up at the library above you. Put out your fingers softly. Press. Nothing. Press again, and the wall thaws, warms, becomes soft as flesh. You dig. Somewhere in there, you know, is a body, his body, waiting to be pulled out. And then you are no longer in the mine. You are digging, with your bare hands, into the bottom of the river, at the place where Michelle fell: at the bottom of that pool. The spines of the books crumble under your touch, leaving only grey silt.

You find him buried there. First his fingers. You uncover the wrist, trace the curve of the forearm. You hesitate to pull too hard: perhaps he will come to pieces in your hands. But you are running out of air. You reach out again, take the shoulders, and his body comes suddenly free, limp, floating upwards. You hold onto his hand. The water surface is far above you, bright but frosted. As you rise towards it, you feel a pulse in his wrist; he twists like a fish, kicks out blindly. He turns to you, his free arm curling around your waist. You place your palm on his palm. Just before you surface, he looks into your eyes.

It's All in a Dream

for Lucy Davis

Even when the flight attendants cleared away the meal service and his neighbours closer to the window reclined their seats to sleep, he still felt uneasy. Across the aisle from him, a mother held up her baby, big-eyed, its hair standing up straight with the static. The child raised its hands in front of its face and wriggled them slowly in puzzlement. He picked up a discarded toy monkey from the aisle and placed it on the seat rest. A gurgle of delight followed, and the mother's eyes turned to meet his. She nodded her thanks.

He tried to pinpoint what disturbed him. Not the baby and the prospect of a sleepless flight. Something closer to a sense of guilt or a nagging regret. He glanced at the screen in front of him. The plane was at cruising altitude and had left the Island far behind. In two hours or so, it would descend, and he would change planes, fly off to that Western City where his wife was waiting for him. Then he remembered. Reaching forward, he pulled out the travel pouch he had carefully stowed in the seat pocket and took out his passport. He thumbed through it, anxiety growing into panic. Something missing. Then he realised the permit he was looking for had fallen out of his passport into the pouch. He fished it out. A blank piece of paper that unfolded to a watermark of a portcullis and chains. A crest, a stamp, and a barcode. Under a title marked "Description of Holder", he read off his Identity Card number and his name.

Three months ago, he had been surprised how easy it seemed to apply for a renewal. When he'd first applied for the permit in the 1990s the process had involved a long paper application form with supporting evidence, then a formal interview in a now long-demolished building. Ten years later, extending it, he had still needed to fill in an application in hard copy and submit it with a letter from his employer. Now he simply logged in and filled out an online form, and at once a reply winked back at him. He would receive an email registering his application, he was told. Confirmation of success or failure was usually given on the next working day. In the meantime, he should note down his unique serial number, in case he had any questions. As simple as that.

After putting in his application that morning a few months ago, he had left the computer on its desk and made coffee. His block of flats and its neighbours were newer than the rest of the housing estate: they clung to the side of a hill like a cliff, all windows facing outwards, away from the razor wire and the guard posts of the army camp that housed the radar array that turned restlessly at night, its single red eye lit up as a warning for low-flying planes. Southwest, away from the hill, lower, older HDB blocks layered up to the horizon. An MRT train snaked by on its elevated track, empty of people now that the rush hour was over but filled up with sunlight. After the previous night's storm, the sky was clear and cloudless; it was early enough for the shadows of his block and its companions to etch themselves over the estate. At noon, the shadows would vanish, and the blocks opposite would flatten out, like a pop-up book opened too far. He would go down to the coffee shop for lunch and, returning, scan the floors above him, layer upon layer of lives stacked on each other up into the sky.

Over the next few days, he fell into a routine. He was busy at the end of the semester: final lectures to give, a talk for the department on an obscure episode in the university's history, and a series of consultations with students. There was something gratifying about these meetings. Some students, of course, were simply concerned about getting the final assignment right and their overall grade in the course. But others were genuinely interested in their research, in making connections between their own lives, the Island's history, and the poems, novels, and plays that they had read. They gave back something to him: they took the materials he had assembled for them and used them in new ways he had never thought of. He was old enough now to meet former students in all walks of life across the Island, surprised by the enthusiasm with which they remembered his classes, recalled discussions or comments that he had long forgotten. *Educate*, from the Latin *educare—to lead out*. Walking a short way with them had led him out into another world. He could take no credit for their successes, but he had been there at perhaps the beginning of something.

Then he remembered the application. He had received nothing in his inbox and logged on to the official website to check. His fingers were clumsy, striking two keys at once, and so he had to solve a barely legible Captcha that would surely defeat most humans as well as a machine. His application, he was told, was in process. He checked the website's description again. *Most applications can be processed within one (1) working day. However, some applications may take a longer time.* So mine, he thought, is one of those.

He had, of course, heard rumours from friends and colleagues. The Island was filling up with people. Permits were not quite so easy to obtain as they had been before. As you aged, you became a greater potential burden on the health system. And then politics. Only last year, he had heard, a colleague had waited seven weeks for his permit, allegedly because of his role in activism outside of the university. In the end, this co-worker had decided to quit his job and leave the Island for good. He had heard the story second-hand from three different friends, the details growing more lurid in each version. Now that the colleague had left, he might never have the chance to ask for a full account. And this permit, to complicate things, was a strange thing. You were never asked to leave. Permanent residency was, as you might expect, permanent. What you applied for was a re-entry permit: a piece of paper that would allow you to keep your residency status upon returning from a trip abroad. If you never left the Island, you would never need it. The choice, as in so many things on the Island, was yours.

As the semester drew to its close, the Island was caught up with the death of a Great Man. Since his wife was away and he was finding sleep difficult, he got up at four in the morning and joined the queue for the lying-in-state. The first challenge was to find the end of the line. People called to each other in confusion under the lights by the river; policemen and NSmen directed them further and further away, beneath the trees and the soft darkness wrapped around the Padang. He found the tail of the queue just across the road from a shuttered shopping centre. The line started moving, coagulated, came to a stop, and started flowing again with surprising swiftness, so that he was on the verge of breaking into a run. They approached piles of water bottles, still nestled in boxes that had almost disintegrated under overnight rain, and he and those who followed him grabbed one each hastily, as marathon runners might. Once a young man tried to cut in front of him and then, realising where he was, suddenly slowed down and let him take his rightful place. They passed under trees with branches lit up yellow by the streetlamps. To the side, the Padang was wrapped up in darkness. At the Cenotaph, weary NSmen hunched over on the steps, the dull twilight washing away race, blurring the edges of each slim, uniformed body. Only when the line returned to the river did the movement slow down and queuing begin in earnest. They passed through scanners, as if in an airport. There were LCD screens, on which images of the Great Man were projected: they heard the sound of his voice for a minute, strident, much younger than in recent memory, and then the queue snaked out of range.

"Twenty minutes to go," a voice behind him said. He was disappointed: he had expected to wait much longer, to compose himself. Another snippet of conversation: "等一下, 很快就有air-con." Everyone was quieter now. They were given pieces of paper on which to write a message, but he could think of nothing. Perhaps I am really here, he thought, not for him but for those we have forgotten. A doorway, and the dazzle of light on the marble floors in Parliament House. He was propelled past a lacquered coffin he could not see inside, with barely time to stop and bow. Outside, in the darkness again, the crowd dispersed, following lines of streetlamps to the river. The MRT was still not yet running. Retirees waited hopefully at bus stops; young men in stiff suits and women in pencil skirts paused in coffee shops before heading to their offices in the financial district. He walked by the river, unsure of why he had come.

Back in his flat, morning coffee in hand, he logged onto the government website. Still in process. He decided to send an email from his work address. This would show he was gainfully employed. He consciously kept things brief and polite. Perhaps the authorities could explain the delay? No doubt the historic events of the past few days had held things up. He would be willing to supply any additional documentation that might be necessary.

After the MRT started up and the sky began to fill with light, he fell asleep. Later in the morning, he was surprised to find a reply. *We note the content of your email. 2 We are processing your application, and we will keep you updated with the outcome in due course. Thanks.* He read the message again slowly. The officer had signed off with her first name, adding a touch of informality. The number 2 was cryptic. Presumably this part of the message had been pasted from a template.

In the afternoon, in his campus office, he began to think about reasons that the permit might be delayed. He had been one of a small group of people organising a public letter from intellectuals and arts workers protesting the denial of tenure to a prominent academic. But that was more than a year ago. He had written letters and articles in the press about the role of the university, implicitly criticising current policies. Yet he'd had favourable feedback from the university administration: he'd been told, in confidence, that he'd articulated things that more senior colleagues would like to and were unable to publicly say. Then there was the talk he had given on alternative histories of the Island. A smartly dressed young man whom no one recognised had been in the audience, taking notes and plenty of photographs of all his slides with an iPad. Yet surely he hadn't been overly critical. What he'd tried to do was appeal to a common past of idealism that had now been forgotten. He had, after all, called into question both accounts that praised the Party without criticism and others that were only critical of it.

A flutter of wings. A pair of creamy white parakeets settled clumsily on the ledge outside his office window, flexing lemon yellow crests. He saw the birds periodically in the sky above the ridge, circling, calling out. Not a local species, a student majoring in Biology had told him: imported birds that had escaped. They did seem awkward, out of place. They bumped into each other, chattered, and took flight again. He returned to his computer screen and to Excel spreadsheets of student marks.

He had always thought that he was safe. Lucky. He had come to the Island two decades ago, drawn by little more than a sense of adventure and the encouragement of a number of friends. He had grown with the universities he worked at, moving from a teaching institution to a "world-class" establishment that rose higher each year in global rankings. He'd always lived off campus, had friends in the community, not the university, got married to one of them. He had found this world that he'd become part of genuinely challenging, naggingly persistent. He realised, slowly, how narrowly culturally centric even much of the progressive scholarship he had read, and indeed which he had written, had been. He found himself leading a strange double life. On the Island, he worked, as well as he was able, inside and outside the university to help establish dialogues for the future and for social change: he developed a form of immanent critique. When he travelled to conferences abroad, he found himself having to correct stereotypical views of the Island. Was it true that chewing gum was banned there? That cars cost $100,000? Wasn't the Great Man, who had stepped down as Prime Minister more than two decades ago, still really in charge behind the scenes? Could he really say, hand on heart, that he had academic freedom? To the last question, taken off guard, he'd replied, *Yes.* Afterwards, he thought he should have said, *Do you?*

When he was much younger, he had been a social worker in that Other Island, far to the north. He had headed a reception centre for refugees fleeing Southeast Asia. The organisation he worked for had organised seminars for staff. At one session, they were gathered in the cold, bare drawing room of a suburban mock Tudor mansion, now entering a second life as a processing centre for the most recently arrived refugees. A winter's morning, frost melting on the lawns outside, the heating system grunting slowly into life. They had sat in a circle, listening to a cassette tape. He remembered the clunk of the buttons, the hiss of the tape, then that voice speaking, hesitant at first. A well-known scientist, whose perfect cut-glass accent and the entitlement that came with it always made him wince. And, then, in an interview that crackled and slipped, a life slowly unwound. This man was not what he seemed to be. He had come as a young adult as a refugee from the Continent in a time of War. Nothing on the Other Island was familiar to him: religion, language, dress, food, the way bodies moved together and then apart. Yet he had thrown himself into the culture of his hosts. He resolved to become better than they were at being themselves. His old self vanished: in the mirror, in the morning, talking to himself, gesturing, shaving, he slowly cut away any last traces that remained.

Later in life, on the Continent, a Wall came down. The scientist could return to the place of his birth. The house in which he had spent the first few years of his life still stood. He connected with something there at a deep, limbic level that was not really part of him. A taste, perhaps, or a smell lingering on a street corner, or the rhythm of a child's voice. But he could not return. At best, the scientist said, his voice crackling and slowing as the tape came to an end, he felt like a fossil, crushed beneath the pressure of layers of rock.

Outside his office window, the parakeets fluttered back to their perches, calling out to one another. Of course he could not quite be like the scientist: he was visibly different here and could not ever vanish. But there had been that same hunger to know this new place. In a cemetery, now threatened by one of the new roads that snaked across the Island, a friend showed him an inscription that might have been written for him. He took a photograph and carefully transcribed it, his crumbling Mandarin shored up by an online dictionary: 埋骨何须故里 盖棺便是吾盧. *Why is it necessary to bury my bones in my ancestral land? The place where my coffin is sealed is my home.* His best home. His old self had already vanished: he was not sure of what he had become. Having fallen out of love with one flag, he could never quite become a patriot again. But at least this new flag, on the Island, had no history of conquest. Not a patriot, he thought to himself, but a citizen, though he had never quite got around to this changing of passports, this shuffling of flags.

He still could not quite believe that his application was deliberately delayed. He counted off a few more days before he checked online again.

Still in process. In conversations with friends over coffee or dinner, he heard again of others who had suffered similar difficulties or worse ones. He had not thought they would be so many. Had he been deliberately looking away all this time? One fellow scholar, indeed, had decided that these cases should not be met with silence: he was monitoring them and other breaches of academic freedom and compiling a history. He arrived early at this friend's office one morning, one of those scheduling mistakes that he seemed to be making more frequently these days. They drank coffee together. His was a minor case. If things went according to form, he would never know, at least not yet. There would be no interview, no formal contact. In due course, after much waiting, the permit might be renewed. Or not.

He leaned back, distracted by the play of sunlight and shadow on the desk in front of him. He was tired, he realised. He hadn't been sleeping well. "But isn't that politically ineffective? What's to stop me from assuming that it's a bureaucratic delay, nothing to do with politics at all? Why would I change the way I behave?"

"Think," his friend said. "What have you been thinking about for the last few weeks? Why are you here?"

Part of him wanted to think it was a misunderstanding. He would write another letter to clear it up. Once, he remembered, he had fallen into conversation with an old man on a bus. Spry, with a starched shirt, scanty hair Brylcreemed back strand by strand. A gold watch, Rolex, and a large golden ring with a green gemstone inlaid at its centre. *Guess how old I am*, the old man had said, and he'd deliberately guessed lower to flatter him.

"Sixty? Sixty-five?"

The man's eyes lit up in triumph. "Seventy-four this year!"

"Wah, and still so youthful!"

"You want to know my secret?" He leaned closer, a silver bangle emerging incongruously from beneath the cuff of his shirt. "I keep my mind active. I still work."

"What do you do, uncle?"

"I'm a letter writer." He drew out a business card from a pocket, as if it were a magic trick. "What does it say?"

He read out the name and the words after it: "Petition Writer."

"I write petitions to important people. Just now, I was asked to write a petition to the President by a family whose son is on death row. An appeal for clemency."

"Isn't it difficult to change the President's mind?"

The petition writer smiled, suddenly conspiratorial. He pulled out a draft letter that looked as though it had been composed on a manual typewriter and began to unfold it.

"That's why they asked me. I know how to persuade him. He's an Indian. Like me. So I must appeal to his beliefs. You see here? And then, I must also show him respect . . ."

He interrupted by reaching up to the buzzer above their heads. "Sorry, this is my stop." The old man coughed and folded the letter again. Just as he was standing up to exit, he pushed the business card firmly into his hand.

He felt like the letter writer now, typing out phrases he had turned over and over in his mind in the past few days. He loved words and the flow of writing. He tried to nuance each of them: to weigh and balance each clause perfectly. *Think of your audience,* he told his students. *Know the people you are writing to.* Yet he was writing to a blank wall or to something crouching there without a face, waiting.

That night, he could not sleep. He slipped out of bed, leaving his wife still sleeping, and went to the kitchen for a glass of water. Opening the windows, he could hear the frogs on the hillside, croaking after rain. To his right, the estate was lit up by a huge gas flare in the industrial area on the horizon, orange-yellow, so bright that it hurt your eyes to look at it. He went to his computer and typed a letter. These were the many things he had done for the Island, in the university and outside of it. He listed them. He had been thinking of applying for citizenship for many years but had delayed it because of family responsibilities, an aged father in the Other Island who might need his care. Perhaps the officer might like to meet him to discuss his application? And to indicate pathways to citizenship? He reworked the letter once, twice, and finally pressed "send". Returning to bed, he slept easily, woken only by the alarm clock and the prospect of a new day's work. In the morning, after his lecture, a reply was waiting in his inbox. He clicked on it.

We note the content of your email. 2 We are processing your application, and we will keep you updated with the outcome in due course. 3 We have forwarded your query on citizenship to Citizen Services, who will contact you in due course. Thanks.

All my life, he thought, I have been lucky. Until now. I thought I would become a citizen of the Island, that my wife and I would die here, together. The place where my coffin is sealed is my home. But now I might be left with nothing, with no claim on this place. I might have to return to the Other Island or go to the Western City. I could blend in there, of course. Soon, no one would know. A lifetime cut away with no visible scar.

He had wanted to go to the Immigration Office alone. *It's my problem,* he said to his wife. *I should deal with it.* But he was glad that she insisted on coming with him. They arrived at the Office before opening time, surprised that the queue was already snaking its way around the back of the building. When the doors were opened, the line dissipated to all corners of the building, and after they took the final escalators to a higher floor, they were by themselves. They approached the receptionist through a maze of taped-off barriers marking out the ghosts of future queues. The young woman asked for his Identity Card number, the number he had known by heart for twenty years. He began to recite it and stopped halfway. It did not sound right. Perhaps he had transposed two numbers? If he could just remember the first digit that came after the S, then he was sure the rest would come. He paused again, until his wife, with a hint of impatience, recited it for him. He took a paper slip with a queue number from the receptionist. The doors hissed open and shut. He sat down, shaken. He had thought he was calm.

The office was just waking up. Only a few of the booths in front of him were lit. Every minute a bell went off, and a new number flashed in red on the screen above them. The same bell that you heard in government offices across the Island. Someone would stand up and scuttle forward. The room was cold. No background music, no smells, as if you were at the bottom of an ocean. He breathed deeply and looked down. After only a little while, his wife touched his arm: their number was flashing on the screen.

The woman at their booth looked up through silver-rimmed glasses, then gestured for them to sit as a phone call came in. She spoke on the phone, switching from English to Mandarin and back again. They waited. She wore the crisp, dark blue blazer that all the immigration staff wore. On the other side of the booth from the phone, the black plastic back of a screen. On her breast pocket, a name tag and picture ID: *Madam Q.* Outside, in the light of day, she must be someone's daughter, somebody's aunt, perhaps someone's mother. There were words that she must use outside: *kachau, manja, sayang.* But not here. Only the scrubbed complexion, the mask of foundation, the eyebrows clipped and trimmed as carefully as her sentences.

When the call was over, she listened to him, courteously but not quite sympathetically, and checked his application with a few strokes on a keyboard, looking at the screen he could not see. At one point, she went back into the office to collect a fat manila file, which she placed on the desk but did not open. She could not comment on his case, she told him. But he could write in on this piece of paper. He could explain his case.

As he wrote, his wife started asking questions, which Madam Q blocked effortlessly, like practice shots before a tennis match, without even moving the manicured nails that she had placed on top of the file in front of her. She was not authorised to comment on individual cases. She did not know when there would be a result. If the permit expired when he was abroad, he would have to come back to the Island with a White Pass. As a visitor, she said, responding to the confusion on their faces. In that case, could he get his permanent residence status back? She paused. Of course he could apply. Explain why. Write in. See what they say.

The pen she had given him was made of transparent plastic yet felt heavy. He was worried that he might press too hard. The piece of paper she had offered him was blank, unruled. A strange sensation of being sent back to school: it had been years, he realised, since he had written a letter long-hand. He began expansively an inch or two from the top, leaving enough room for a salutation that he could return to later. Yet in a few minutes, he realised he was cramping his lines together, reducing the size of the letters, fearful of running out of paper. When he finished, he asked who he should address the letter to. *To Whom It May Concern.* He looked over what he had written again, surprised at the spidery writing, the scratchy phrasing.

He passed her the letter. For a moment, he thought that she was going to go through it, correct the grammar, and hand it back. But she simply took it and filed it, after checking that his email address was written clearly. She shifted in her seat. The interview was coming to an end. His wife had run out of questions. A few seconds, only, to find a way through.

"I've been writing in about this for a month."

She nodded.

"I've had replies." He mentioned the first name of the officer who had replied to him, the one who loved to paste from templates.

"Miss X?" It was the first time he had encountered a surname.

"Yes."

"Wait a minute."

She took the hard copy file from the desk and vanished through the doors. They waited a minute, then another. She returned.

"The officer's not in yet. Would you like to wait?"

They waited. His wife went off in search of food and returned with teh-C and a 菜包. A sign warned them not to eat or drink in the office, so each took turns to go outside and to stare back through the glass windows into the room at the flashing numbers, listening for the muted chimes of bells. When they were called forward, they found Miss X formally dressed in something close to a police uniform. Yet conversation was much easier now. She was younger, very kind, very understanding. She listened carefully. She was, she reassured them, working hard on the case. They should not worry. She smiled, leaning back in her chair, pushing back a stray strand of hair. She might have been one of his students, a few years after graduation. Afterwards, they could not agree on exactly what they had said to her. They were, his wife thought, very close to asking why the renewal of the permit was taking so long, but a sense of politeness prevented them from doing so. Or perhaps they had raised the topic, and the officer had brushed their concerns away as delicately as she brushed her hair, so lightly so as to leave no trace in the memory.

They left feeling relieved, with a lightness in their steps down the long escalators and into the bright sunlight of the car park. The officer was on their side. Surely this was a mistake, after all? When a week later he received notification of the renewal of the permit, he was elated. He logged on to check the details and was brought back to reality again: renewal not for ten years or five but for one year only. He was being put on notice.

The aircraft cabin was hushed now, with only the murmur of the air conditioning. The baby was asleep in its bassinette, tucked up in a blanket. His companions nearer the window had fallen asleep too, mouths open, hands stroked by sunlight. The plane was flying over a blank seam of cloud he could see through the window: even when he twisted his head, he could not see the sea below. The cabin staff had vanished, and for a moment he thought he might be on a ghost plane, flying on autopilot, its passengers and crew unconscious. For all he knew they might be falling towards the sea. Then a patter of footsteps behind him, the sound of a curtain being pushed aside. Reassured, he put the seat back, plumped his pillow, and allowed himself to fall asleep.

He was woken by a buzzer, then a woman's voice in English, Mandarin, and Hokkien, announcing the beginning of the descent. He had been dreaming, he realised. He had been on a road on the Island, one he drove down every day. But he was walking this time, north, uphill, in the heat. Behind him, rising as high as his shoulder from the horizon, was smoke. The city was burning. The mother from the plane had entrusted her big-eyed baby to him. He cradled it upright against his chest, so that it looked back over his shoulder. The sun was hot, and the road narrowed to a path leading into the forest. The baby's hair tickled him as he walked.

They were being followed. He looked for somewhere to hide the baby and escape the approaching fire. To his right, a hill of towers. A cemetery, with its mounds and tombstones climbing up the hillside into a canopy of trees. He turned towards the two white pillars that marked its entrance. Near its gate, the ground had been disturbed. A section had been cordoned off with metal hoardings, and the roadside was littered with broken gravestones. He passed them and went inside. He had only taken a few steps when the baby wriggled like a fish and escaped from his grasp, crawling away into the undergrowth. He looked back. He could smell burning, see the smoke rising above the trees. Whatever was following him, he felt sure, was gaining on him. He did not have much time.

He needed to find the child quickly, to hide it. Behind the first grave, he could hear something crawling, pushing leaves aside. When he got there, there was nothing: only the trace of a path or a tiny green tunnel in the long grass. Above him, a pair of cream-white birds fluttered and settled on a branch. He listened. Nothing. The scrabbling sound was repeated, further up the hill. The second grave he reached was larger, squat pillars with those familiar couplets flanking the tombstone, the mound rising behind it like a marital bed. One of the pillars was broken, and at its foot was a hole; looking inside, he could see the glistening edge of a lacquered coffin. He could hear the child's gurgling laughter, underground now. He reached down, parting grass as soft as baby's hair. A hand reached out from the hole towards his, a baby's hand at first, then swelling to adult size, pulling him down into soft darkness among the roots of trees.

The buzzer again. When he landed, he would transfer planes, walking the corridors of the airport for a couple of hours before he went to the gate. On the next flight, to the Western City, he would fall asleep, and he could re-enter the dream. If not, on the next night, in his wife's arms, in the Western City. Surely.

Mudskippers

Early on the morning before she is due to fly to London, Kathy and Jian Wei go to Sungei Buloh. They are among the day's first visitors to the wetland reserve. Fifty and greying at the temples, Kathy's husband seems to her—at these moments at least—still curiously boyish. He has prepared for the expedition like a Boy Scout, squirrelling away umbrellas, insect repellent, water, and other treasures in his backpack. When he marches ahead onto the boardwalk, she wants to tell him to slow down, not to brush cobwebs aside without noticing the golden orb spiders suspended at each web's centre, big enough to span a palm. At the river, she points out the crocodile under the bridge, almost entirely submerged in water, and he grunts in acknowledgement. She feels a certain relish in showing him something that he's missed. This comes, no doubt, from a companionable sourness in the way they relate to each other that is found in all old married couples, especially childless ones. You put on all the bug repellent you want, but you still walk with a companion whom it cannot quite guard against, who knows all the tender places on the body, how easy it is to draw blood.

"You'll miss me?" she asks with a faint hint of remorse.

"Of course. But make sure you ask your dad this time?"

"You don't mind if he comes to Singapore to live with us?"

"Of course not. We've been over this. 自己人, what. He should be with family, with his own people."

They *have* been over this, many times. But it's easy for you, she thinks. You'll come back from work and share a beer with him, tussle over the English Premier League scores. Some minor male bonding, another round of stories about his posting at Seletar Airbase in the 1950s. The excuse of late hours at the office if his presence gets out of hand. Meanwhile, for me . . .

"We can get a helper," he says. "It won't be too much of a burden on you."

"But all his friends are in England. He wouldn't adapt. He'd just hole himself up in the flat all day."

"We've talked about this. That's for him to decide. Don't ask him, and you'll never know."

They wander further. The boardwalk ends in a gravel path leading to another bridge and a viewing platform built out over the narrow estuary, with stairs spiralling upwards into an onion-shaped dome of staves. The leaflet they consult calls the structure a "pod"; it's pretty enough in the mist but strangely purposeless. The wooden slats are too far apart for it to serve as a hide, and there is no roof to offer protection from the rain. They look out at the rising tide spooling across the mud.

A flash of movement. She points. "Mudskipper. See it?"

After a minute they see dozens of them, each the exact grey of the mud, some in the water, letting the tide pull them slowly higher, others glistening on mudbanks between the channels. It's easier to spot them when they move: when the cheeks puff up or the mouth gapes, or when, after doing push-ups slowly across the mud surface, they twitch suddenly, flick their tails into the water.

"Eeee," he says, childlike, but he's right in finding something disgusting in them, halfway between a frog and a fish but with the logic of neither. Creatures assembled from leftover parts, the bulbous eyes and the clumsy, heavy head grafted awkwardly onto that supple, tapered tail. And then that tall dorsal fin, raised suddenly, perfect but incongruous, like a sail stranded miles inland.

They breathe through pores in their skin, he tells her, and keep air stored up in sacs, like a scuba diver, in their gills. The skin surface must be kept continuously moist; they must always be in water or, when the tide is out, must burrow down deep into pockets in the mud. Yet they have left open water behind for good: some species, if completely submerged, will drown.

She watches them slither and twitch a little longer, then begins to climb the stairs. He's close behind her, so that when their feet slip on the wet surface of the tread, they catch each other in their arms. She likes this sudden contact, this pressing together of bodies. Early in their marriage, he would have held onto her for a long time; now he pushes her away a little too quickly. She could turn to him and say, "Do I disgust you that much?" Of course it would just be a joke. But there's the difficulty of weighting the voice for such a question: light, of course, with a hint of depth but no trace of a break. Even if she could get it pitch-perfect, she knows what would happen: a puzzled smile, protestations, and then, on the boardwalk as they walk back, a sly hand reaching out, held in hers for a self-conscious minute.

"You're okay?"

"Fine," she says, clutching at the handrail.

The flight from Singapore is the same as it always is. Overhead luggage bins bulge with last-minute airport shopping, and Kathy has to work hard to find a space for her modest carry-on. She has booked the aisle seat to have more room, but her neighbour to her left jams his elbow against hers on their shared armrest and turns away so that she cannot catch his eye. She watches films fitfully, breaking off to the route map of a yellow plane inching its way across continents. New Delhi. After the meal, she sleeps and wakes to a baby's sharp cries. Ankara. Something hot brushes past her face. A lobster-pink arm, fresh from a tropical beach, followed by a muttered apology and the flapping of slippers in the darkened aisle. Paris, then the English Channel.

On arrival, she realises what has changed. The new passport she fishes out at immigration is thicker than before and red, not burgundy. She can no longer use the citizens' queue but must wait in a much longer line with all the others. The booths ahead of her at the end of the hall are newly refurbished, all steel and dark glass. There's something hard-edged about this country, not like the softness of the light at Changi, the *welcome home* recited by immigrant officers when her passport is returned. Touch the wrong place on the edge of this cold, northern island, and you might cut yourself and begin to bleed.

When she is called to the counter, the officer looks down at the passport, then up again at her. "How long are you here for?"

"Ten days," she squeaks.

He squints at the Singapore passport.

She clears her throat to speak. When she and Jian Wei meet English people socially, they sidle up to him afterwards. Where is his wife from? Holland, Scandinavia, Eastern Europe? *From Mars*, he says, rolling his eyes. At these moments of arrival, she has to trim vowels, plump up consonants, feel her way back into a forgotten accent.

"I'm visiting my father."

He looks at her again, wrinkles his nose with that peculiar gesture only the English can make, and waves her through. After customs, she collects her luggage and calls her father to let him know she's landed. The phone rings and rings: then his voice, flustered, lilting, just before the answerphone clicks in. "No worries," she tells him. "I'll just pick up the car and be on my way."

—

She takes her time to drive to her father's house. In the airport parking lot, she checks the rental car in the morning chill. No dents. A single scratch on the driver's door. Inside, a faint smell of cigarette smoke and the momentary puzzle of the gear lever, with its gate and rubbery clutch. She breathes deeply. Depress the clutch. Turn the key. Shift up into first. Then her body remembers. She drives out through a maze of slip roads onto the motorway, through landscape just waking up, blanketed in mist.

After an hour, halfway on her journey, she stops at a service station for a breakfast she doesn't really need, a bitter coffee and a limp croissant bought with shiny, unfamiliar coins. In the market town near where her father lives, she takes another unnecessary detour to the supermarket, wandering, jet-lagged now, through aisles of cook-chill foods, her basket growing heavier with each step. There are some things she cannot find here. Chicken on the bone she can get from the butcher's. Green beans, at a pinch, will fill in for long beans.

When she reaches the village, a few streets away from his house, she finds herself pausing again. She pulls into a side road next to a new block of flats. From here she can look out over the valley, over the flat roof of the primary school. She remembers when it first opened: how she and her classmates, in their new blue-checked uniforms, walked past the old school and continued up the hill, into a new life. Her family's movement from the north to the south of England also felt like a movement in time. No more high Victorian windows or wrought-iron railings: everything was soft, low-slung, streamlined, white ceiling tiles mirroring those on the floor. A central pond, where the class cultured frogspawn, watching tadpoles bud, wriggle free, and grow into tiny frogs, inching their way out of the water.

Pinpricks on her forehead. A thin rain is falling, as soft as fur, catching in her hair. She turns to the car, glancing at the red brick of the new flats stacked up behind a discreet signpost: Sheltered Housing. She recognises the building now from photographs her father held up over Skype calls: this is a place he likes, that he wants to look at more closely.

He has said he'll leave the house unlocked, but the door will not open. She presses the doorbell and hears it echo deep within the house. Silence. She fishes in her bag for a key that turns smoothly in the lock, but the door remains stubbornly closed, even when she pushes with all her weight. Again, something deep in her body remembers: she turns the key back and pushes up as she turns the doorknob so that the bolt clicks open. Then the door is pulled inwards, and her father is standing there, still unnervingly tall, still structurally solid, this ruin of a man.

He leads her to the lounge. There's a lamp lit at the table by the window and a pen at rest next to the easel. He has sat here waiting for her, working, fingers crinkling over a tiny, postage-stamp-size piece of drawing paper.

He sits. "Kath. How was your flight?"

"Fine."

"And the drive down?"

"Don't get up," she says. "I'll just get my things and put them in the bedroom. And then tea?"

"Cup of tea," he repeats but does not move.

The room is like a cave, its walls papered with his prints. A sketch of a young man in a hammock under a palm tree. The covers from the books he illustrated in London in the 1960s and the later work, the free-flowing abstract designs. In the last few years, arthritis has meant he can no longer work on such a large scale. He makes small, postage-stamp-size drawings and has them blown up at a printer to the size of magazine covers. The newest are prominently displayed. Pen lines wriggle together, then apart. If she looks closely, she sometimes thinks she can glimpse the trace of a human form: the angle of an elbow or the remembered curve of a waist that his hands can still trace.

On the coffee table by the window are the brochures from the sheltered living developments and residential homes she has helped him order. He has, in an unusual gesture of neatness, arranged them in a pile, topped with a small red notebook and a pen. This should reassure her, but it does not. The pile is hard, angular, bright with smiling photographs. There is no art to these brochures: they should not be in the house. In the passageway, then on the narrow stairs, carrying her suitcase up to her room, she feels suddenly numb. Like that moment on a childhood beach, years ago, when she stubbed her toe against a rock. When she looked down and then up again to golden sands running out forever to the sky and clutched her father's hand, waiting for pain to come.

Over the next day or two, they fall into a rhythm. The house is stuffy, especially in the evening and early night. Her father has no fans, even on the upper storey, and he keeps the double-glazed windows tightly shut. Before she sleeps, she opens one and so wakes to billowing curtains and a morning chill on her face, to traffic and the voices of children on their way to school. Her father's room is next to hers, but she leaves the old-fashioned bathroom with its iron tub and chequerboard tiles to him and showers downstairs. In the morning she writes, messages Jian Wei, or dips into the work emails that never stop coming. After a time, she hears him stirring through the wall. Drawers open, and the wardrobe door clicks shut. She keeps her own door ajar, so that she can hear him pad slowly to the bathroom. Running water, then the gurgle of the cistern.

After about half an hour, she descends to the living room and opens the curtains. Sunlight dapples the sketches and prints on the wall. When the wind stirs the trees in the garden, it whisks the light into strands, always in motion. Only the brochures sit still in their neat row on the coffee table, and she thinks of that unasked question about Singapore. She goes to the kitchen and makes tea. Milk for him, not directly from the bottle but from the milk jug he keeps in the fridge. Add hot water, so that it's not too strong. Filter the water from the kettle, to remove the limescale. There are other rules to remember in this house, habits to unlearn. In Singapore, she fills the kettle and boils water for the day; here, he says, it's best to only boil enough water for a single cup. Later, when she washes the plates in the sink, he will tell her that there's no need to rinse them, no need to waste water.

For an artist who thrives on chaos, he has made surprising efforts to impose order on his life. He has bought a pill box for medication, which he fills up once a week, a clear plastic wheel with segments for each day's dose. She has been over each pill and capsule with him, thinking to help. But he knows each dosage and what the medication is for. She is the one who forgets and whose bustling presence jostles him out of the rhythms and rituals he has set for himself. He makes his own breakfast, and they sit opposite each other, mugs of tea in hand.

On the third day of her visit, the conversation begins with her usual question. "How did you sleep?"

"The usual." He smiles. "I've never been a great sleeper."

She thinks of her mother, how she'd once been very tired after a long drive and said the next morning that she'd slept so well, just as you sleep as a child. But for Kathy now, what she remembers from childhood are those sleepless nights when she was thinking, when she couldn't sleep because of all that delicious knowledge, when her mind was racing round and round, rubbing over new things. *You think a lot,* her form teacher had said to her one day. *I bet you find it difficult to sleep at night.* Kathy had laughed in relief, at the recognition that there was someone else out there like her: that, in this, if in nothing else, she and this thin, birdlike woman were one of a kind.

"I was looking at the albums in my room last night," she says.

He looks up from his tea.

"The one from Seletar Camp, when you were stationed there. Shall we look through it together some time?"

He nods and suddenly she finds herself saying, "Dad, we need to talk. About the future. You know . . ."

He turns to picking at a capsule with clumsy fingers. Is he wearing his hearing aid? He has refused, out of vanity, the standard National Health Service ones, with the thick, kidney-shaped pieces of plastic behind the ear. He has gone private and chosen tiny silver pearls that nestle inside the ear canal. Perhaps he has forgotten to put them in or the batteries have run out. Has he heard her? He swallows his pills one by one and drinks his tea. She can hear her voice slowing down, flickering, fading out. Then he begins to talk. The troopship out. The cantonment outside Seletar Camp gates. Firecrackers at New Year. The heat made his hands sweat, so he found it difficult to sketch. In Jalan Kayu, there was a curry shop he and his mates went to, where you could get your curry with bread in mess tins. Will she cook curry for him this time? Later, when he is in the sitting room, she will search for the capsule she knows he has dropped on the floor, tidying up the crumbs he let fall on the carpet.

Each morning, they visit places on the list they have put together, places busy with bright euphemisms: *shelter, respite, home.* They make a good team, father and daughter. Each place is different. Some are clearly mistakes. One of the first is an old Victorian mansion, hidden behind overgrown trees at the end of a long drive. In its sitting room, empty rows of plastic chairs line a wall opposite a blaring television. Most of the patients, the manager tells them, are resting in their rooms, then corrects himself. Most *residents*. The halls are lined with linoleum and smell of soap: every now and then, there is a sign forbidding staff to use mobile phones. When they leave, the manager unlocks the door and locks it again behind them. They stand in the driveway, looking up at the pebble-dashed gables, the blank dormer windows high among the pine trees. They shake their heads at exactly the same time and smile conspiratorially.

After each visit, they go for a pub lunch, driving off into the country. They cannot quite find what they are looking for. There are gastropubs, their bars refitted in light, unvarnished wood. They serve organic local produce on wooden platters, on stripped tables on which traces of paint artfully linger. He finds the new seats uncomfortable, blinks in the unexpected sunlight, and comments on the small portions and high prices. Other pubs at first seem less changed. Sepia photographs on the walls, a smokeless fire that pub staff keep forgetting to bank, a menu of roasts and puddings. There's a thinness here, as if the whole building were a stage set that, standing up, you could peer behind. He makes the orders, uncomplaining but somehow going through the motions. If you pray long enough, her mother once said to her after she had stopped going to church, you might come to believe. What does he miss now? Bars fusty with cigarette and pipe smoke, a cast iron grate clogged with embers. Plump and lumpy jacquard cushions on the chairs, walls lined haphazardly with etchings and horse brasses, faux leather menus stamped with gold letters, tacky in the hands. In the next few days, they range further but are never quite satisfied.

On these drives, she thinks, he wants to arrive at a place that no longer exists. He has told her of it, and she has been there as a child. An imagined England, in those decades after the War. His brothers and sisters left that

Northern country town to go out into the world. Of all of them, he went the farthest, to Singapore. A life lived in black and white, he told her. Then suddenly colour arrived. *I had my fun, of course, before you were thought of.* He returned after his posting to the capital city. He worked hard. He had talent: he could draw and make things with his hands. Everything had its place, its own logic. He was part of a larger story. He met someone like him, a young woman from another Northern city. Kathy sees the two of them in the photograph albums he keeps upstairs, smiling in front of a new car or a new house. After a time, she is also in the photographs, a chubby, golden-haired child. It is always sunny. If she looks more closely, her face is overexposed, its contours bleached out, with scratches for eyes.

When she closes the album, she can find only hints of this world he has left behind, faint as the crumbs he leaves on the carpet. The parade of shops in the village is full of banks, chain stores, or charity shops: not the butcher, baker, and fishmonger of her childhood. After the book club he attends at the library, retirees gather and talk wistfully of topics she imagined were long forgotten: Empire, cricket, the monarchy. At times, he too is irritated. They haven't travelled, he tells her. They haven't seen the city or the world. So it isn't here, this place they want to find again to share. Not in the clatter of coffee cups, the whispers about immigrants and outsiders that she hears both here and in Singapore. The world she finds at times in Singapore, yes, a sudden treasure plucked out of the sediment of everyday life. When Jian Wei's father places what he calls a *shilling*, warm to the touch, into her hand. Or their discovery of Khong Guan iced gem biscuits, in great golden tins, in a provision store.

"How did you eat them?" she'd asked Jian Wei, and he explained how he'd always tried, with milk teeth coming loose, to prise that tiny cone of icing away from the biscuit, whole, and let it melt in the mouth.

"Me too."

Soulmates, she thought. *In all the world, at last, there is someone like me.*

—

They look at sheltered housing next. The next place impresses them at first. An old red sandstone Catholic school that has been rebuilt into something like a condominium, with padded, noiseless lifts. The manager is a young man with glasses, crisply professional, arms full of leaflets and folders, tripping himself up with statistics. He gives them a tour. There's a garden with raised beds for easy access—no bending down!—a library, a games room, even a gym. Better than a condo, her father jokes with her, and she can see he's tempted.

The apartments are small but neatly furnished, with double-glazed windows, a galley kitchen, and a bathroom with grab rails and a bathtub that opens at the side, like a car door. There's a shared dining room, their guide says, in the other block. For later. They have coffee in the library downstairs, a converted chapel, thickly carpeted, with narrow stained-glass windows and sofas you can't quite settle back in, a magazine rack, and a coffee urn.

"I'll leave you here," the manager tells them. "Any questions, just call me."

Her father stands up, cup and saucer cradled carefully in his hand. He doesn't care for the artwork on the walls. From China, he tells her, mass-produced on a production line of workers, each one added a few scripted brushstrokes. Something else is niggling at him too.

"You can afford it, Dad. We've done the sums."

He shrugs, swings his arms, trying to pluck words out of the air. She takes the cup and saucer from his hand and places them on the coffee table. It's all a little too beautiful, he tells her. Quiet. Like a museum. He would be well taken care of. But he would be an exhibit, brought out of storage each morning, dusted, and displayed.

On the third day of their house hunting, the development he's talked about before, next to the school, proves better. It's smaller than it seemed to her that time she paused on the way to the house. Less raw and new too: more intimately aged. The manager bustles cheerfully through the sitting room, introducing her father to the residents. They already know him from his previous visits; they are more curious about her. She finds herself drawn into a long conversation, or rather presented with a monologue, by a gentleman in a tweed jacket, about the fall of Singapore to the Japanese, that fortress with its guns facing outwards. She listens, irritated but not having the heart to correct him. The woman sitting next to him catches her eye and raises her eyebrows knowingly. After an hour, she pries her father away, and they walk in what seems like triumph down the drive to the car.

That night she cooks curry for him. Easy enough, with the Prima Taste packets she's brought, full of sachets she lines up on the kitchen counter. All his knives are blunt, and she sharpens one to chop the chicken, searches high and low to find the colander he hasn't used for months. After that, things are easier. Low heat on the stove, and the sauce thickens, velvety, its smell stealing into every corner of the house. He comes to the kitchen table early, sets the table with spoons and forks, and slices a baguette, his brow furrowed, hands clumsy as mittens. Like father, like daughter.

When they eat, he spoons up the curry greedily, a little too fast, then coughs.

"Water?"

He's tearing, but he waves her offer away.

When he finishes, his bowl is wiped clean without a trace of sauce, the bones placed carefully on a side plate. The bread, too, is gone. He still follows that injunction to clean your plate, drummed into him as a boy in school eighty years ago. A small boy just like the one in those book covers on his living room wall, sketched out in only a few lines: in a smart coat, freckles clustering like bees on his face.

"Was it good, Dad?"

"Yes."

"Remind you of Jalan Kayu?"

He nods but still does not look at her. A private smile.

Now surely is the time to talk. "You wouldn't want to come to Singapore, Dad? To live with us." She is not sure whether she has made a statement or asked a question. Something in her voice is already pulling back. "I mean, you could come to stay, but everything would be different for you. And you'd miss your friends."

"Kath."

That shortening of her name, which no one else ever does, pulling her back into childhood.

"Dad."

He looks directly at her. "That was a long, long time ago."

He takes a sip of beer, then he's off somewhere else, on to another memory. Outside the barracks at Seletar, a young Indian man would cut the grass. They were about the same age: they would share cigarettes, the young man speaking a beautiful, modulated English. "Better than yours, he told me once, you know. And he was right!"

Should she read these digressions as refusals? In a way, they are enough. She can return. She can say to Jian Wei, to friends, even to taxi drivers in casual conversation, *My father is still in England. I worry about him. We asked him to come here, but he'd rather stay in England. Really. What to do?*

In the evening, it stays light until eight, and her father, after the meal, goes back to work on those tiny pieces of paper under the glare of a silver Anglepoise lamp. Shoulders hunched over the easel, he seems almost to be burrowing blindly into the paper, finding his way through the touch of his broken hands alone. What is he searching for?

There is little to occupy her. She can go out for a walk, of course, into the park at the end of the road, on to the footpath along the old railway line, or wander along the single street of shops that have already closed, trying to summon up interest in country bungalows or package flights to Malta, Ibiza, or Thailand. Yet all routes lead eventually back to her father's door. If he's paused, she'll coax him into conversation and make tea. At nine o'clock, he'll tidy everything up and wish her goodnight, climb those narrow, precarious stairs up to his bedroom. She'll linger in the sitting room, thumb through his brochures and magazines, and then, after brushing her teeth, admit defeat. In bed, she tries to read a novel but defaults to checking social media on her handphone. A text from Jian Wei, ending with the inevitable question. *So, did you ask him yet?* She does not reply.

In dreams, she ranges further than she does in her waking hours. She is in the garden at the back of the house, walking down the steps under the wisteria trellis and onto the stone-flagged path. It is much longer than she remembers, and eventually she comes to the rusty corrugated iron garden shed where her father keeps his tools. The door is locked, but she notices something she has never seen before: a flight of concrete steps to a cellar. She descends. They are lined with books from her childhood, that set of leather-bound encyclopaedias inherited from her grandfather which she would look through, fascinated, on rainy afternoons. She squats down and opens one to a map of Malaya and a photograph of a beach with palm trees. The paper crinkles, and that peculiar smell she remembers from childhood flies out, dry, of camphor and pressed flowers, forgotten leaves. The smell puzzles her. *I am fifty now. I am no longer a child.* Then she feels a tug on her hand. Dad. He has joined her.

They climb the stairs together. He moves with difficulty, apologising for his age. At the top of the stairs, the garden is covered over with mud, soft, grey, glistening, stretching away for miles to the horizon. On the last step, he stumbles, and she grabs hold of him before he falls. As she does so, his body begins to twitch, to slip not down but upwards, his arms dissolving into something close to fins, his torso flapping and spilling through her hands. She holds onto him, her head braced against his back, so that she can no longer see his face. And then he tells her—and she is not sure whether he says this or whether it is made clear to her without words—*Let me go, Kathy. I want to be with her: why do I have to wait so long?* She holds onto him, even as his body falls from her hands yet remains somehow mudbound, tethered by its weight. The mud sucks at her ankles. If she releases him, she feels, he will still not be able to float free. She does not let go.

The day before she is due to leave, they go on a longer drive to the coast, to a little village with its fishing harbour and a long expanse of beach beyond. It's hot, and her father surprises her by bringing out a jaunty Panama hat. He's got a cravat around his neck too. He hasn't quite managed to fasten it correctly, and as she helps him out of the car, she has an urge to reach up and straighten it out. She resists: she will not become her mother. At the end of the path to the beach, he points to a bench. She can go on the sand, and he will wait for her. He's quite happy to admire the view.

She walks forward, past crumbling concrete fortifications and the rocky outcrop on her right, teeming with intertidal life. She takes off what she now calls her slippers. What her father calls her *sandals*. The sand is coarse and gritty, then smooth. It goes on and on to the horizon, mingling with sea and sky. The water, when she reaches it, laps against her toes and her calves, surprisingly warm. She wades further in. Words begin to return to her. She *paddles*. She thinks the water will be colder further out. But it's still warm. Like tea, while it's brewing. While it's *steeping*. Words only we share. 自己人. One's own people. She should ask him again, properly.

She knows she should not stay on the beach too long. The tide returns elliptically, through hidden runnels and channels that snake insidiously behind you. You think you have your retreat prepared, but you might easily be cut off by this deepening of water, with no way back to land. When she returns, he has found a friend: one of the fishermen from the village who now crews the lifeboat. They are swapping sea stories. Another chance to talk closes up.

They walk back up the hill to the car park. At an ice cream stall, she sees his eyes light up, and she buys two cones, one for each of them, not forgetting to take plenty of tissues. There must have been a time, she thinks, when he did the same for her, forty-five years ago. She has looked through old photographs of beach outings in albums he keeps in the room she now sleeps in. His body was tall, like a wall above her. Even then, she had looked forward to adulthood, to venturing out. She had not thought then about how you return, half a century later, to childhood, with your future closing in ahead of you. This moment should be perfect. The sun declining on the hill, the high grass waving, like hair, and, very faint, the sound of the sea on shells, tinkling.

"Kath." He's looking at her with concern.

"Hay fever. Grass pollen," she says, sniffing, rubbing her eyes.

That evening he's suddenly talkative, reminiscing about London in the 1960s, the kaleidoscope of Carnaby Street. He remembers some drawings he'd like to show her and gets up with effort. Still tall, his body: thin, with that ruined, persistent beauty. He lumbers upstairs. She follows him, trying to stay back, not to rush him, but he still hurries himself, and she finds herself pressing behind him, caught up in his enthusiasm. Her foot slips fractionally, and she notices for the first time since arriving the bubbled carpet, the stair rods that have worked their way loose. She'll fix them before she leaves. Halfway up the stairs, the carpet slips again, further this time. His hand reaches out for the banister but only plucks at it and flaps away. He begins to fall backwards, very slowly. She is also falling, forward. There's a cracking noise. She cannot breathe. Her ears are ringing, as though the air has been sucked out of the house. She tries to brace herself and reaches out. They will catch each other. She will not let him fall. Not this time, surely.

The Strange Machine of Dr Goh

Father, I'm not sure how to tell this story. It's not been long since you passed, and often I find myself still thinking of you. We didn't talk much in those last years of your life. Or rather, we didn't talk *about* much, beyond those everyday greetings—*How did you sleep? Have you eaten yet?*—that quickly turned to scolding and shaming. There was so much we didn't say.

So let me write something to you now, something like a letter I'll send out in the hope that you'll catch hold of my words somewhere, grasp these keystrokes that scratch the screen in front of me and dissolve into air, become waves of atoms, enter undersea wires, and come to rest again on a server on another continent, thousands of miles away.

This all started with my annual review. You remember my anxiety at this university ritual where I'm hauled up before the Head of Department and two senior faculty members and asked to account for my work in the past twelve months. Going in I was quite confident. My teaching feedback was, as usual, excellent. My research had flagged a little, but my essay, "Taking Stock: BRAND's Essence of Chicken, Transgressive Appetites, and Liquid Consumption in Colonial Singapore", was out for review. For my administration component, I'd done sterling work on two job search committees and also volunteered to oversee the selection process for the Sikit

Pandai Undergraduate Intelligence Award. I knocked on my Head of Department's office door, notebook and folder in hand, and was pleased when his even-toned voice shouted, "Come in."

The three committee members were ranged around the far side of a large circular table, the window behind them. I was offered a seat near the door. I noticed that the table was on castors, so that even the slightest pressure pushed it forward until it was met with resistance from the bodies on its other side. I reached out to shake hands with the panel members, realised that the table was too big, made a vaguely supplicative gesture instead, and sat down. In the centre sat my HoD, with an expression that I presumed was meant to be a smile but which seemed closer to a grimace. On his right, Professor Q, a recent import from a highly ranked US university. On his left, Associate Professor K, my kopi kaki and surely my ally.

HoD peered intently at the screen of the iPad propped up in front of him. Professor K began, no doubt following a pre-arranged strategy. My teaching feedback was impressive as usual, with excellent scores and warm responses from the students. What was my secret? I stammered out a reply about empathy, about taking time to understand where students were coming from. This seemed to go down well, then Professor Q took over. One of the students in my Singapore history classes, praising my classroom management style, had written that I was "the very embodiment of (post)colonial Singapore." What did that mean? I replied something to the effect that my classes were evidently teaching my students the art of strategic ambiguity and backhanded compliments that would serve them very well in the Civil Service. This produced a quickly stifled smirk from Dr K. At this point HoD made an automatic swallowing noise and told me that unfortunately I would not be considered for this year's Departmental Teaching Award. It would be better to give one of my younger colleagues the opportunity for recognition. Dr K looked directly at me and made a small, squeezing gesture with her left hand. *Slow down. Don't let him get to you.*

Things went from bad to worse. My administrative contributions were highly valued, but had I thought of taking on a more major role? That would be necessary as I prepared my dossier for promotion. And research . . . At this point my HoD paused, and Professor Q took the opportunity to get a word in again.

"Kay Kee, how would you evaluate your own research output?"

I'd rehearsed a response to this inevitable question. I acknowledged that I had not been as productive as many of my colleagues, but this in fact showed my long-term commitment to in-depth research. BRAND's Essence of Chicken might seem a trivial topic, but it was connected to a hybrid cosmology of self-care in our city-state that extended from Traditional Chinese Medicine to Ayurvedic rituals. My archival research and interviews with traditional practitioners could not be rushed and also offered the possibility of training a number of undergraduate and graduate research assistants. My—

"How many tier one research articles have you published in the last three years?" HoD asked.

"Not many . . . 1 . . ."

"Precisely zero."

"That may be true, but . . ."

I'd hoped for some support from Dr K, but she looked down, refusing to meet my eyes. The sun had come out, and the members of the panel were reduced to silhouettes against the window behind them, like a row of robots speaking an algorithmically generated script.

Dr Q attempted another tack. "Kay Kee, have you considered other research topics? Something . . ."

"Less provocative," my HoD added.

"More popular," suggested Dr K.

"A little less obscure," Professor Q continued.

Before I could reply, my HoD made that swallowing noise again and continued. Truth to tell, the History Department was under pressure. Student numbers were declining: most young people were interested in the future, not the past. In TikTok and Instagram, not in the archives. There was a concern that some of our research wasn't quite—he searched for a word here—*mainstream* enough. Had I heard the recent speech by the Minister for Education about the "sly civility" of "armchair critics"? He'd heard on good authority that this was a reference to one of our more prominent colleagues. A number of key anniversaries would come up in the next few years: self-rule, independence, the founding of the Party. Couldn't each of us adapt our strategic research areas to focus on these topics and re-establish our Department's national pre-eminence?

"You're suggesting whitewashing?" I asked.

They all replied at once. "No . . ."

"Not at all."

"Kay Kee, that's not what we want here. Think a bit about what HoD is saying. How can you add value to the Department?"

HoD began to push against the big round table that separated us. Its leading edge bit into my midriff, which admittedly had gained more padding in the last few years. The back of my chair was against the wall, and I was the meat in a sandwich—or perhaps the filling in a curry puff—that was being inexorably compressed. I had a vision of a swarm of drones surging towards me. I panicked. I wanted to shout, *Gostan, reverse, go back.* But all that came out was:

"Go . . . Go."

HoD looked at me, puzzled, while Dr Q's face broke out in a broad smile. "Of course," she said. "What a wonderful topic!"

We looked at her in consternation.

"Dr Goh Keng Swee. Singapore's economic architect. I always thought that our focus on Lee Kuan Yew means that others have been neglected."

I nodded, still processing. HoD looked at me quizzically.

Dr Q continued, "We could commit substantial research funds to this. It really does fit with our strategic objectives."

Dr K made a series of small, almost imperceptible, nods. *Go for it. Take this opportunity.*

I cleared my throat. "I think I could take this on."

The rest of the meeting passed in a haze of mutual self-congratulation. When I was released, I rushed to the staff pantry and, to celebrate my relief and assuage the traces of new anxieties, feasted on Lipton tea, mochi, and laopo piah.

Father, wherever you are, I find writing like this freeing. I don't have to translate for you. I don't feel you looking over my shoulder and judging me. I don't put up that wall of duty between us. I can let you into my world, and the language I use is no longer a weapon. I can laugh at others and, most of all, at myself. I can relax. Are you surprised at what your son is sharing with you? At what was hidden behind those walls of habit?

The week after the meeting, I carved out some time to do preliminary work on Dr Goh. The results were discouraging. I was surprised to find no trace of his oral history in the National Archives, and while the oral histories of others did refer to him, this was mostly in passing and in an official capacity. I thought that the Institute of Singapore Studies or some other library or archive might hold his papers, but they were nowhere to be found. Next, I tried biographies. The first, by his daughter-in-law, Tan Siok Sun, was very much a series of personal reminiscences drawing on unpublished private sources. Perhaps there was scope for an intellectual history, a more detailed examination of the man, his life, and his thought?

Dr Ooi Kee Beng had beaten me to it with his magisterial *In Lieu of Ideology: An Intellectual Biography of Goh Keng Swee.* Dr Ooi had read every single article or speech Dr Goh had ever written. He also had warnings for future researchers in his introduction. "Useful documented sources" about Dr Goh, Dr Ooi noted, "were a scarcity." Writing a biographical account of Dr Goh's life necessitated relying "on interviews with an ever-diminishing group of ageing insiders and on limited access to official documents." It was now more than ten years since Dr Goh had passed, and the group of insiders had diminished much further while access to official documents had not greatly increased. I cast my net further to less well-known sources, such as O. Kosong's *GKS: Wine, Women and Song,* and Wu Zhili's 吴庆瑞: 说曹操曹操就到—perhaps best translated as *Goh Keng Swee: Talk of the Devil and He Will Appear*—but the books were full of unsubstantiated gossip and of no use to a serious historian such as myself.

I wracked my brain to come up with a new approach. Perhaps there was something interesting in Dr Goh's early thought, before he entered government and had to toe the Party line? Here, too, I'd been forestalled by Ho Chi Tim's wonderful University of Hawai'i thesis, *The Origins, Building, and Impact of a Social Welfare State in Late Colonial Singapore.* I reached out to the archivists I knew at the National Archives at Fort Canning. Did they have any new material? They replied that a few of Dr Goh's personal effects had come into their possession. His pipe, for instance. I wouldn't be able to look at the object in person, but they'd recently developed a virtual reality viewer through which I could examine it in detail, as though it was right in front of me on my desk. Would I like to try it out? After several attempts, I installed the software and, helped by my Singpass, negotiated various levels of security clearances. The viewer was indeed remarkable. I was briefly excited by the possibility that the scratches on the rim and bowl were some form of code or hieroglyphics but had to eventually concede, on closer inspection, that sometimes a pipe is just a pipe.

In my department, though, things were looking up. I used to dread bumping into my HoD in the corridor in the morning. I'd bleat a greeting as he passed me in the corridor, and he'd studiously ignore me. Now, though, when he caught me in the pantry, rifling through the olive sachets of packaged meals one of our junior colleagues had brought back from reservist training, he ignored my pilfering and beamed with enthusiasm. How was the research on Dr Goh going? He'd been talking it up in the recent Dean's meeting. If I wanted to make an archival trip overseas to get things moving, he could arrange small projects grant funding. I smiled and assured him that things were going very well. Laying the groundwork, of course, would take time. He nodded in agreement. I'd keep him updated, though? No pressure, naturally. Again that expression on his face, teeth clenched and lips pulled back, a pained grimace that tried so very hard to be a smile.

With growing anxiety, I spread my net wider. I let colleagues and friends know about my work, and I posted a note on the social media groups about Singapore history and heritage that I was part of. Soon, I'd wake up in the morning to find the home screen of my phone pockmarked by the red bubbles of notifications. The problem here was not too little information but too much. Everyone had a Goh Keng Swee story, but most were quite trivial. Some remembered Dr Goh visiting their childhood school as Education Minister and their excitement in getting ready to put on a performance for him; others remembered his sterling work as an MP in Kreta Ayer. One or two had laboured under him in various ministries and playfully suggested they might have revealing stories to tell. When I approached them, however, they cited the long arm of the Official Secrets Act, and our online conversations petered out. I'd copied a photograph of Dr Goh, framed it, and placed it on my desk to inspire me. Each morning he smiled back at me with his chubby face and receding hairline. I'd thought of him as a muse, but he remained an affectionate, mercurial, and ultimately unknowable Sphinx.

It was about this time that I decided to go back to basics. I retreated to the Institute of Singapore Studies Library, cool, deserted, and suitably distant from my department. I thought I would consult those books that Dr Goh had read early in his intellectual career. I began with A.C. Pigou's *Socialism Versus Capitalism*, which Dr Ooi's biography suggested had been an important formative influence. Curiously, the book was not on the open shelves but needed to be ordered from the closed stacks. After putting in the order, I waited in the researchers' common room, where I drank a Nespresso and ate two rather dry crispy chicken biscuits offered by a researcher from Penang.

When I picked up Pigou's book from the front desk, I was surprised how worn the copy was. It had been rebound in black cloth in the 1980s by someone from the Handicaps Welfare Association, but the pages themselves seemed much older. The paper had become brittle and darkened to an unpleasant shade of brown, and the glue in the spine had begun to disintegrate. The first few pages were stuck together and difficult to separate. I skipped over them and went on to the first chapter. Pigou's style was, to say the least, laboured, and Economics never was my strongest subject. After a few pages, I lost the thread of argument and began flipping through the text. That was when I noticed marks on several of the pages, words underlined, and every now and then a hand-drawn star in the margins. Could this be Dr Goh's personal copy of the book? How might it have come here? I went back to the first pages of the book and gently prised them apart. At the top of the second page was a small inscription: *Ex Libris GKS. December, 1948.* He'd acquired this copy on his first visit to London as an undergraduate, then, although he would have known of it much earlier, in his studies at Raffles College in Singapore before the War.

The book itself wasn't very helpful: a few scribbles were not enough to base a research paper on. From the ISS librarian, however, I was able to confirm that two further volumes, like Pigou's book, had been donated to the library by Dr Goh's son after his father's death: John Maynard Keynes's *General Theory of Employment, Interest and Money* and James Puthucheary's *Ownership and Control of the Malayan Economy.*

The Puthucheary text, perhaps gifted to him by the author, was entirely unmarked. The Keynes volume was a different story. It had been annotated heavily in black ink. In addition to the underlined passages, there were frequent written comments. I took photographs and transcribed them. *An overly optimistic scenario?—Rubbish!—That could never work for a trading economy!* Clearly Dr Goh was not impressed with Keynes's notion of deficit spending.

The volume had not been rebound and was covered in faded red cloth, fraying at the edges. After I finished making notes and put it down on the desk, I noticed that the top board refused to remain completely flat. There was a slit on the inside of the back cover, and the endpaper bulged upwards in a large blister. After a little manoeuvring with my pencil, I extracted an envelope, apparently made of the same, aged paper as the rest of the book. It had been opened and clumsily resealed. I turned it over. On the front were the two words *Keng Swee* in cursive writing that I knew from the annotations in the book was not Dr Goh's hand. I turned it over again and tried to open it. The seal refused to give, and I did not want to tear the paper.

The library's closing time was approaching. This would have to wait for another day. I stacked my books and placed a yellow reservation card next to them on my desk. A rainstorm was threatening, and I took my folding umbrella out of my backpack for the long trek to the bus stop. I heard the sound of distant thunder, but the rain held off. At the bus stop, I refastened the umbrella and put it back in my pack. That's when I saw the letter in its yellowed, brittle envelope, nestled carefully in an inside pocket in my bag.

Father, all this must be new to you. Not just the story I'm telling you, but its central character. I've let myself run on deep into this world of books and a kind of language that you never quite knew. I can see this now, for the first time: how both love of what I did and the anxiety to prove myself pulled me further and further into this world, away from you.

But some things you surely know about your son. I'm responsible. I follow the rules. I'm still not sure how the letter came to me like that. I don't recall picking it up. I was certain I'd slipped it back into its pocket in the endpaper and left it in the book in the library. On the long bus ride home, I was conscious of it burning a hole in my backpack or, more likely, slowly disintegrating into a cloud of illegible paper flakes. When I got back to the flat I would hide it, I decided, so well that you would never find it and ask me how it had come to be there. When I opened the door, you were not in your usual place, sitting in the chair by the window reading the newspaper or asleep. I almost called out, then I felt the dead weight of silence in the flat and remembered again you were gone. I went back down to the eating house, bought cai png in a squeaky Styrofoam container, and ate quickly at the living room table, barely tasting my food. I half thought I might have imagined the letter's presence, but it was still in my bag when I checked.

I placed it on my study desk and turned it over in my hands. I could take it back tomorrow, of course, slip it back into its place in the book, and let the librarians know about my discovery. Yet I was worried they might take it away to be examined, preserved, and catalogued before making it available to a scholar such as myself. It might vanish for months and years, and time was running out for me. In my department, whispers had started about the progress of my research. Only yesterday, one of our best honours students had approached me to supervise her thesis, shyly telling me that she, too, would like to research the life of Dr Goh from a decolonial perspective, given my rumoured expertise. I'd nodded non-committally and subtly deflected her scholarly interest to alimentary matters, offering her a piece of pineapple cake from my recent visit to Taiwan. Her approach had unnerved me, making me conscious of the thinness of my knowledge. So, after dinner, I tried something that you taught me when I was in primary school. Do you remember how you collected stamps and showed me how to steam them off envelopes with a kettle? I boiled water and held the envelope over the steam until I could ease the seal open with my fingers.

Inside, a single page of notepaper, folded in two. When I opened it, I could smell a faint but cloying scent of heavy flowers, like chrysanthemums at a wake.

4 December 1954

Dear Keng Swee,

This is just a note to say thank you for arranging for me to go and see Dr Phillips at LSE and to see the demonstration of his machine. To think that he was in Singapore during the War and imprisoned by the Japanese. How he must have suffered! The machine was impressive, I must say, even though a few valves weren't quite functioning correctly. As you say, you will certainly be able to improve on it with your newer version.

Remember what I told you. Machines are all very well, but surely there is a place for the human heart? Didn't it occur to you that the machine looked very much like those diagrams of our bodies, with its red fluid going round and round? Perhaps you will find this all rather whimsical, typical of a student of English Literature. We look for images: we search out metaphors. But can a new nation be built only through a mechanical process? Is there no place for poetry? Is there no place for something that does not move forward but rather recirculates—and so seems to stand still?

Don't worry, I won't mention our "tour" to Alice the next time I see her.

Yours,
Primrose Perera

Alice, I knew, was Dr Goh's first wife. The letter was written during Dr Goh's second sojourn in London, when he was studying for his doctorate. I had no idea who Primrose Perera might be, but I could find out. This was a tenuous lead, but for the first time I had something to work with, a series of faint footprints leading back into the jungle of the past.

The next day, I had no classes and decided to work from home. Father, it was at times like this that I missed you most. We shared a rhythm on those mornings when I did not have to leave early for work. I slowed down, and you tried your best to speed up. I cooked oats and left them to cool in the pot on the stove until you were ready to eat. I took slices of Gardenia bread, still cold, from their bag in the fridge, to toast when you sat down. I folded the English and Chinese newspapers and placed them at the breakfast table, ready for you. If I remembered, I brought the butter out to soften. Also kaya and Nutella, which you insisted should not be put in the fridge overnight, but which I sometimes forgot.

I was never quite sure what distractions would delay you. You might first fumble with the blood pressure monitor, cuffed above your elbow, recording its readings on paper in hand-drawn tables with a crazy logic that you claimed to understand but that I could never figure out. You might shower and change clothes. Or you might, with infinite slowness, set up a row of pills and capsules next to your plate, assembled from blister packs and plastic canisters. You refused to use the pill box I had bought for you, telling me it was too confusing. After all these detours, you'd sit down, and I could heat up the oats, put on the bread to toast, sometimes fry an egg as a supplement. We would finally eat, but by this time I would be checking and checking my watch.

At those times, I remembered the slowness of the old estate we'd been moved from after Mother passed. The warmth of the red bricks on the point blocks, held in a lattice of white-painted concrete. When I was a toddler, the elevators only stopped at every third floor: we would climb one storey rather than come down two, because I found it easier to go upstairs rather than down. In the morning, mynahs seethed in the trees. In the evening, especially after rain, swallows swooped in lazy loops through the darkening sky. During the Seventh Month, crowds would gather at a getai stage set up at the back of the estate. There was a Post Office Savings Bank branch, a sundry shop, two eating houses, and a wet market with an attached hawker centre. This wet market later acquired a dubious claim to fame: it was the place where a minister of the ruling Party, on an election walkabout, was said to have flinched when a fishmonger went to shake her hand, and she rushed off to wash it immediately after. She'd lost the election to an opposition candidate, and for some years the estate's inhabitants had been besieged by governmental initiatives to win them back.

In the end, much to your reluctance, we were offered a new estate and had to move. By then, Mother had died. The new estate had much better facilities. The blocks were taller and much more modern. The lifts stopped at every floor. Glass windows on the doors allowed you to see who was inside before you entered. There was a covered walkway to the MRT station, and you could make your way there without an umbrella without getting wet, even in the heaviest tropical downpour. The car park was covered, protecting vehicles not only from the rain but from the mynahs' leavings after their nightly feast of rotten fruit.

The new estate was an improvement on its predecessor, but you felt something was lacking. Many older hawkers whom you knew by name had taken the opportunity to retire. The bank was replaced by a single ATM across the road, and the nearest wet market was a fifteen-minute walk away. In the small eating house downstairs, stallholders staged elaborate openings, then went out of business six months later, complaining about the high rents. Provision and hardware stores were replaced by pet salons and tuition centres, rows of overstocked open shelves giving way to etched frosted glass windows and closed doors. Every now and then, I thought that something natural was growing again, like the tiny ferns that sprouted in gutters or in decorative creases in the wall, or the lizards that gathered under fluorescent strip lights at night to feast on the circling insects. But after a day of fogging for mosquitoes or the application of a new coat of paint, the estate would revert to its original pristine cleanliness. I wondered if the planners at times thought of human beings as a kind of infestation, like the weeds and the insects and the lizards, marring the symmetry of the towering blocks, the smooth pathways between them, and the carefully pruned trees. You thought of it differently, you told me once. It was as if you had gone into exile without migrating, finding yourself lost in a beautiful but unfamiliar city, never quite able to find your way home.

I came back to the present, to the desk in front of me with the computer and the letter, and I tried to find my way out of the fog of memories, to search further, and to write.

In the next few days, I followed those faint traces of Primrose Perera, Dr Phillips, and his machine. Phillips was easy to find. In the late 1940s at the London School of Economics, he'd built a hydraulic device to simulate the flow of money in a country's economy. The machine, as I understood it, was not simply a model but also capable of simulating policy interventions: increased taxation or investments, for example, could be mimicked by opening corresponding taps wider. Pictures showed a confusing mass of plastic pipes and tanks, through which coloured water flowed. I could understand the association that Primrose Perera had made. The machine seemed less like the cool curves of the graphs I associated with economics and more like a human body—or a child's attempt to copy one. I thought of the frogs we'd been made to dissect at school, bellies opened to show the dark lobes of the liver and the roots of arteries that snaked off under as-yet-undisturbed skin.

Primrose was more difficult to locate. In a reel from the library's microfilm collection, I discovered two drily witty letters she had written to *Suara Merdeka*, the newsletter for Malayan students in London in the 1950s, criticising the boorish behaviour of the male leaders of the student-run Malayan Forum, who included Dr Goh among their number. Online searches of newspapers yielded only a notice that she'd received the Queen's Scholarship to study in England in 1951. Perhaps she had never returned to Singapore.

The semester was ending, and there was a brief pause between my last lectures and tutorials and the due date for final assignments. My HoD smiled now when he saw me in the corridor in the morning, and I fed him tidbits about my research which he gulped down eagerly, like a fat koi in a pond. The machine in particular fascinated him. Perhaps I could offer an interdisciplinary undergraduate research opportunity for selected students from History, Economics, and Engineering? We could use the class to build a replica of Dr Goh's improved machine for the upcoming Founders' Day celebrations. He'd already been in touch with the Office of University Communications about a social media campaign. I only had to say the word, and they'd get started.

I tried to respond to his enthusiasm, but in truth I'd begun to put my research on hold. At the end of semester, with marking still to come, I felt fatigued. It wasn't just that I wasn't sleeping well. I went for my annual health check-up. My body was scanned, prodded, poked, and various fluids sampled. At fifty, I was told, everything seemed to be in good working order. I could play with inputs and outputs, of course: a little less alcohol and fatty food, more vitamin D and exercise. Overall, though, things were running smoothly: the cause of my exhaustion lay elsewhere.

Father, I've never really shared this with you, this feeling of fatigue that came over me in the last few years. Even when you were still with me in our flat, I had episodes of sleeplessness. I'd go into the living room, switch on the ceiling fan, lie on the couch, and check my phone, be sucked quickly into a whirlpool of messages on Facebook, WhatsApp, and LinkedIn. Once or twice I remember you came out of your room, unaware of me in the darkness, and groped your way slowly along the wall to the toilet, pausing, hands splayed out onto the wall like a lizard's, then continuing on. Light would pool in a corner of the room through the frosted bathroom door. After a minute or two and a flush of water, darkness would come again. I'd sense more than see you grope your way back to your room and close the door, still unaware of my presence.

I didn't enter that room of yours often: you were protective of it, only opening up to our Malaysian cleaning lady who came each Sunday, mildly amused by this father and son, a widower and a bachelor, living awkwardly together. Most of the flat was orderly and, save for my bookshelves, bare, but your room was stuffed full of things that you'd brought from our old home. She'd asked me once, when you were out, should I clean inside the drawers and the cupboards? She showed me their contents. Trophies, medals, and certificates, now tarnished or yellowed with age. Photograph albums made of clammy plastic, their leaves stuck together. Mottled old T-shirts from trips abroad or community centre outings, folded up and put away long ago, crinkling when touched. *Leave them*, I said. *Just mop the floor.*

I remember going into your room on another occasion, when you did not wake as usual in the morning. I opened the door very softly, just enough so I could see the bed. You were lying like a child on your side, your legs wrapped round your bolster. Unmoving. Frozen. Were you still breathing? I watched over you for several minutes. To my relief, you turned over in your sleep. I closed the door as quietly as I could, but the click must have woken you. After a few minutes, you emerged, shabby, blinking in the light, shaking your head, and glancing at the clock. I began to toast the bread and heat the oats again, and you pushed me away. 不必. *No need. Go to work.*

And then there was that other day I crept into your room, and you did not turn over, even when I reached out to shake you. Softly, first, then much harder.

Returning home on another evening after work, I checked the submissions folder for early assignments from students. Three had arrived, but I couldn't summon the concentration to read them. After twenty years of teaching, I found marking more and more of a burden. In the classroom, in conversation, ideas flowed, and students voiced novel readings and intriguing responses that came from the heart. Yet when they wrote their final assignments, I sensed a creeping sclerosis, a growing rigidity of thought in all but the best essays. I looked at my watch. The deadline was at midnight. Tomorrow, I resolved, I would get up early and begin the task of marking.

I checked my email and social media, then a couple of alternative news sites I followed. On a whim, I logged into Ancestry.com and signed up for a month's free trial. That's where I found her, in London, in the Civil Registration Marriage Index.

Name: Primrose Perera

Registration Date: Jan 1954

Registration District: Hampstead

Inferred County: London

Spouse: Chew Jin Keong

Primrose Perera, then, had become Primrose Chew, the famous principal of Banyan Girls School and policymaker at the Ministry of Education. She had been hiding from me in plain sight.

Over the next few days, I ground my way through the marking. Four essays at a time, then a break. On a particularly difficult day, I went to my university office to force myself to focus. It was on the spine of a ridge, its windows looking out over the wharves of Pasir Panjang where monstrous cranes moved silently back and forth in the sunlight, plucking up shipping containers and depositing them on land. At lunchtime I went to the canteen. I looked for Professor K and other colleagues, but no one was in their offices, and the whole campus was silent and bare. On the steps up to the canteen the great flame of the forest tree had come into flower, and its orange-red blossoms, brought down by overnight rain, lay scattered in my path.

After lunch, I found it difficult to return to the student essays. I began daydreaming of what Dr Goh's improved version of the machine might look like. It would be larger, tidier, with a stainless steel backboard and carefully moulded tanks and pipes. Everything would gleam. And it would be much more complex. Singapore's experience taught Dr Goh that no national economy could exist in splendid isolation. There would need to be a series of valves attached to cannulas linking his machine to other machines. I might not find the machine itself, but a sketch might survive or a series of plans?

I was following an admittedly tenuous trail. Primrose Chew had passed away ten years ago, a year after her husband's death. From the obituary, I'd found the name of a daughter, Penelope Chew Yi Ling. A government scholar and educator like her mother, sent abroad to Cambridge and returning to work in the teaching service. Then, in her thirties, like her mother before her, Penny Chew had also vanished.

After working my way through a few more student essays, I let myself search online for Penny Chew as a reward. She was not as difficult to trace as her mother had been. In the past, it had been easy to hide or to be forgotten. From the 1990s, with the internet, we had become joined up to each other, linked by undersea cables first made of copper and then filled up with light, dematerialising even as their capacity grew. Online I came across a plethora of Penny Chews, from a Malaysian environmental activist to an Australian media influencer. Narrowing my search, following the pieces of a biography I already knew, I found her. She'd left Singapore for Canada, moving first to Toronto, then to Vancouver. She'd retrained as a librarian, achieved some success, and given her career up again. Now she was an artist, running a small non-profit called Penelope's Loom. They were weavers, but they offered no products for sale. Their website seemed to have been drafted in a fit of early enthusiasm, then neglected; the Instagram posts were infrequent.

I waited until I finished grading to draft an email explaining my project and asking Penny whether she'd kept any of her mother's correspondence. I considered again this house of cards I'd built for myself on the evidence of a single note left within the covers of a book. What if Dr Goh had never built the machine? Was it really worth following so speculative a lead? Then I remembered my HoD's hands drumming on this office desk, that table at the annual review pushed into the softness of my stomach. The acid taste of anxiety in my mouth that might also have come from overeating. I clicked "send."

Her reply came back before I left the office. She was still in Vancouver. She had a box of her mother's correspondence, taken from the family home after she passed. We switched to WhatsApp, texting each other frantically. She'd gone through the papers after her mother's death, looking for something very different from the object of my search, trying to find a woman she had never quite been able to know. Dr Goh? There was a diary in which he was mentioned and some letters, she thought. Anything about a machine? She hadn't noticed, but she hadn't been looking hard.

Could she copy the contents of the box for me? No. But I was welcome to look at the material on my next trip to North America. Did I know Vancouver? Yes, I'd been on a faculty exchange to the University of British Columbia a few years ago. She gave an address near the intersection of Barclay and Nicola Streets, in the heart of the West End. I asked if I could come soon, and she replied with the scream emoji. *You remind me of my old ministry colleagues. Slow down and you'll see more. I'm not going anywhere. You can come when you like.*

—

My HoD was as good as his word. I spent a long evening filling out a grant application, which was approved post-haste. Two weeks later, in the middle of May, I found myself in the West End in Vancouver after a long trans-Pacific flight. The air was clear, like natural air conditioning. After I checked into my hotel, I walked in Stanley Park to try to stay awake until sunset, at least, on this long, early summer day. I passed the bowling greens, then flower beds and the rhododendron garden, bushes already in bloom, and worked my way into the wider section of the park. By the side of the path, water flowed, and skunk cabbage and horsetails had sprung up. In the lower canopy, the vine maples were still green, thin branches reaching everywhere, their leaves a constellation of tiny green stars. Above me, the skeletons of huge cedar trees, the bark and the trunks twisted, with broken crowns and candelabra branches that reached up beyond the limits of sight. It felt like I might be in the wilderness, miles from anywhere, then I'd hear the throbbing of a float-plane's engine and see the aircraft pass overhead like a shadow as it came in to land.

At night, I slept soundly for the first time in months. When I woke in the queen-size bed with its soft cotton sheets, I did not know where I was. Through the window, I saw the sunlight turning the tips of the tower blocks in the street outside yellow. I got up, brushed my teeth, and began to prepare for my meeting with Penny Chew.

She had said that I should only come at two o'clock. After breakfast, I walked up Barclay to her apartment complex to check out the lay of the land. Something had shifted since I arrived. The sun was orange now, and the patches of snow on the mountains had a purple tint. I coughed: a hint of smoke in the air, of wood burning. I'd read about the forest fires in the interior of the province. When I first came here a decade ago, I'd escaped from a

Singapore choked by smoke from peat fires in Sumatra and landed in Vancouver to air that was clear as crystal. Now the fires had followed me, spreading across the globe.

The apartment building where Penny lived was a relic from the 1930s, three stories of red brick topped by a mock Tudor facade, its black beams and white plaster reminding me of the black-and-white walk-up flats on Portsdown Road at home. Above the porch, carved into stone, was its name: Maple Court.

By afternoon it was raining, and the temperature had dropped. *Junuary*—I remembered that word from my Vancouver days to describe a summer that never quite arrives. I pressed the buzzer for her apartment, and a voice chirped back at me, its familiar clipped accent not quite erased by long Canadian vowels and rolling Rs. The lift seemed out of order, or at least very slow to respond, so I took the stairs. The carpet was thick, olive, with a design of golden tendrils that reached upwards and out of the frame. On the edges of the treads and on the landings, it had worn threadbare, so that a grid of fibres showed through. I slipped once and steadied myself against the wooden banisters, covered with a century of scratches and layers of varnish. On the third floor, I looked down the corridor and saw a small figure at an open door, waving to me. Penny.

Her apartment was bigger than I expected. She led me past a galley kitchen and through a short passageway that widened to a long living room with a wall of leaded windows, through which a green light was filtered by a sea of trees in leaf. Near the window, a low table at which we sat down. At the back of the room, her loom, like a monstrous sea creature with an open mouth, rows of vertical white threads like baleen and, where the threads met, a strip of brilliant cloth, deep red hatched with white, like a truncated tongue. Laid down at the side was the shuttle, its wood smooth with the passing of hands—like the bui in the temples you used to take me to in childhood, Father, those worn, wooden half-moons you'd throw and throw again, seeking answers to our questions and the shape of our lives ahead.

She served tea. I'd brought a small bag of gifts: Prima Taste laksa paste, kaya, a packet of salted egg fish skin: the things you get for Singaporeans overseas. She simply thanked me and put the bag aside. Later, when I tried to recall her face, I could not remember it. I could have passed her in the street and not recognised her again. But I remember her hands, the fingers long and spindly, swelling into pads at the tip, like a lizard's feet. Her feet were bare, their knuckle joints swollen, and they made me think again of you.

I found you once sitting in the chair next to the kitchen door, head bowed. I was brave enough to ask if you felt tired or unhappy, and you said, brightly, no, you were looking for a grain of uncooked rice that had fallen on the floor. We searched for it, me squatting next to your chair, but it was invisible among the flecks on the cream tiles. I noticed your toes, their joints as swollen as Penny's were, the nails overly long and hooked over, like the claws of a huge bird of prey. Somehow this brought to mind a couplet you'd written out for me on my graduation, all those years ago when I'd said I wanted to continue my studies, something about a sea of knowledge and a 鲲鹏, a roc, a great bird that could fly ten thousand miles. But all I said to you was, *You should cut those nails soon.*

I asked Penny about the box, and she said she had it ready in her study, the room through the doorway over there. Could I take photographs? Of course. Surely I must be impatient to start, to find out the truth about Dr Goh and his machine?

She showed me to the place she'd made for me at her desk in the study. The box was on a side table: an old, black cardboard shoebox, oversize, bulging, and held together by twine—too small for something on which my career would depend. After she left me, I could hear her scuffling in the other room, then the sound of the loom, the hiss of the reed bringing the rows of warp threads together, the clicks of the treadles, and the shuttle passing back and forth.

Before I left in the early evening, she asked if I'd found what I was looking for. I told her I wasn't sure. Given the quantity of material, I'd taken photographs mostly, not notes. At times I'd slowed down, focused, and read passages in detail. I thought I was beginning to understand, but I needed to look more closely. I'd thank her, of course, in the acknowledgements for my research. I felt awkward saying goodbye, as if I'd taken something and given nothing in return. As I passed through the living room, I noticed that the loom was bare, and there was a coil of red thread next to the shuttle.

In the long evening, at the desk in my hotel suite, I began to process the photographs on my laptop, filing and organising them while snacking on a packet of salted egg fish skin that had mysteriously manifested itself in my bag. I took a couple of days to put the files in order and read them, before I flew back on that direct flight, those long hours across the Pacific. Hunched up at my tray table, I cut and pasted text, my fingers moving over the keyboard, and you came to my mind again, pecking at your keyboard with a single finger. How in your world, in Dr Goh's world, each of the gestures I now performed had been not virtual but physical. You'd open the creaking drawers of the rusted filing cabinet in your room, push apart the flutter of hanging files, and struggle to insert small pieces of cardboard you'd marked up into the label holder. I'd watched you type an article with an electric typewriter, cut out paragraphs from the sheet of paper with scissors, spray their backs, and paste them carefully onto a new sheet marked with a faint grid of blue lines.

In Singapore, the first thing I wanted to do was to go to Bright Hill to see your urn, to tell you what I'd found. At the columbarium, it was stiflingly hot after Vancouver, with that heaviness of the air that comes before rain. In the Ancestral Hall, I searched for your photograph in a crowd of tiny faces behind glass that stretched from the level of my eyes up to the eaves. I counted off the rows until I found you both: two portraits framed together like a pair of spectacles. Mother's had faded, yours still was clear. Although I do not believe, I prayed. Then I went down the stairs, crossed the courtyard, and entered the cool of the columbarium. Mother's urn I found easily, but I struggled to locate yours among the maze of niches.

After checking off the number on my phone, I turned into the last row of urns, much as a taxi turns into a lane between HDB blocks. You were above eye level, with two small blue tags on each side of the niche door to indicate that it was not the most expensive choice, differentiated from the orange, yellow, and green tags below. Your photograph, the one I'd asked them to use, seemed very small, your face thin. You were wearing a jacket, and I wondered if the picture had been taken just before you retired or on a holiday in a colder country. It felt incomplete, a mere trace of you, like a thumbprint. I read your name running downward, the character 君, and the date of your death in both lunar and solar calendars. I spoke to you softly. I reached up and touched your face. I told you: These papers I have assembled are a kind of offering to you. I cannot burn them: they have changed their form into atoms on my hard drive and in the cloud; they rest somewhere across the oceans, miles away. But when I return to the flat at night, I can summon them out of air through those wires that bind us all together, shape them into a solid form again. Air becomes pixels becomes paper becomes air. So think of these fragments as offerings to you, in that distant country, wherever you are.

1. A journal entry in a manila notebook, with substantial foxing on the inside covers.

3 December 1954

Keng Swee invited me to see Dr Phillips and his machine. I think I've mentioned it before. The machine itself is the size of a door, a linked series of Perspex tanks, through which coloured liquid circulates. It can model the economy, and it is thus a perfect image of the world. I went with him to the lecture at LSE today. Dr Phillips waited for us to settle down, his suit hanging on his thin, skeletal frame. A jutting chin and thinning hair. Push him, I thought, and he might dissolve. You would be left with a heap of clothes. He was imprisoned by the Japanese in the War, KS whispers, after the fall of Singapore. Perhaps his body retains some memory of that time in its stubborn refusal to fatten and put on flesh.

Dr Phillips chain-smokes as we students gather in the theatre, the clatter of seats being unfolded and coats being removed. He seems nervous, glancing at his notes. But when he begins, he is all enthusiasm, starting up his machine, showing how the red liquid falls from one Perspex tank to another and how the valves, which stand for parameters, can be adjusted. Income flows in from the top. A small pipe siphons off taxation, and the income tank fills up. From there, there are two pipes, one for savings, one for consumption. At this point he loses me. He writes in hieroglyphics on the board. Next to me, KS nods in excitement and copies the equations.

There is a way, KS whispers to me in a less frenetic moment, that the machine can record the simulations it produces and draw graphs to measure various outcomes on paper. Of course, the process here is speeded up. In the machine, circulation happens in a minute or less; in the real world, it may take three to four months. Yet perhaps the world can be thought of as a machine. If it is, think what the future holds for us in Malaya. We need to think not just of rubber or tin, those mainstays of the colonial economy, but the manufacture of goods. New inputs: opened taps. What we might do for the common good.

He turns back to the lecture, anxious to miss nothing. But I cannot concentrate on what Dr Phillips is saying. I sit back and look at the performance. From a distance, things look different. Those excited gestures, that incessant smoking, the churning of the water in the machine. Might these not be science and logic but a kind of madness or shell shock, a traumatised twitching of disobedient limbs? If that's true, I'm the only one who thinks so. The audience listens, rapt.

At the end of the lecture, Dr Phillips allows questions, shambling in front of the blackboard. There are objections from students with crisp English accents, attempts to point out the machine's shortcomings, which he swats away impatiently. Of course there are limitations, but the solution is surely to build a better machine.

Then KS raises his hand. "Dr Phillips, why is it so bloody cold in here?"

There's a shuffling and muttering in the hall, a turning of pink, overboiled faces in our direction. How will Dr Phillips react?

He lights the inevitable cigarette. "Mr Goh, that's the first intelligent question I've had all morning."

He draws, on the blackboard, a diagram illustrating the workings of the heating system, its choke points, and what is broken. Just another example of the circulation of fluid. Just another machine.

2. An extract from a letter, in a folder marked, "To be Given to Penelope on My Death," dated 3 March 1956.

Dear Keng Swee,

I understand what you are saying. You will focus on your doctoral studies in London and graduate as soon as possible. Time presses. There is much to be done. You will only work on your improved version of Dr Phillips's machine after you return to Singapore.

Is this wise? Think how quickly history is moving. Mr Marshall is Chief Minister; he is opening constitutional talks. Colonialism's days are numbered. When you return to Singapore you will be thrust into the political arena. You will have little free time, little chance to reflect. The time to work on the machine is surely now . . .

3. An extract from a second letter from the same folder, dated 15 November 1958.

Dear Keng Swee,

It seems strange for me to write to you since we're now both back in Singapore. Of course you're so busy, and I haven't had the chance to see you. You will drop me a line from time to time? I wanted to tell you I have a daughter, only three months old. Your son must be older now, almost a teenager, as the Americans say. He was born at a difficult moment, in the War; Penelope has come into a world of so much hope.

Forgive me if I still harp about the machine. You spoke of it with such vision. You say you'll build it after the elections, but if you are busy now, surely you will be even more busy if you do take office . . .

4. An extract from a third letter from the same folder, dated 3 September 1968.

. . . I understand now, at last. The whole island is your new machine. Money flows from land and from outside, from catheters to other machines. It collects in the income tank. From there it goes into the infrastructure pipe. You are building homes, schools, and factories, and the fluid returns from them, by a labyrinthine route, into the income tank. The tap in the welfare pipe is closed.

I can find poetry in this. Each day, at school, I watch as we raise our flag, with its stars and crescent moon. The stars are the sparks of a welder's torch, the moon a swelling strip of reclaimed land. The families of the children in my school move into the new flats that go up and up into the sky. Everything is clean and freshly painted. Each day, their parents, working shifts in the flatted factories you have built, make televisions, radios, and cameras that flow out of our port, and income flows back in. Your colleague, Mr Rajaratnam, even thinks culture can be made in the same way. Stop up those old, frayed tubes that link us to the past. Tighten the taps on what comes in from the West. Let the liquid in the tank of national income slowly rise.

This poetry speaks to me but not to my daughter. She is stubborn. The more I push, the more she pushes back. Even as a small child she would undo what she had made. She would delight in toppling a tower of bricks or pouring paint on a landscape of flowers she'd spent a whole morning drawing. Was Kian Chee also like this as a child?

5. An extract from the last letter in the same folder, dated 20 January 1990.

Keng Swee,

Why do you no longer reply to me? I know things must be difficult for you. You've stepped down from Cabinet, and you and Alice have been through what must have been a painful divorce. You seem to be keeping yourself busy, though. My life has also been difficult. Jin Keong has been unwell. Penny has told us that she will leave her job and return to Canada. She will not be coming back. It may be better for her there, but I've found myself taking old photo albums out of the cupboard and looking through them. She was such a happy baby, so playful and so fat! I had such high hopes of this world we would make for her. I turn the album pages. I press my finger to her face. At this age, the tears come quickly.

Keng Swee, in these later years of my life, I worry about the machine you have built. Each year it seems to become more complicated. You add new pipes and new tanks. You reinforce the joints. The liquid flows at a much greater speed. I think you said you thought that a time might come where things became calmer, when the flow settled down, not a torrent but a broad, slow stream. Why do you think that this has not happened? Why has your machine grown to fill the whole world?

Each of us has also become a machine. Money flows in, if we are lucky, into our CPF accounts, out into housing and the expenses of everyday living. The young move faster and faster. Everyone wears armour; everyone carries weapons. Will we ever stop? Surely we do not need simply to be fed, for our appetites to be stimulated by more and more delicacies? We are not simply the sum of what has been put into us. We are more. In the classroom at times, especially in those early years of teaching, I felt that something spoke through me that was not limited to me. Just like that mad logic of Dr Phillips at LSE all those years ago. I sensed this all along, but I could not quite grasp it, until my own body began to slow. Old age reaches out a hand to us, pulls us back, shakes us, makes us stay still. But then it is too late to warn others. This is what my body tells me. This is what I believe.

CODA

Questions for a National Therapy Session, 9 August 2030

It's your 65th birthday, that last gateway to pass through on the slow journey into old age. At 45, you were officially allowed to use those exercise machines next to the void deck in your HDB estate, although you'd actually used them for years. At 55, you could collect the money from your CPF Ordinary Account, but you left it there, gathering interest, just to be safe. At 60, you were given a PAssion Card that entitled you to discounts on public transport and more. Today, your CPF Life payments will start, money trickling into your bank account each month. Your employer suggested that you stop working, but you told her you want to carry on. You've worked hard. You've saved. Your flat is long paid off. But you're still not absolutely secure. Prices are rising, and the world is uncertain: your MediSave is draining away, despite the periodic top-ups the government gives you. Besides, you've said, who would respect me if I had no job? How would I fill my time after a lifetime of work?

Perhaps this is what brought you to the counsellor's office. You hesitate. The door at street level is plate glass, and you fumble with the keypad to input the code you've been given. You climb the narrow stairs to the second floor of the shophouse. Your knees creak. Everything around you is trim, clean, newly painted. In the anteroom, where you've been asked to wait, you sit down gratefully. Dark, new slate tiles on the floor, a strip of LED lights on the ceiling, the walls covered in artful black-and-white photographs of vanished street scenes. Something stirs inside. You take out a coin and scratch the wall just next to the couch, in a place no one will notice. Layer upon layer of paint, of different colours and textures even, each one completely covering up the one beneath.

You remember what your children said. When you enter here, you no longer have to keep your guard up. You'll be like an onion, peeling off layer after layer. There is nothing worth hiding now. Yet you don't know where to begin. Your story isn't a simple story: there are many ways of telling it, many ways of speaking truth and falsehood mixed together.

Let's call your therapist History. She welcomes you in. Her face seems familiar, and you want to greet her. Her name is on the tip of your tongue. Then, as happens increasingly nowadays, you begin to doubt yourself. Perhaps she is not the person you thought you recognised. A stranger who looks very similar to a friend you once knew. You take off your glasses. Her face is now a blur, perhaps a deep well with no apparent bottom. Or simply a reflection of yourself. As if you were in one of those new restaurants with glass all along one wall that might or might not be a mirror, and you are not sure whether you're looking at the room in which you are sitting from a new angle or at another completely unknown room.

These are the questions she asks you.

I notice you are breathing hard. You have told me before you often feel the pressure to be on time. You are always running in a race that seems to have no end. When did this start? How did it develop? Can you tell me more about the reasons that you feel this way?

You told me in your emails that you've been thinking of the past. You describe your birth in 1965 as traumatic. You say you were abandoned. Could you tell me a little more about this?

You've talked about trauma, how that wound of abandonment has marked your life. What would happen if we were to allow that wound to heal, to become a scar rather than remaining open? I get the sense that if you let that happen you could tell the story of your birth in a different way. A story of forgotten invention and of suppressed joy. Above all, of transformation and change. If you did, where would you start? How would that change the way you see yourself now?

You've told me about your relationship with Colonialism. I hear you when you say you're glad you broke things off with him. He certainly got the message, and when you kicked him out of the house you thought he'd gone for good. But I'm curious why you kept so many mementoes of him. What do you feel when you look at them now?

You kept him out, of course. You were fiercely proud and self-reliant. But you suspect he has changed his name or his form. At first you thought he'd crept back in, a presence in your house like a mouse or a rat, scuttling between the chair legs, leaving droppings, eating crumbs. You put down traps but caught nothing. Now you tell me you think he is haunting you. Perhaps, you tell me, he can enter your body, possess you, speak through your lips in a different voice. How would you recognise him? What would you say to him? What practices of exorcism might you learn and put to use?

You also say you like living with Capitalism right now. He's given you many things: the chill of air conditioning, the soft chair on which you rest your aching limbs, the fat electronic watch on your wrist, that feeling of always being full. From what you've told me, though, he seems to be rather controlling.

You tell me you are sure he will change, that he will not be like this for-ever. In your experience, have people close to you actually changed when they are in a relationship with you? At what point, do you think, does con-trolling behaviour shade into abuse?

Inequality has also come to have a much greater role in your life in the last few decades. When you were young, you hated her. Now she and Capitalism are your friends, and you tell me you sometimes catch them whispering to each other. You wonder what secrets they are sharing. Inequality insists that there is no future without her. You must accept her as she is. What do you think of being given this kind of ultimatum?

You miss Socialism, you say. They used to be your best friend, but they seem to have vanished from your life. Let me challenge you now, since we know each other better. Did they really leave of their own free will, as you say, or did you push them out? Where do you think they went? Why are you still frightened that they might return?

It's fine to sit in silence. Don't feel the pressure to talk.

I notice that when you're silent and when you talk about sad things, you smile a lot, especially when I look at you. When we talk about the past and it weighs too heavily on you, you break off. When you do this, you suddenly talk about the future, of those wonderful plans you have rather than what you remember. Why is that? What is going on inside? What do you feel now?

It seems to me that when you use the word *feel* you really mean I *think*. What do you actually feel? Right now. Not in your head, but in your body. A tightness, you say, like a band. Something that isn't just to do with age. Hard, like a stone. Sim tia. The heart hurts. Sakit hati. Just there, you say. You have cupped your hand across your chest, just above your heart. You are looking upwards. Let's just be aware of this for now. Let's return to this moment later.

You have mentioned the man you call your father. I notice that when you say his name your expression changes. You sit upright; your body stiffens. You tell me you fear him, but you also love him. Can you tell me more about this relationship?

You also talk about your uncles. I feel I know them well from our conversations. The two who stayed, the round-faced economic genius and the sharp-tongued journalist. And the other uncle, the youthful, handsome one, the one your father forced to leave, the one whose name it still hurts you to mention. What would it look like to see these people not as fathers or uncles, not as heroes or villains, but as human beings, as flawed as we are?

You mentioned your mother for the first time. Could you tell me more about her? Your sisters or your aunties? What about all those other people in your life? Am I right that your father and uncles have somehow crowded them out? The stories you tell of your father and uncles seem thin. Do you also sense this? How might the story thicken? What sediments might you dig into? Is there a way, in talking about the past, you can move from your head to your body? From thoughts to sensations. The taste of food in the mouth. The texture of a child's fingers, interlaced with yours. The soft line of hair on a lover's body, just where the shoulder runs up into the neck. The pads of your fingertips held together in prayer. Anger that fills the body like a tide, then recedes.

You tell me you work very hard. You're always running very fast, but you are only standing still. You want the very best for your children. But you find that they are slipping away. They do not live with you now. The more you give them, the more they want. Their mouths are always open, like the mouths of young birds demanding food. You cannot talk to them. They speak a different language, one you are not quite fluent in. It sticks to your tongue. You cannot get the words out.

You're shaking your head. What I said wasn't quite right. It's not that the language they speak is wrong. You would like to learn it. But you wish they would learn yours too, the language that you have almost forgotten. Is this what you wish to tell me?

Let me challenge you again. I notice that although you are quite old, you always insist on telling me how young you are. You are sure you are not yet ready, not mature enough. I'm interested why that should be the case.

You also say that you are forgetful now. The past is frozen, even in this heat. You hack and hack at it, and it remains frozen. Is there a way you might allow it to melt?

Here are tissues. I'm curious why you are worried about tearing up.

Let me sum up. You told me a story about how you became what you are now. You remember a morning, still, beautiful, cool, when the sun had not yet risen over the sea. You could see the horizon and make out five stars and a tiny, thin, crescent moon. Then the day got brighter. The sun came up. Buildings pushed skywards. You couldn't see the stars anymore. Even at night there is so much light that you cannot see anything in the sky. Sometimes you do catch a glimpse of the moon between the buildings, but it's full, swollen, pressed down close to the earth. Too big to support. Too heavy to hold up. Life is hard.

But you've also told me that there is something there, at the beginning of the story, a wild fierce joy that might speak to the present, if only you could catch hold of it.

Next time we meet, I would be honoured if you would tell me more of this story. Take me back to the beginning, to that moment. How did it feel to be there, at that time when you were most happy? What strengths did you draw on? What were your values? And what was there that you can still remember and begin to tell others and use now in this changed world?

Acknowledgements

Many of these stories have been published previously. Most were collected in the original edition of *Heaven Has Eyes* (Epigram Books, 2016). Of these, "September Ghosts" was originally published in *Prism International* 44.3 (Spring 2006). "Two Among Many" came out in *Cha* 4 (August 2008) and was reprinted in Dzanc Books' *Best of the Web 2009*. An earlier version of "Penguins on the Perimeter" was published in *Quarterly Literary Review Singapore* 13.4 (October 2014) and republished in *Quiet Loving, Ravaging Search: 20 Years of Quarterly Literary Review Singapore* (Dakota Books, 2021). The title story, "Heaven Has Eyes", was one of a number of short stories chosen by *Wasafiri* to celebrate the journal's thirtieth anniversary in 2014 and published on the journal's website. "Aeroplane" was written for the anthology *In Transit*, edited by Zhang Ruihe and Yu-Mei Balasingamchow (Math Paper Press, 2016), while "Library" was included in *The Epigram Books Collection of Best New Singaporean Short Stories Volume 3* (2017), edited by Cyril Wong. "Pigeons and Doves" was written in response to a call for historical fiction about Lim Chin Siong by *New Naratif* and Singapore Unbound in 2024. An earlier version of "Questions for a National Therapy Session, 9 August 2030" appeared in *The Birthday Book: 20/20 Seeing Clearly*, edited by Chua Jun Yan and Selina Chong (Birthday Collective, 2020). I'd like to thank the editors of all these publications for their thoughtful responses and suggestions for revision.

Several of the stories make use of archival or published material. "Forbidden Cities" cannibalises accounts of Lee Kuan Yew's visit to the University of British Columbia in 1968, available in back numbers of *The Ubyssey* in the Rare Books and Special Collections, University of British Columbia Library. "When Pierre Met Harry" makes use of Lee's speech, "The Returned Student", made at Malaya Hall, London, in January 1950. "Mudskippers" is informed by oral history accounts of British servicemen at Seletar Camp, available in the National Archives of Singapore. "Pigeons and Doves" makes use of and at times quotes from material on Lim Chin Siong from the David Marshall Private Papers and Alex Josey Private Papers, Institute of Southeast Asian Studies, Singapore. "Letters from London" emerges from a research project on Sinnathamby Rajaratnam's London years. Sources used include the S. Rajaratnam Private Papers at ISEAS, the S. Rajaratnam Photograph Collection at the National Archives of Singapore, and the *1939 Register* at the National Archives, Kew, UK. I would also like to thank Dorcas and Norman Cumming for hosting my visit to Raja's former boarding house at Steele's Road in London, and Fergus McLeod and David Jonathan and their families for helping me figure out precisely which flat Raja and Piroska Feher (Piri in the story) lived in in Priory Road. Finally, "It's All in a Dream" responds to and follows the structure of Lee Kok Liang's story of the same name, first published in the literary journal *Tumasek* in 1964.

The stories in the collection emerge from my life in Singapore and a number of important friendships. Among those I'd like to thank, either for direct comments on my writing or for more general discussions that influenced the stories in some way, are Matilda Gabrielpillai, Wee Wan-ling, Teo You Yenn, Chan Cheow Thia, Tan Dan Feng, Zhang Ruihe, and Lydia Kwa. Thanks, too, to Hajera Rostam and Renée Lemieux for their help with one particularly troublesome story. I'm grateful to the perspectives on Singapore literature and society from my students over the years and to the participants in the Guided Autobiography groups I've run with NUS College alumni in recent years, who have taught me much about listening.

Reflecting on the content of the book, I realise that I have had two important teachers later in my life: my father, Cedric Holden, and my mother-in-law, Kuo Ching Yun. My partner, Ng Yun Sian, has been and remains the most important formative influence on my life and the writing that comes from it. I'd also like to thank Edmund Wee and Jason Lundberg at Epigram Books for their work on the first edition of *Heaven Has Eyes*, and Koh Jee Leong, Yu-Mei Balasingamchow, and others at Gaudy Boy who have encouraged me in the writing of new stories and revision of older ones for this new edition of the collection.

About the Author

PHILIP HOLDEN's life has spanned three continents, with its centre of gravity in Singapore, where he taught and researched Singapore and Southeast Asian writing at university in a three-decade-long career. He is the author of critical, historical, biographical, and fictional writing, exploring the connections between social and historical narratives and questions of identity, belonging, and agency. Before his academic career he worked in children's theatre, as a union organizer, and as a residential social worker with refugees. Now a registered clinical counsellor, he explores the intersections of storytelling and mental health through work in Guided Autobiography and in facilitating lived-experience stories. Philip leads a migratory life between Singapore and Vancouver, Canada, and shares its ever-changing story at www.pulauujong.org.

From the Latin *gaudium*, meaning "joy," Gaudy Boy publishes books that delight readers with the various powers of art. The name is taken from the poem "Gaudy Turnout," by Singaporean poet Arthur Yap, about his time abroad in Leeds, the United Kingdom. Similarly inspired by such diasporic wanderings and migrations, Gaudy Boy brings literary works by authors of Asian heritage to the attention of an American audience and beyond. Established in 2018 as the imprint of the New York City–based literary nonprofit Singapore Unbound, we publish poetry, fiction, and literary nonfiction.

Visit our website at www.singaporeunbound.org/gaudyboy.

Poetry

Fablemaker: Poems
by Mandy Moe Pwint Tu

Eke: Poems
by Wahidah Tambee

Interrogation Records: Poems
by Jeddie Sophronius

Waking Up to the Pattern Left by a Snail Overnight: Poems
by Jim Pascual Agustin

Time Regime: Poems
by Jhani Randhawa

Object Permanence: Poems
by Nica Bengzon

Play for Time: Poems
by Paula Mendoza

Autobiography of Horse: A Poem
by Jenifer Sang Eun Park

The Experiment of the Tropics: Poems
by Lawrence Lacambra Ypil

Fiction and Nonfiction

Heaven Has Eyes: Stories
by Philip Holden

The Unrepentant: Stories
by Sharmini Aphrodite

The Way You Want to Be Loved: Short Stories
by Aruni Kashyap

Lovelier, Lonelier: A Novel
by Daryl Qilin Yam

Bengal Hound: A Novel
by Rahad Abir

The Infinite Library and Other Stories
by Victor Fernando R. Ocampo

The Sweetest Fruits: A Novel
by Monique Truong

And the Walls Come Crumbling Down
by Tania De Rozario

The Foley Artist: Stories
by Ricco Villanueva Siasoco

Malay Sketches: Stories
by Alfian Sa'at

Other Series

New Singapore Poetries
edited by Marylyn Tan and Jee Leong Koh

Suspect: Volume 1, Year 1
edited by Jee Leong Koh

From Gaudy Boy Translates

Memorial Club: A Novel
by Mozid Mahmud

Picking off new shoots will not stop the spring:
Witness Poems and Essays from Burma/Myanmar 1988–2021
edited by Ko Ko Thett and Brian Haman

Amanat: Women's Writing from Kazakhstan
edited by Zaure Batayeva and Shelley Fairweather-Vega

Ulirát: Best Contemporary Stories in Translation from the Philippines
edited by Tilde Acuña, John Bengan, Daryll Delgado, Amado Anthony G.
Mendoza III, and Kristine Ong Muslim

Books by our other imprint, Bench Press

Sample and Loop: A Simple History of Singaporeans in America
by Jee Leong Koh

Snow at 5 PM: Translations of an Insignificant Japanese Poet
by Jee Leong Koh

Seven Studies for a Self-Portrait: Poems
by Jee Leong Koh

Equal to the Earth: Poems
by Jee Leong Koh

Lightly in the Good of Day: Poems
by Bob Hart

Try to Have Your Writing Make Sense:
The Quintessential PFFA Anthology: Poems
edited by Donna Smith and Howard Miller